ARTHUR M

FOCUS

PENGUIN BOOKS

For Mary and Jane Ellen

PENGUIN BOOKS

Published by the Penguin Group
27 Wrights Lane, London W8 5TZ, England
Viking Penguin Inc., 40 West 23rd Street, New York, New York 10010, USA
Penguin Books Australia Ltd, Ringwood, Victoria, Australia
Penguin Books Canada Ltd, 2801 John Street, Markham, Ontario, Canada L3R 1B4
Penguin Books (NZ) Ltd, 182–190 Wairau Road, Auckland 10, New Zealand

Penguin Books Ltd, Registered Offices: Harmondsworth, Middlesex, England

First published in the United States of America by Reynal and Hitchcock 1945
First published in Great Britain by Victor Gollancz 1949
Published in Great Britain by Martin Secker and Warburg 1974
Published in Penguin Books in the United States of America by arrangement
with Harcourt Brace Jovanovich, Inc.
Published in Penguin Books 1978
Reprinted with an Introduction by Arthur Miller 1986
3 5 7 9 10 8 6 4 2

Printed and bound in Great Britain by
Cox & Wyman Ltd, Reading

INTRODUCTION
BY THE AUTHOR

Some part of the genesis of this book must lie in the Brooklyn
Navy Yard, where I worked the night shift in the shipfitting
department during World War II, one of some sixty thousand
men and a few women from every ethnic group in New York. It is
no longer possible to decide whether it was my own Hitler-
begotten sensitivity or the anti-Semitism itself that so often made
me wonder whether, when peace came, we were to be launched
into a raw politics of race and religion, and not in the South but in
New York. In any case, whatever the actual level of hostility to
Jews that I was witnessing, it was vastly exacerbated in my mind
by the threatening existence of Nazism and the near absence
among the men I worked with fourteen hours a day of any
comprehension of what Nazism meant – we were fighting Ger-
many essentially because she had allied herself with the Japanese
who had attacked us at Pearl Harbor. Moreover, it was by no
means an uncommon remark that we had been maneuvered into
this war by powerful Jews who secretly controlled the federal
government. Not until Allied troops had broken into the German
concentration camps and the newspapers published photos of the
mounds of emaciated and sometimes partially burned bodies was
Nazism really disgraced among decent people and our own
casualties justified. (It is a fiction, in my opinion, that national
unity around the war reached very deep in a great many people in
those times.)

I cannot glance through this novel without once again feeling
the sense of emergency that surrounded the writing of it. As far as
I knew at the time, anti-Semitism in America was a closed if not
forbidden topic for fiction – certainly no novel had taken it as a

main theme, let alone the existence within the Catholic priesthood of militants whose duty and pleasure was to stoke up Jew-hate. When one is tempted to say that everything in the world has gotten worse, here is one shining exception.

I was reminded of this only recently when quite by chance I happened to tune in on a local Connecticut radio station and heard a Catholic priest trying to reason an obviously anti-Semitic man out of laying the blame for several bombings of Jewish homes and synagogues in the Hartford area upon the Jews themselves. There was a widespread search going on for the perpetrators, so the man had called into the priest's talk program to offer his ideas as to who might have been responsible. He had no doubt it was somebody whom a Jew had mistreated, either one of his employees, or somebody who had bought some defective item from him, or someone he had bilked out of money, or maybe it was the work of the client of a Jewish lawyer outraged at having been defrauded. There were, he thought, all sorts of interesting possibilities since the Jews, as everyone knew, have a habit of defrauding and exploiting their workers, and in general have no respect for right and wrong and feel responsible only to one another. (The arsonist was caught some weeks later – a mentally disturbed young Jew.)

I had not heard this litany since the thirties and early forties. Not since before the photos of the bodies were published in the papers. But here it was again, as though freshly minted, brand new discoveries that the caller was supremely confident everyone knew perfectly well but thought it bad manners to talk about in public. And such was the confidence of his manner that he soon had the poor priest on the ropes and could assert with utmost self assurance that he was simply being factual and not anti-Semitic.

The differences now, of course, are that no Hitler stands at the head of the greatest armed force in the world vowing the destruction of the Jewish people, and there is an Israel, which, notwithstanding all the futility of much of its present vision, is still capable of defending the right of Jews to exist. This book, in short, was written when a sensible person could wonder if such a right had reality at all.

It is inevitable that one should wonder whether anything like the situation in this novel could recur, and it is a question no one can answer. In the fifties and sixties I might have persuaded myself that its recrudescence was not likely, and I would have based such reasoning on what had begun to seem a truly profound shift in the world's conception of the Jew. For one thing, anti-Semitism, linked as it was to totalitarianism, was being viewed as one of the keys to the dismantling of democracy and at least in its political forms was no longer an option for people who, whatever their private grievance against Jews, were still committed to the liberal state. This conjunction between mere private prejudice and public calamity had not even been broached when this book was written, and it is the centerpiece of its shape and action. By the end of World War II anti-Semitism was no longer a purely personal matter.

But there was also the shift, however paradoxical, in the perception of the Jew as a consequence of the first successful decades of Israel's life as a state. In a word, the Jew was no longer a shadowy, ghettoized mystery, but a farmer, a pilot, a worker. Throwing off the role of victim he stood up and was suddenly comprehensible as one of the world's dangerous peoples – dangerous in the conventional military and characterological sense. He was like everybody else now and for a time it would be difficult to imagine the traditional anti-Semitic attitudes feeding themselves on warriors rather than passive victims. For a time Israeli technical and military missions were spread across Africa and her example seemed about to become an inspiration for any poor country attempting to enter this century.

This exemplary condition was not to last. An irony so gigantic as to sweep the mind into the explications of mysticism moved Israel partially in fact, entirely in the world's perception, from a land settled by pastoral socialists and internationalist soldier-

3

farmers, into a bellicose armed camp whose adamant tribal defensiveness has inevitably hardened against neighboring peoples to the point of fanaticism. Jewish aloneness is back, but now it is armed. One more impersonation has been added to the long historic list that supplied so many contradictory images: Einstein and Freud and/or Meyer Lansky or another gangster; Karl Marx and/or Rothschild; the Prague Communist chief Slansky running Czechoslovakia for Stalin, and/or the Jew Slansky hanging by the neck as tribute to Stalin's paranoid anti-Semitism.

Focus is much involved with impersonations. Its central image is the turning lens of the mind of an anti-Semitic man forced by his circumstances to see anew his own relationships to the Jew. To a certain degree, it seems to me that Newman's step toward his human identification with some part of the Jewish situation has indeed occurred, at least in sectors of the democratic world, since the mid-forties, and so the projection of such a change as occurs in this story was not altogether romantic and unlikely.

But in the four decades since writing *Focus* certain new perspectives on the Jewish situation have opened up from surprising angles. In particular the attitudes of some Asian peoples toward certain successful strangers settled in their midst, for example the Chinese in Thailand and the Vietnamese in the Cambodia of Sihanouk before the Vietnamese occupation of that country. It used to amuse me to hear descriptions in Bangkok of the local Chinese, which were so exactly similar to what people used to say about Jews, and doubtless still do in the West. 'The Chinese really have only one loyalty, to one another. They are very clever, study harder in school, always try to be first in their studies. There are lots of Chinese bankers in Thailand, too many; in fact, it was a real mistake to give Chinese Thai citizenship, because they have secretly taken control of the banking system. Besides, they are spies for China, or would be in time of war. Actually, what they are after is a revolution in Thailand [despite their being bankers

4

and capitalists] so that we would end up as dependents of China.'

Many of the same contradictory things were being said about Vietnamese who had been settled in Cambodia for generations, and they too were more industrious than the natives, of doubtful loyalty, on the verge of being spies for Communist Vietnam despite their being fervent capitalists, and so on. Two striking similarities exist in these instances – the Chinese in Thailand and the Vietnamese in Cambodia were very frequently visible as merchants, landlords of stores and small houses, peddlers, and an inordinate number of them were teachers and lawyers and intellectuals, enviable in a peasant country. They, so to speak, visibly administered the injustices of life as far as the average Thai or Cambodian could see, since it was to them one paid the rent or the limitlessly inflated prices of food and other necessities of life, and one could see with one's own eyes how soft a life they led as intellectuals.

It is important also that the host people were self-characterized as somehow more naive than these strangers, less interested in money making and more 'natural' – that is, less likely to become intellectuals. In the Soviet Union and the lands ruled by her arms and culture in Eastern Europe the same sort of accusations are made openly or implicitly. *Focus* is a view of anti-Semitism that is deeply social in this particular sense: the Jew is seen by the anti-Semitic mind as the carrier of that same alienation that the indigenous people resent and fear, the same conniving exploitation. I would only add that they fear it because it is an alienation they feel in themselves, a not-belonging, a helplessly antisocial individualism that belies fervent desires to be a serving part of the mythic whole, the sublime national essence. They fear the Jew as they fear the real, it often seems. And perhaps this is why it is too much to expect a true end of anti-Semitic feelings. In the mirror of reality, of the unbeautiful world, it is hardly reassuring and requires much strength of character to look and see oneself.

CHAPTER ONE

HE had gone to sleep exhausted by the heat; his bones hurt. For a long time he lay there purposely seeking a dream that might draw him off to unconsciousness. And seeking it he fell asleep, and a dream arose.

He was in some sort of amusement park. A crowd was listening to a barker whose face was pouring perspiration. He moved away from the crowd and walked aimlessly. The ocean was nearby. Then before him stood a large carousel, strangely colored in green and purple patches. Somehow there were no people there. It was deserted for acres around him. And yet the carousel was moving. The brightly colored carriages, all empty, were going in a circle. And then they stopped, and went backwards. They stopped again and went forwards. He stood there perplexed, watching the shuttling of the carousel, and then he knew that underneath, below the ground, there was a gigantic machine operating: a factory, he realized. Something was being manufactured beneath the carousel, and trying to imagine what it was he grew frightened. The empty carousel kept going forwards and backwards, and he began moving away from it. Then for the first time he heard a noise coming from it, a growing sound, a cry . . . 'Aleese! Aleese! Aleese!'

With a shock he awoke. It had sounded like a woman. How sharp! He was panting. With open eyes he lay on his bed listening.

The night was quiet. A slow summer breeze was swaying the curtains pleasantly. He looked at his window and regretted having left it open so wide. Suddenly the cries came again. 'Aleese! Aleese!' His fleshy arms jerked down to his sides. He lay perfectly still. Again the sounds pierced his room. 'Aleese!' They

7

were coming from the street. Was he still dreaming? He tried lifting a leg. It worked. He got out of bed and walked barefoot out of the room and along the corridor to the front bedroom windows. Silently he raised the venetian blinds.

Near the lamp post across the street he could sense two moving figures. The cry went up again, but this time Mr Newman could make out what it said: *'Police! Police! Please, police!'* He strained to see through the darkness, and crouched very still at the window. A woman seemed to be out there struggling with what looked like a large man. Now Mr Newman could hear the man's voice. It was growling threateningly, drunkenly bass. The woman broke away from him now and ran into the street toward Mr Newman's house. On the manhole cover in the middle of the street the man caught up with her and slammed his arm against her head. The manhole cover clanked under his weight. As he held her she broke forth in a shrill tirade of something that sounded like Spanish. Probably Puerto Rican, Mr Newman decided. The man's sounds were English, however, he recognized with relief. The drunk's free arm came up again as though to strike at the woman and again she screamed for the police. But now she was pleading for them, weeping to the darkness around her. Mr Newman, twenty yards from her, could hear the frantic breath rushing out of her body as she screamed for the police. She turned in the direction of his window now. She must have noticed that his blinds had come up only a moment before. Mr Newman quickly stepped back into the room. *'Police!'* He thought of his bare feet; without his slippers he could not be expected to go out and stop this. Nobody else on the block was out there anyway. If he called the police the woman and the man would probably be gone by the time they arrived, and he would be embarrassed to explain why he had made such a fuss. The pair were struggling no more than ten feet from the edge of his little front lawn now. He could not see the woman's face

8

because the street light was behind her, but in the night, and awakened rudely from sleep, he thought he saw her eyes. The whites were bright against the dark skin, and she was darting helpless glances at his and all the other houses from which people were undoubtedly watching her. But he backed away from the window, the woman screaming 'Police! Police!' in her accent. He turned in the dark and went out of the room.

'Police!' In his bedroom he lowered his window until it was too far closed to allow anyone to creep in. Lying on his back he listened. The night was silent again. He waited a long time. From six blocks away the elevated grumbled and stamped on toward Manhattan. There was no sound from the street any more. In bed he shook his head, trying to imagine what sort of woman would be out at this time of night, and alone. Or if not alone, then with that kind of man. Possibly she was returning from a night shift and had been molested by the man, a stranger. Improbable. Her accent satisfied Mr Newman that she was abroad at night for no good purpose, and it somehow convinced him that she could take care of herself because she was used to this sort of treatment. Puerto Ricans were, he knew.

Exhausted, dull again, hardly realizing he had been awake at all, he closed his eyes and tried to sleep. Slowly his round little fingers opened and his lips parted and sucked like the lips of a fish, for his sharp nose could not pass enough air into him. As always he lay flat on his back with one hand resting on the rise of his belly, his short, slightly bowed legs stretched out with the toes tenting the sheet. Even in sleep he seemed to cling to his sense of propriety, for when the breeze died in a little while his hand gently folded the sheet away from his body and then moved back to its place on his warm belly. When he awakened there would hardly be a crease in the bedding and his reddish hair, trained flat from the part on the left side, would really not need combing.

9

CHAPTER TWO

THERE had been a time – until a few weeks ago – when he enjoyed emerging from his house in the morning. He would come out onto his high front porch with the quick vigor of a bird, and descending the brick stoop would scan his ten square feet of front lawn for any scraps of paper the night might have blown up. Then, rapidly picking up the rubbish and dropping it into his garbage can at the curb, he would give his house a quick but warm glance and head for the subway. He had a fast, forward-leaning way of walking, like certain dogs which come down a street looking neither right nor left. He was a man who seemed afraid of being seen loitering.

But when he stepped onto his porch this morning the heat struck his fair, childishly puffed cheeks, reminding him of his body and his trouble, and for a moment he felt weakened and afraid. He walked to the top of the stoop, and halted when he heard a crackling under his shoe. Bending way over from the waist he peered at the brick floor of the porch and lifted his shined, round-toed shoe and saw a piece of cellophane. He picked it up between two fingers and went down the stoop and along his little cement walk to the curb, where he opened the garbage can and deposited the cellophane. For a moment he stood smoothing his navy blue summer jacket down over his belly – which was beginning to make a coastline, as he said – and felt perspiration inside his starched collar. Blankly he looked at the house.

A stranger on the block could never have noticed any difference between Mr Newman's house and the others. They stood in a flat-topped line, attached two-story brick, with the garages built in beneath the high front porches. Before each house grew a slender elm which was neither thicker nor much thinner than its neighbor, all of them having been planted in the same week some seven years ago when the development was finished. To Mr Newman, however, there were certain vital differences. Standing for a moment beside his garbage can, he glanced up at his shutters which he had painted a light green. The other houses all had dark green shutters. Then his eye moved to his window screens, which he had hinged at the sides so that they opened like doors instead of swinging out from the top as the others on the block did. Many times he had wished, improvidently, that the house had been built of wood so that there would be more surface to paint. As it was, he could only work around his car which stood on concrete blocks in the garage. On Sundays before the war he would take the car out and go over it lightly with a waxed cloth, brush out the interior, and drive his mother to church. Without admitting it, however, he enjoyed the car much more now when it was on blocks, for it is well known that rust is a terrible menace to an unused machine. On these war Sundays he took the immaculate storage battery, which he kept in the basement, and installed it in the car and ran the engine for a few moments. And then he disconnected the battery and hauled it back into the cellar, and walked round the car looking for rust spots, and turned the wheels a little with his hands to keep the bearing grease mobile, and generally did each Sunday what the manufacturer had advised doing twice a year. At the end of the day he enjoyed washing his hands with Gre-Solvent, and sitting down to a good dinner, feeling the presence of his muscles and his good health.

Glancing at the garbage can now to be sure it was covered tightly, he walked down the street in his earnest way. But despite his even stride and the confident, straight-ahead set of his head, he felt his insides moving and to quiet himself he thought of his mother, who was sitting now in his kitchen waiting for the day maid to arrive and make her breakfast. She was paralyzed below the hips and spoke of nothing but pain and California. He tried to involve his mind in her, but as he neared the subway his abdomen became quite taut and he was glad for the necessity of halting a moment at the corner candy store where he bought his paper. He said good morning to the proprietor and paid his nickel, careful not to touch the man's hands with his own. He would not have been especially horrified to have touched them but he did not like the idea of it. He fancied a certain odor of old cooking coming from Mr Finkelstein. He did not want to touch the odor. Mr Finkelstein said good morning as usual and Mr Newman walked the few yards around the corner, paused an instant to firmly grasp the handrail of the subway stairs and made his way down.

He had another nickel ready for the turnstile and inserted it after expertly feeling for the slot, although had he seen fit to lower his head he could easily have made it out. He did not like to be seen lowering his head.

Coming onto the platform he turned left and strolled leisurely, noting as he went that as usual most of the people were crowded together at the platform's center. He always went to the front end – as they should if they had the sense to observe that the first car was always emptiest. When a stretch of some twenty yards lay between him and the waiting people, he gradually slowed and came to a halt beside a steel pillar. He turned toward it unobtrusively, and stood with his face a hand's width from the indented center of the steel I-beam.

With an acute squint he screwed the pupils of his eyes into focus. Raising and lowering his head he searched the white-painted surface of the pillar. Then his movements stopped. Someone had written here. As he read, his skin began to warm with anticipation. In a pencilled scrawl, hastily written between the arrival and departure of trains, was *Come LA 4-4409 beautifull and dumb*. As he had many times before, he stood wondering now whether this was actually an advertisement or a wishful joke. A breath of adventure touched him, and he visualized an apartment somewhere ... dark and scented with women ...

His eyes searched farther down. A well-drawn ear. Several √ √ marks. It was a fairly fruitful pillar, he felt. Often they were washed clean before he arrived in the morning. *My name IS NOT ELSIE* caught him for a moment and he shook his head and nearly smiled. How angrily Elsie – or whatever her name was – had written that. Why were they calling her Elsie? he wondered. And where was this Elsie now? Was she asleep somewhere? Or on her way to work. Was she happy now or regretful? Mr Newman felt a tie, an attachment with the people who wrote on these pillars, for it seemed to him that they said only what they meant. It was like opening someone's mail ...

His head stopped moving. Above his eyes was carefully printed, *Kikes started WAR*. Below it, *Kill kikes kill ki.* Apparently the author had been interrupted by the arrival of his train. Mr Newman swallowed and stared as though caught in the beam of a hypnotizing light. Above the fierce slogan stood the exclamation, *Fascists!*, with an arrow pointing down at the call to murder.

He turned from the pillar and stood looking down at the tracks. His heart had grown larger, his breathing came faster as a titillation of danger danced upon his mind. It was as though he had just seen a bloody fistfight. Around this pillar the air had witnessed a silent but terrible contest.. While above on the street the traffic had calmly moved and people had slept through the night, here below a wild current had flowed darkly and had left its marks and was gone.

He stood unmoving, caught. Nothing he ever read gripped him so powerfully as did these scrawled threats. To him they were a kind of mute record that the city automatically inscribed in her sleep; a secret newspaper publishing what the people really thought, undiluted by fears of propriety and selfish interest. It was like finding the elusive eyes of the city and staring into her true mind. The first rumblings of an approaching train roused him.

As to a severed limb he turned again toward the pillar, and stopped when two women smelling of cherry soap halted near him. He glanced over at them. Why, he wondered, must these things always be written by such obviously ignorant hands? These two women, now — they share that slogan-writer's indignation and yet it is left for the lowest people to step forward and spell out the truth. Air began to whirl and rise around his legs as the train thrust like a piston into the cylindrical station. Mr Newman stepped back a yard and his elbow brushed the dress of one of the women. The cherry smell was strong for an instant, and he was glad she was a well-kept woman. He liked to travel with people who were well kept.

The doors hissed open and the women went in. Mr Newman waited an instant and then followed carefully, remembering how a week before he had started in before the doors had been fully withdrawn and had collided with them. As he reached up and grasped an overhead porcelain handle his face grew pinker at the memory of that moment. His blood began to pump rapidly. He brought his arm down as the train started, and drew his white cuff out under the edge of his jacket sleeve. The train sped toward Manhattan. Relentlessly, mercilessly it carried him toward that island, and he closed his eyes for a moment as though to contain himself and his fear.

His paper was still tucked under his arm. Remembering it, he opened it and pretended to read. There was no banner headline. Everything crawled beneath his eyes. Holding the paper as though engrossed in it, he looked over its edge at the passenger seated in front of him. Ukrainian-Polish, he registered without thinking. He studied the man as well as he could. Worker's

14

cap. Soiled windbreaker. He could not make out the man's eyes. Probably small, he supplied. Ukrainian-Polish . . . taciturn, hardworking, inclined toward strong drink and stupidity.

His eyes moved to the man sitting next to the worker. Negro. His eyes continued to the next, and held there. Contriving to move a step closer, he lost all sense of his surroundings. There sat a man whose type to him was like a rare clock to a collector. The man was staidly reading the *Times*. His skin was fair, the back of his neck flat and straight, his hair was probably blond beneath the new hat, and on squinting, Mr Newman caught a glimpse of the Hindenburg bags under the subject's eyes. The mouth he could not see clearly, so he supplied it – broad and full-lipped. He relaxed with a certain satisfaction that always came to him when he played this secret game going to work. Probably he alone on this train knew that this gentleman with the square head and the fair skin was neither Swede, nor German, nor Norwegian, but a Jew.

He glanced again at the Negro and stared. Some day, he thought – as he always did when a Negro face confronted him – some day he must look into the various types of niggers. It was academic, he knew, for he did not need the information for his work, but still . . .

A hand touched his shoulder. Instantly his body stiffened as he turned.

'Hullo, Newman. Just looked up and seen you.'

With the expression of affable condescension which changed his face whenever he encountered Fred, he asked, 'How was it in your house, warm last night?'

'We always get a breeze through the back windows.' Fred lived next door. 'Didn't you get a breeze?' he asked, as though he lived in a breezier part of town.

'Oh certainly,' Mr Newman said, 'I slept with a blanket.'

'I'm putting a cot down cellar,' Fred said, prodding New-

15

man's arm. 'Now that I got it all finished off down there it's cool as hell.'

Newman considered. 'Probably be damp down there.'

'Not since it's finished off,' Fred said, definitely.

Mr Newman looked away inconclusively. For one thing Fred worked in the maintenance department of the same company, although in a different building, and wore his overalls to work as well as his overall manners. As he often did when confronted by Fred, Mr Newman felt an irritated resolve to have his own cellar finished off whether he could afford it or not. He could never understand how this lumbering boar could be worth twice what he was to the same company, considering the importance of his own work and the exceptional nature of his talents. Neither did he enjoy being seen on the subway with Fred, who invariably jabbed him with his finger when he spoke.

'How'd you like the row on the street last night?' Fred asked. There was a suppressed smile of the risqué on his heavy jaw, which was attached to his face by two long, deep creases on either side.

'I heard it. How'd it wind up?' Mr Newman asked, his handsome lower lip protruding judiciously as it did when he became intent.

'Oh, we went out and got Petey to bed. Boy, he was crocked.'

'Was that Ahearn out there?' he whispered in surprise.

'Yeh, he was comin' home with a load on and he seen this Spic woman. She wasn't bad from what I seen of her.' Fred had a habit of glancing behind him as he spoke.

'Did the police come?'

'Naa, we kicked her off the block and put Pete to bed.'

The train stopped at a station and they were separated for a moment. When the doors closed Fred came back to Mr Newman. They stood silent for several minutes. Mr Newman kept looking up at Fred's hairy wrist which was very thick and probably powerful. He remembered how well Fred used to bowl last summer. It was strange how sometimes he enjoyed being with Fred and Fred's gang on the block and then at times like this could not bear him around. He remembered a picnic they had had at Marine Park and the fight Fred had . . .

'How do you like what's goin' on?' Fred's smile had gone but the two long creases remained like scars in his cheeks. He searched Newman's face with his puffed slit eyes.

'Going on how?' Newman asked.

'The neighborhood. They'll be movin' niggers in on us next.'

'That's the way it goes, I guess.'

'Everybody's been talking about the new element movin' around.'

'That so.'

'Only reason most of the block moved way out here was to get away from that element, and now they're trailin' us out here. You know that Finkelstein?'

'The candy store?'

'He's got all his relatives movin' into the house on the corner. The left-hand side next to the store.' He glanced behind him.

This was what fascinated him about Fred. You wished he would speak more softly, but you somehow wanted him to go on for he said things you felt and dared not say. A foreboding of some sort of action always descended on him as Fred spoke. It was the same feeling he got around the pillars – something was building up inside the city, something thunderous and exhilarating.

'We're thinking of gettin' up a meeting. Jerry Buhl was talking to Petey about it.'

'I thought that outfit was out.'

'Out, nothin',' Fred said proudly, drawing down the corners of his mouth. In the mornings especially his lids were so puffed they nearly closed over his eyes. 'Soon as the war's over

17

and the boys get back you're goin' to see fireworks like there never was around here. We're just layin' low till the boys come home. This meetin' looks like the first start, y'know? Can't tell, the war might be over any day, the way it looks. We want to be on our feet and ready. Y'know?' He seemed to need Newman's confirmation, for his expression became uncertain.

'Uh huh,' Newman muttered, waiting for him to speak on.

'You want to come? I'd take you along in the car.'

'I'll leave the meetings to you fellows,' Mr Newman smiled encouragingly, as though deferring to Fred's powerful build. But actually he did not like the type of people at those meetings. Half of them were cracked and the other half looked like they hadn't had a new suit of clothes in years. 'I'm not much good for meetings.'

Fred nodded, unimpressed. His tongue slid over his cigar-worn teeth and he looked out a window at the lights rocketing by.

'All right,' he said, blinking his eyes, rather hurt, 'I thought I'd ask you. We just want to clean out the neighborhood, that's all. I thought you'd be interested. All we gotta do is make it hot for them and they'll pack up.'

'Who?' Mr Newman prompted avidly, his round face pleasantly interested.

'The Jews on our block. And then we'll help the boys across the avenue with the Spics. There'll be pushcarts on the streets before you know it.' He seemed indignant at Newman. He had a pocked chin which now showed little red bumps.

Again the titillating of danger caught Mr Newman. He was about to reply when he looked down and saw the Hindenburg Jew studying him. The man seemed about to get up and push him or something. He turned to Fred.

'I'll let you know. I may have to work late Thursday,' he said quietly, turning his back on the Jew. The train was coming into his station. Fred touched his arm and said OK. The doors opened and Mr Newman quickly stepped onto the platform. Instantly upon facing in the direction of his stairway his body began again to tremble inside. The train pulled away and he walked toward his exit, careful about his distance from the platform edge, and climbed the stairs.

On the sunny sidewalk he stood still for a moment and caught his wind. As he raised his arm to press his Panama more firmly onto his head, a cool drop of sweat fell from his armpit to his ribs. Every day of the past weeks he had halted on this corner, dreading what might await him in the office, and as always during these pauses his skin became creamy in the heat of the sun and his imagining. Walking neatly now, watchfully along the already baking sidewalk, he tried to think of his block and the houses all identical standing there like pickets on a fence. The memory of their sameness soothed his yearning for order, and he walked toward his building judiciously gathering the full force of his wits.

CHAPTER THREE

WITH a few aged exceptions he had hired every one of the seventy girls who worked at the seventy desks on the sixteenth floor of that building.

A block away from it he looked distracted, his lips moving spasmodically as though to find a place of compòsure on his face. Passing through the Gothic entrance of the Corporation's skyscraper his lips seemed to die and become still; as the elevator lifted him upward his lips hardened, and when the doors opened and he stepped out onto the sixteenth floor his mouth was set as severely as if he were refusing food.

The transformation was much older than his recent fear. For twenty years and more the mammoth size of the company had forced it upon him. He knew that the company owned a hundred skyscrapers like this, in nearly every state and foreign nation, and the thought of its size had depressed him, had become a weight upon him whenever the possibility arose that he might have to defend himself against it. He had seen other men trying to defend themselves against it, and he had seen them crushed, and so he stepped onto the sixteenth floor with his features set in a mask of responsibility, as though to display to anyone who might be watching that he was already concerned about the morning's work. It was the face of a pastor moving toward the altar on a high occasion, and the girls at their desks responded by glancing away and hushing as the ceremony was about to begin.

He crossed the width of the desk-rowed floor and entered his office. Immediately on hanging up his hat a profound irritation began scratching inside him. He went to his desk and sat down. As though about to utter a curse, he refused to look either right or left and kept his eyes lowered. A horrible joke had been played upon him, and he was the one who had played it.

Several years ago, in his zeal to serve his employers as they had never before been served, he had conceived of an office with glass walls to be set on one side of the floor. The arrangement was adopted, and from then on he could work at his desk and simply look up to tell at a glance whether the whole floor was in order. When a girl had a question to ask she could no longer leave her desk, make a half-hour detour through the ladies' room and eventually arrive at his office to ask him a point of information. Now she need only raise her hand and in a moment he would be at her side. The innovation had cured one of the office's most serious ills. For he had noticed that no sooner had one girl left her desk than another would follow, and by noon the floor was restless with the coming and going of a railroad terminal.

His glass-enclosed office had been a great satisfaction to him. It was the thing he had done here. It had drawn comment from a vice-president some nine years ago. Often during the depression he felt sure that his salary had not been cut only because the higher officials realized that the kind of man who could originate such an idea should not be penalized under any circumstances.

But lately it had become a terrorizing experience to sit in full view of the stenographers. For when he raised his eyes he could see nothing through the glass. At this moment someone might be beckoning to him out there, and getting no response. His days were spent in walking up and down the rows of desks as though on errands of importance, while in fact he was desperately trying to be where he could be summoned by voice. So he sat behind his desk this morning waiting for a respectable amount of time to elapse before venturing out on the floor on one of his weighty errands. And he knew that the girls were laughing at him for the pretense. But he would go out among them anyway. It was horrible but he would go, for as the weeks passed he felt the ineffable shape of a gigantic blunder forming on this floor. A mistake on the part of certain girls here could mount up until, by the time it had passed through the labyrinthine intestine of the Corporation, it might well explode in a catastrophe that would leave him standing on the sidewalk downstairs, out of a job.

Pretending to study a sheaf of papers on his desk, he was about to rise and head toward the northwest corner of the floor when the phone buzzer vibrated his desk. It was toned down very soft so as not to disturb the girls. He picked up the phone just as though it were quite ordinary for him to receive a call five minutes after he had arrived in the morning. But it was not ordinary and his throat was already closing against the quickening beat of his heart.

'Mr Newman.'

'Miss Keller speaking.'

'Yes, Miss Keller.'

'Mr Gargan would like to see you in his office. Right away, if you can. He's got an early appointment.'

'I'll be right in.'

He hung up the phone. It was impossible to deny that he was frightened. He got up and walked the length of the floor to a door painted cream. Through this he entered Miss Keller's office. She nodded him past her with a bright smile, and he came to another cream door. This he opened and walked into Mr Gargan's office. Mr Gargan was sitting behind his long desk with his back to a wide window which looked out upon the river. Mr Gargan had a full head of black hair, parted in the center, and it shone under the morning light from the window. The only signs of Mr Gargan's importance were the two photographs on his desk; no one else was permitted to have any personal objects on his desk. One picture was of Mr Gargan's small motorboat, which he kept at Oyster Bay, Long Island, and the other was of his two schnauzer dogs. In the background behind the dogs was his six-room house where he lived with his wife near Elizabeth, New Jersey. When Mr Newman entered Mr Gargan was doing nothing but looking at the river. He turned to Mr Newman.

'Morning,' he said, and nothing more.

'How are you this morning, Mr Gargan?'

'Pretty good. Have a chair.'

Mr Newman sat in a leather chair beside Mr Gargan's desk. He did not like to sink down so deep. It always distressed him to lose height. Mr Gargan picked up a newspaper which he seemed to have been reading and tossed it over to Mr Newman's side of the desk.

'How do you like that news?'

Mr Newman, anxious to give an intelligent reply, instantly bent toward the paper. 'I hadn't noticed the paper this morning. What . . .?'

'You can't read it, can you?'

Mr Newman stopped moving. He looked at Mr Gargan's eyes which were piercing now and deeply angered.

'Why in the world don't you get yourself a pair of glasses? Good God, man!' Mr Gargan exclaimed, exasperated.

Mr Newman heard nothing but understood everything. Sweat was pouring from his body.

'Can you see me now, for God's sake?'

Anger stung Mr Newman. 'I'm not that bad, I'm only . . .'

'But you are that bad. You are. I doubt that you can see me clearly.' Mr Gargan leaned forward challengingly.

'I do, I see you. I'm only a little . . .'

'Did you give this Miss Kapp a personal interview? The one you hired last Friday?'

They were speaking faster.

'I always give everybody a personal interview. I never took anybody on without one.'

23

'Then you can't be seeing me clearly now.' Mr Gargan leaned back, convinced.

Mr Newman strained to see him. He did look a little blurred around the mouth, but the light in here was shining into his eyes . . .

'Miss Kapp is obviously not our type of person, Newman. I mean she's obvious. Her name must be Kapinsky or something.'

'But she can't be, I . . .'

'I can't sit here arguing with you . . .'

'No sir, I'm not arguing. I just can't believe she . . .'

'You can't *see*, Newman. Will you tell me why in the world you don't get glasses?' Suddenly Mr Gargan's tone changed. 'It's nothing serious, is it? I don't mean to be . . .'

'No, I just haven't had the time, that's all. Drops and everything. It puts you out for a day or two . . .' Mr Newman tilted his head to the side and started to smile away the importance of his failure to get glasses.

'Well, take the time. Because you know what this kind of thing does. It throws the whole office off, having somebody like that around. The girls spend half their time in the rest room talking about her. And you know the job it is getting rid of them. I don't want it to happen again. We just aren't set up to take that kind of person.'

'Oh, I know . . .'

Gargan broadened his neck, leaned his head closer to Newman, and smiled charmingly.

'Well, don't let it happen again, will you?'

'I won't. I'll attend to her today.'

'That's all right, I'll take care of it this time,' he said, satisfied, and rose. 'I think I can do a better job of explaining. The wrong kind is liable to take off out of here and make some kind of a story for the newspapers or something. I'll attend to it.'

Mr Newman nodded. They were together again as of old – in

24

league, as it were. The less said the better now. He felt a
certain importance and instead of smiling with the joy that was
in him, he peaked his brows. At the door Mr Gargan looked
down at him.

'Because we really don't want that happening. You know
what I mean.'

'Oh, certainly. I'll see the doctor tonight.'

'Take the day if you have to.'

'Too much work on the desk. I'll go about four.'

'Fine.' The door opened under Mr Gargan's hand. 'You
don't feel it's anything personal, do you?'

'Oh, God, no,' Mr Newman laughed.

Smiling, he made his rapid, short-stepped way through Miss
Keller's office and out onto the floor. Once out of the office the
feeling of comradeship he had known with Mr Gargan dropped
away, and with it his smile. He walked quietly to his cubicle
and entered. He sat a long time staring. It was impossible to
work. Finally he moved, brought his watch up to his nose and
studied it. Only seven hours to go. The watch slid out of his
hand and hit the desk. He picked it up and held it to his ear
and then studied the crystal, which was slimy with perspiration.

CHAPTER FOUR

HE did not go at four. He waited until five.

The optometrist's office was one flight up over a fancy leather goods store. Mr Newman found the large square waiting-room empty. At one end of the room was a doorway masked by a large black curtain. Behind this the examinations were made. He sat on a chair beside the wide store window at the front of the waiting-room, and with his second handkerchief of the day wiped the sweatband of his hat and set it on his head again, horizontally, as was his preference. (His skull being flat at the sides he could never wear a hat tilted, as it always slid over to the horizontal after a few minutes anyway. In time he had come to believe, and obdurately advised others, that tilting a hat on the head put it out of shape.)

Carefully so as not to dampen the crease in his trousers he laid his hands upon his thighs and through the wide window looked down toward the street below. The heat of the day had dulled him. For many many days now he had become parched with dread at the prospect of sitting like this and waiting for the optometrist. But like a plant to the sun, he rose to occasions once the light of authority was directed upon him. Gargan had said to come here and he was here, and the horror that lay within him could not rise and take shape so long as he kept on doing as he was told. He waited, staring through the window and seeing blurs. Thoughts formed chains leading away and he followed, remembering the men who had bucked off for themselves only to flounder about, while he had stayed on with the company, underpaid but dignified, and had worked right through the depression, right through the war. Because he had toed the line, done his duty, carried off the ceaseless indignities that came from above. He was safe, would always be. Perhaps, when this whole monstrous war was over, he might even find a woman and get married. Perhaps his mother might be persuaded to go to her brother's in Syracuse. Perhaps . . .

As he sat in the quiet room staring down at a street that was hazy to his eyes, a rare but persistent vision returned to him – the shape of a woman. She was large, almost fat, and she had no face that he could make out, but he knew she was congenial to him. She was an old inhabitant of his mind and seemed to arise before him most readily at times like this when duty pressed him. And her body in his sight now recalled, as it always did, the first time she had come to him. He was sitting in a trench near the border of France and he had been sitting there in water for three days. Colonel Taffrey came into the trench that night and said they were to go into attack when morning came, and then went away. It was during those few hours before the dawn that she formed herself for Mr Newman, her thighs and her hollows nearly touching his hand. And when the time came and he climbed the parapet he swore to keep his longing for her and all she meant to him, for it was the most beautiful desire he had known in his life. If he ever got home he would find a good job and work until he had a nice house, like the ones they advertised, and then he would have her, a woman with her form and her congeniality. But when he got home he sat with his mother in their parlor in Brooklyn, and she told him quietly and with the shades drawn that she was losing the motion of her legs . . .

Voices in the room startled him into turning. He could see no one. Now he realized the voices were coming from behind the black curtain at the far end of the room. His ears were growing frighteningly sharp . . .

He turned back to the window. His body was throbbing. What would happen, he wondered, if a man, a man like himself simply walked out into the street and disappeared? Never arrived again where he was expected. Simply moved around the country searching for happiness, for ... well, for the right woman? Supposing right now, through that door ...

A presence entered the room. He turned quickly to see the optometrist coming toward him. Someone – a woman? – was going out the door. He stood up, wishing to God that he could be happy, and forgot whether to call the optometrist doctor or mister.

'Well! I've been wondering what's kept you, Mr Newman. Managed to get along all right?'

'Well enough. Are my ...?'

'Been ready three weeks now,' the optometrist's voice was coming from around a desk across the room. Mr Newman walked to it and saw the man fingering through a drawer filled with envelopes in which glasses were packed. He came to Mr Newman's and picked them out and drew them from the envelope.

'Here, sit down.' The optometrist indicated a chair in front of the desk and started to draw one up for himself.

'I'm in a hurry, doctor, I ...'

'Only take a minute, I'll see if they fit you.'

'It's all right. I tried the frames the last time,' he said impatiently. The optometrist started to speak again but Mr Newman had taken the glasses from his hand and was saying, 'I really have to go right away. They were eighteen, weren't they?' He handed the optometrist two ten-dollar bills which he had rolled together in the office.

The optometrist looked at him, then turned and went into the examination room with the bills in his hand.

There was a round mirror on the wall beside the desk. The optometrist had hardly disappeared behind the black curtains when Mr Newman stepped silently to the mirror and put on the glasses. He could see nothing but a watery world of mercury with the colors of his blue tie washed into it. Hearing the optometrist's step behind the curtain he pulled the glasses off his face and thrust them into his handkerchief pocket.

'I've been thinking about your case,' the optometrist said, as he handed Mr Newman his change.

'You have, eh?' Mr Newman said, suppressing his new interest.

As he spoke, the optometrist leaned over and from the desk drawer took a little box and picked two cupped pieces of plastic out of it. He placed them in the palm of one hand and held the hand flat open before his stomach, and leaning back, said, 'The time will come when nobody will wear exterior glasses, Mr Newman . . .'

'I know, but . . .'

'You haven't given them a fair trial. A man as interested in the cosmetic angle of glasses owes it to himself to give contact lenses a fair trial.'

As though he had heard this many times, Mr Newman shifted to go, and said, 'I wore them every night for four weeks. I just can't stand them.'

'That's what a lot of people say till they get used to them,' the optometrist almost whined. 'The eyeball naturally resents any foreign material touching it, but the eye is a muscle, and muscles . . .'

The man's overbearing manner forced Mr Newman toward the door. 'You don't have to . . .'

'I'm not selling you anything, I'm just saying . . .

'I can't stand them,' Mr Newman said, shaking his head with real sadness. 'When I put them in, every time I blink my eyes I get upset. It doesn't seem natural to be sticking them into your eyes every morning and putting in that liquid every three hours . . . I . . . well, it just unnerves me. They seem to *move* in my eyes.'

'But they can't move . . .

'Well they do.' He spoke now with some of the terrible disappointment he had suffered during the weeks he had sat in his room trying to accustom his eyes to the touch of the lenses. He had walked alone at night with them in his eyes and once he had gone to the movies to find out if he could get his mind off them while he had them in. 'I even went to the movies wearing them,' he was saying, 'I tried everything, but I just can't take my mind off them when I've got them on. I mean you touch your eyelid and there's no sensation under it. It . . . it unnerves me.'

'Well,' said the optometrist, closing his palm over the tiny cups and lowering his hand, 'you're the first one with that reaction.'

'I've heard of others,' Mr Newman said. 'If these things ever get so millions of people use them you'll find out there are people who can't bear them.'

'Well, enjoy your glasses anyway,' the optometrist said, walking him to the door.

'Thank you,' Mr Newman said and opened the door.

'See?' the optometrist laughed, dropping one of the contact lenses to the floor. 'Bounces like a ping-pong ball.' He stood pointing at the lens which had bounced and was clattering to a stop on the floor.

Luckily he found a seat on the subway. It would have been beyond his strength to stand all the way to Queens tonight. In his spasm of excitement the odor of the packed passengers, to which he was peculiarly sensitive, would have sickened him. Even seated he felt weak. The new glasses lay in his pocket like a small living animal. As though racing with the homeward rush of the train he kept trying to imagine an alternative to wearing glasses, but the closer he came to his station the more inevitable became the realization that without them he would soon find himself unable even to leave his house. To relieve his anxiety he tried to summon up the image of the faceless woman in his recurring vision of happiness, but she faded as soon as she appeared and all he could see clearly and most constantly was the mirror over the sink in his bathroom.

He got out at his station and climbed to the street, seeing only the mirror. Without noticing Mr Finkelstein, who was sitting in front of his candy store taking the warm night air, he crossed over to his side of the street and turned up the path that bisected his tiny front lawn. The screen door was unlocked and the door was open. Forgetting to take off his hat he passed his mother where she sat by the radio in the living room, and went upstairs rapidly, for he knew these stairs. He called good evening down to her as he entered the bathroom and turned on the light. He set his hat upon the flat rim of the bathtub and took out the glasses. The stems opened stiffly in his hands and he was careful not to force them. He put the glasses on and looked into the mirror. The mercurial blur swirled before his eyes again, grained by the colors of his tie. He stared into this mass of silver. He blinked his eyes and looked again. On the right side he began to see the frame of the mirror. It became very sharp. Now the left side cleared. The whole frame of the mirror became astonishingly clear, so much so that he forgot his purpose and looked around at the bathroom. It suddenly seemed as though he had let out a breath which he had been holding for many years. The bristles of his toothbrush . . . how definite they were! The tile on the floor, the weave of the towels . . . And then he remembered . . .

A long time he stood staring at himself, at his forehead, his chin, his nose. It took many moments of detailed inspection of his parts before he could see himself whole. And he felt as though rising off the floor. The beating of his heart caused his head to nod slightly in rhythm. Saliva filled a little pool in his throat and he coughed. In the mirror in his bathroom, the bathroom he had used for nearly seven years, he was looking at what might very properly be called the face of a Jew. A Jew, in effect, had gotten into his bathroom. The glasses did just what he had feared they would do to his face, but this was worse because this was real. It was shockingly worse than at the optometrist's three weeks ago when he had tried on the frames alone. Then they seemed to make him more like the Hindenburg Jew type, for he did have flat vertical cheeks and a squarish head and very fair skin, and – most telling – suggestions of bags under his eyes, the stern Hindenburg pouches. And that would have been bad but not impossible, not like this. Now with the lenses magnifying his eyeballs, the bags, being colorless, lost prominence and the eyes fairly popped, glared. The frames seemed to draw his flat, shiny-haired skull lower and set off his nose, so that where it had once appeared a trifle sharp it now beaked forth from the nosepiece. He took the glasses off and slowly put them on again to observe the distortion. He tried his smile. It was the smile of one who is forced to pose before a camera, but he held it and it was no longer his smile. Under such bulbous eyes it was a grin, and his teeth which had always been irregular now seemed to insult the smile and warped it into a cunning, insincere mockery of a smile, an expression whose attempt at simulating joy was belied, in his opinion, by the Semitic prominence of his nose, the bulging set of his eyes, the listening posture of his ears. His face was drawn forward, he fancied, like the face of a fish.

He took the glasses down from his face. Now he could see less clearly than ever and his eyes roved dizzily for a moment. He walked weak-kneed out of the bathroom along the corridor to the closet where he hung up his jacket, then down the stairs into the living room. His mother, with the Brooklyn *Eagle* in her lap, had turned on the bridge lamp behind her, which she did only after he came in at night, and sat looking at him in the doorway waiting to start the short evening conversation that was equivalent to hello.

He could smell his dinner on the stove. He knew where every

32

piece of furniture stood and how much it had cost and how long it would be before he would have to paint the ceiling again. It was his house, his home, and this old woman sitting in the wheelchair by the silent radio was his mother, and yet he moved as stiffly as if he were a stranger here. He sat on the couch before her and they talked.

'Did you hang up your jacket? Was it very hot in the city today? Did they push you in the train? Were you busy? How is Mr Gargan?'

And he answered the questions and went in and ate his supper which the day maid had left for him. Tasting nothing and digesting nothing, he finished nothing. When he was through he washed his face at the kitchen sink and dried it with a towel which he kept down there for that purpose. Strangely, all he could think of was how clearly he had seen the bristles of his toothbrush. He took his paper of the previous night which he had not finished – he always finished last night's before starting on tonight's – and sat again on the couch under the lamp, and put on his glasses. Feeling pressure around his arms he slipped off his black sleeve garters and placed them beside him. His mother called his name. He looked up and turned his full face to her. She studied him, gradually leaning forward in her chair. He smiled weakly, just as he did when he bought a new suit.

'Why,' she laughed at last, 'you almost look like a Jew.'

He laughed with her, feeling that his teeth were sticking out.

'Couldn't you get the rimless kind?'

'I tried them on. They all do the same thing to me. These are better than any on that account.'

'I don't suppose anyone will notice,' she said, and picked up her *Eagle* and held it high to catch the light.

'I guess not,' he said, and picked up his *Eagle*. His body was wet and his face dry and cool. A breeze was moving through the house from the back yard. From the street came a quick swell

33

of children's shouts which faded as they chased each other away. Annoyed, he exchanged a scandalized look with his mother at this infraction of the block's peaceful tone. The traditional feel of the moment was like a breath of sanity, reassuring him. He turned to his paper and for the first time ever, it seemed, he could read it comfortably. Ordinarily, because his eyes had tired so quickly, he studied through little else but the lead story about the war, often losing his way among memories of his own bleak year in France. Tonight, however, he even delved into the little squibs at the bottom of the pages. And one of these he read perhaps five times. It was a short note. It said that vandals had invaded a Jewish cemetery the night before and overturned three headstones and marked the swastika over others. Reading it engrossed him as detective stories once had. There was a tang of violence to the story, the same threat of dark deeds and ruthless force that flowed out to him from the subway pillars. His eyes kept massaging the two paragraphs as though to draw out the last wave of emotion from them.

A deep stillness settled upon him, the tides of his body seemed to settle in a glassy pool. And his dream of the carousel flowered in his mind. '*Police! Police!*' He saw the empty carriages moving forward, then suddenly backward, then forward again. What in the world was being manufactured under the ground there? What had he been thinking to dream such a thing? In his mind's eye he got into one of the empty carriages, a large ornate yellow swan. He rode forward, then was pulled back, then forward ... He could feel the hum and power of engines under him below the ground. A dark texture of fear flapped upon his neck and in anger he banished the carousel and concentrated on the paper ... the editorial commending the fire department, another about morale, then a story about diamonds as they were used in the making of war equipment. But as he read, the words dropped out of his head and all that remained was a vision of tombstones toppling and vandals with

34

crowbars and heavy irons in their hands breaking marble Stars of David in the dirt.

When his mother had finished her *Eagle* she rolled her chair over to him. He was asleep. She shook him. He opened the couch for her and helped her to bed. Then he went upstairs and got undressed. His hat remained on the rim of the bathtub. It had never before spent the night out of its oval box.

CHAPTER FIVE

THE next morning he went to work as usual, returned home, had his dinner, and went to bed at his accustomed early hour. The second day passed, and the third. On the fourth day, in the afternoon, he sat at his desk behind the glass walls of his office and felt even the smallest spasm of glee. It was a rare mood for him.

No one had noticed anything different about him. This alone would have been enough to lift the heavy clothing of fear in which he had lived for so long. But there were other things; new and strong sensations had begun to vibrate in his quiet world. For three days he had been interviewing girls for the job just vacated by Miss Kapp – née Kapinsky – and although several of the applicants might have satisfied Mr Newman in the old days, now he turned them all down. He could see so sharply now that he wanted to present Mr Gargan with something unusual, something which, in a sense, would represent the apotheosis of his powers of selection. The rhythms of his body quickened as though to a challenge – his job itself seemed new. Besides, he felt a new admiration – almost a feeling of brotherhood – for Mr Gargan now. For the man had forced him to see, had taken things in hand and made him shake off the misery of his existence. The girl he hired would make up for all his misconduct of the past, including the hiring of the Kapinsky person. The girl had to be perfect.

More so, since for the past two days Mr George Lorsch had been spending a great many hours in the building. Mr Lorsch was the vice-president of the company in charge of operations. His picture often appeared in the society pages of the newspapers. And because he spent only a few busy days of the year in the building, inspecting and going over the efficiency of the various departments, Mr Newman could easily imagine Mr Gargan's gratitude at the hiring of an exceptional employee at this particular time. For it was Mr Lorsch who, according to well founded rumor, had laid down the original specifications for the type of person to be employed by the company. The man never walked onto a floor without thoughtfully scanning the girls as he made his way from office to office. In the past two days he had twice looked squarely into Mr Newman's face as he passed the cubicle and once had smiled in at him. Mr Newman bent to the quest for the perfect girl.

He looked down at the three remaining job applications on his desk. The name at the top of one form pleased him. Gertrude Hart, age thirty-six, three years of high school. Unmarried, Episcopalian. Born in Rochester, New York. He called the receptionist's desk through his phone and asked for Gertrude Hart to be sent in.

She arrived before his desk quite strangely. Girls applying to him rarely smelled even of cologne; her perfume hung heavy in the air around her. Never did they arrive with flowers in their hair; she had a real pink rose pinned atop her upswept brown crest. And yet she was stately, quite erect and refined. She was resting her hands loosely and gracefully upon the chair back as she stood there looking at him, and she had a way of lounging on one hip that was not suggestive, but only a posture of abounding ease. Most startling of all – even above that black and glossy dress – was her smile, which raised her left eyebrow a fraction higher than the other: without uncurving her full lips she was smiling. Mr Newman heard his voice saying, 'Please sit down.'

His stomach twitched as she swung closer to him and sat beside his desk. When she rested her arm on the edge of the top he went dry, as though she had reached over and smoothed his face, for his desk was as personal and alive a part of him as a member of his body. Suddenly he was aware of the astonishing curve of her legs and her thighs, one of which was touching his desk. His neck, his chest, his arms felt bloated.

He looked down as though to study her application form. The words on the sheet turned grey and then vanished. Not daring to look up at her, he tried to remember what her face had looked like. It further astonished him, now as he stared at the application form, that he had not taken in any facts about her face. She was like the woman of his vision – an odor and thighs and an erect back. And he looked up and found her face.

'How long were you with this Markwell company?'

She spoke. He heard nothing after her first phrase. 'Well, I was there about three years and then . . .'

Rochester! He gaped at her mouth forming the horrible stiff lipped drawl of Brooklyn. The shiny black dress that had seemed to sheathe the body of an unapproachably dignified woman from upstate now became a specially bought get-up for this interview; now it seemed to have cost about five ninety-five.

She kept talking. And gradually another reversal of impression shook him. Despite her snarl of an accent she really was dignified. For the first time he was able to inspect her face. What intrigued him was the arch of her left eyebrow. It had made her seem on the point of smiling, but now he knew she was not smiling. She was studying him, and somewhere in her brown eyes he had lost control of the interview.

She stopped talking, her eyebrow remaining relentlessly raised. He got to his feet and stood behind his chair – something he had never done in the presence of an applicant. But he could not direct things with his eyes on a level with hers.

She had a long face, he saw now, and it was made to seem longer by the upswept pile of hair. But it was not a thin face. The lips were full – and red – and the neck was broad and it rounded softly into the side curves of the jaw. The upper lids of the deep-set eyes were naturally dark and he imagined that

38

when she slept her eyes looked slightly popped. Her forehead however, was what distracted him when he tried to decide about her face. It was so high and it curved out to such a width of powdered skin that her hair seemed almost to be receding from it; he kept trying to destroy the feeling that her forehead was occupying the whole office.

But for the forehead, he thought, she was quite beautiful. He had not met such a woman in his life, and yet he knew her for the effect she would have on him, for he had dreamed part of her – the part that heated him and broke into the even rhythm of his breathing. The part of her that had made the interview personal instantly on her entrance . . . The thing that now made him so certain that she was accessible to him. She was. He knew it.

'Have you ever used an electric typewriter?' he asked, as though it were of terrible moment to him.

'Once in a while we had a chance to, but there was only one in the whole office. It wasn't like this place,' she said with some little awe. And indicating 'this place,' she turned her head toward the floor of girls behind her. Mr Newman stopped any movement. She turned her face full to him again and he walked over to the filing cabinet, from where he could again see her profile. She waited a respectful moment, as though to give him time to look into a drawer, but hearing no sound she jerked her head to see him standing there looking down at her.

Her eyebrow lowered abruptly. Mr Newman quickly returned to his chair at the desk and sat down as her face flamed.

For a long moment he did not dare raise his eyes to hers. He knew she was watching and he kept his expression immobile. Not a glimmer of his indignation and his disappointment so much as reddened his skin.

'As you probably know,' he said complacently, 'we must have people with electric typing experience. I assumed you had it.'

He looked up with his cultivated air of dismissal. She turned her head around extravagantly toward the floor full of girls typing at standard machines and then, in her own time, looked at him and waited.

'We're replacing those as fast as possible,' he explained. 'The war's held up production on them, but we intend to use them exclusively in this department . . .'

His brave words collapsed at the warping of her face. Her lips had parted and her brows peaked upward slightly and she seemed either about to implore him or to spit in his face, he wasn't sure which.

'I can run one perfect with a day's practice. There's nothing to running them if you already know typing as good as me.' She looked theatrical, he thought, leaning over his desk that way.

'We prefer people who . . .'

Her smooth pink chin was closing in toward him. 'I was born Episcopalian, Mr Newman,' she said sibilantly, and a furious little splotch of red appeared on her skin next to her nose.

There was nothing in what she said that was new to him. It was a standard speech which he had heard many times before (except that most of them chose to be Unitarians – on their way up in the elevator). And yet he felt his heart growing cold as he stared at her furious face. A fright was coming over him and he did not know why. There was something in her eyes . . . in the way she sat so angrily confident waiting for him to reply. She was not moving, glaring at him . . . The intimacy . . . that's what frightened him . . . yes, the intimacy was new. Her malevolence was intimate. She sat there as though she knew everything about him, as though . . .

She was taking him for a Jew.

His lips parted. He wanted to run out of the office, and then he wanted to hit at her. She must not do that with her eyes!

He sat there unable to speak to her through his hate. And yet the perspiration on the palms of his hands was to him the sign of embarrassment also, for he was polite to an extreme and he could not say that he was not Jewish without coloring the word with his repugnance for it, and thus for her. And in his inability to speak, in his embarrassment she seemed to see conclusive proof, and strangely – quite insanely – he helplessly conceded that it was almost proof. For to him Jew had always meant impostor. Since the beginning. It was the one thing it had always meant. The poor Jews pretended they were poorer than they were, the rich richer. He had never been able to pass a Jewish neighborhood without seeing behind the dingy curtains hidden sums of money. He had never seen a Jew driving an expensive car without likening him to a nigger driving an expensive car. To him they had no tradition of nobility such as they attempted to flaunt. Had he had an expensive car he would instantly have appeared as one who had been born to it. Any gentile would. Never a Jew. Their houses smelled, and when they did not it was only because they wanted to seem like gentiles. For him, whatever they did that was pleasing was never done naturally, but out of a desire to ingratiate themselves. This knowledge was as old as his life which had begun on a street in Brooklyn one block away from the Jewish neighborhood. Then as now, he could not think of them without a sense of power and self-purification. Listening to reports of their avarice insensibly brought him closer to an appreciation of his own liberality, which seemed proven by the simple fact that he was not a Jew. And when he encountered an open-handed Jew his own parsimonious nature was outraged, and since he saw all men only through his own eyes, in the Jew's open-handedness he saw only trickery or self-display. Pretenders, impostors. Always.

And now in his embarrassment she was reading the proof of that pretense, he thought. The challenging sneer in her eyes was unbearable and yet he still could not speak. He sought pleasantries and could not evoke them. He turned away from

41

her impatiently and turned back. It only took a moment, and then he knew for the first time in his life that it was not politeness choking back his words. He was sitting there in the guilt of the fact that the evil nature of the Jews and their numberless deceits, especially their sensuous lust for women – of which fact he had daily proof in the dark folds of their eyes and their swarthy skin – all were the reflections of his own desires with which he had invested them. For this moment he knew it and perhaps never again, for in this moment her eyes had made a Jew of him; and his monstrous desire was holding back his denial. He found himself wanting her to believe it of him just for this moment, here alone in the office, wanting her to let him dip into that dark pool whose depths he had often searched, only to turn away. Just for this private moment to descend, and find out . . .

In disgust with himself he got up. His jaw clenched against the pain of his own corruption, and she saw it and seemed to take it for an expression of anger. With her large purse clapping against her thigh she got noisily to her feet.

'You know what they ought to do with people like you?' she threatened. 'They ought to hang yiz!'

She was straining for an argument. Staring, he thought her face looked almost Irish when it thrust forward that way . . .

'Every place I go it's the same stupidity. I've had secretarial jobs where I didn't even *have* to type! I had jobs that . . .'

He was not hearing any more, for as she glanced over her shoulder to see if someone was coming to interrupt her he saw the Hebrew dip to the nose and the sad-eyed gloom over the upper face . . . Turning back to him she leaned forward and dug stiff fingers into the desk top, and they quivered before him like ten red-tipped arrows. 'One of these days they're going to hang you!' she screamed in a heaving whisper, demanding that he reply in kind.

His spine was exploding with chills. Not since his mother had screamed at him when he was a boy had he been alone with a woman in such throes. He could not blot out the sheen of her dress and the dazzling pin she wore between her breasts, and the bared emotion in her tearing eyes lured him while it fed his fright.

To himself, to his confusion and hateful longing, he muttered 'I'm sorry,' and shook his head in refusal.

She swung around, threw open his glass door and crossed the floor through an aisle of desks. She had the vitriol of the Hebrews, he thought, and their lack of taste. He watched her calves go. She was overdressed, overpainted. As she went he noticed for the first time the furpiece swinging from her arm. In a way that clinched it: it was a very hot day. As she vanished into the reception room he saw the tail of the fur brush against her leg . . .

Exhausted, he let himself into his chair. He felt loose, lubricated. A sense of evil hung over him. Reaching under his hot jacket he pulled his sleeve garters down and felt the blood circulating into his cold hands. Delicately he removed his glasses and slipped them into his handkerchief pocket and stared at nothing. The rough music of her voice rang in his ears and her perfume still hung in the air.

When time and place once more flowed into his mind his hand jerked quickly in surprise; he was looking into the solid back wall of the cubicle. Angrily he swung about and sat facing the glass walls and through them, the floor full of girls. In a moment he picked up the phone, and ordered, 'Please send in . . .' He broke off, and impatiently grabbed up the application under Miss Hart's. The words blurred intolerably. His little chin curled furiously under his lips as he drew the paper up to his nose. From the receiver in his hand the operator's voice crackled. He set the application on the desk and reached into his pocket and took out his glasses and put them on.

43

'Miss Blanche Bolland,' he said quietly, and hung up. Until he heard the approaching steps of Miss Bolland he kept looking down at her application, as though studying it.

He really did not *see* the others who came to his desk and told their stories that day; he hired an inoffensive-looking girl with black hair and a skinny face. The perfume of Gertrude Hart flowed through his afternoon, and the vision of her thighs. And slowly her face faded from his image of her until only her real body remained to fill out the faceless one of his dream. During that day he found himself looking toward the door of the receptionist's room as though to retrace and treasure every movement she had made. At times he dreamed of the trench in France, and for one moment he caught again the full, excrutiating desire he had known in that dawn ... And dreaming, he noticed Mr Lorsch standing just outside his office, shaking Mr Gargan's hand. Mr Lorsch said something, and then moved away across the floor and disappeared toward the elevators. Mr Gargan waited until the vice-president was out of sight. Then he turned toward Mr Newman and entered his office. He had his chin thrust upwards and was scratching his neck in thought.

CHAPTER SIX

'LAWRENCE' he began . . .

Mr Newman clasped his hands together on the desk. Mr Gargan had never before called him by his first name.

Mr Gargan finished scratching his neck. He looked only once at Mr Newman and drummed once on the desk with his fingers, indulging his manner of tilting his head down and looking off past his own shoulder, which he did whenever he was thinking with precision. He kept that position as he spoke.

'Mr Lorsch has been laying out a bit of a reorganization.' He sniffed tiredly through his Jersey-clogged nose. 'I won't go into all the details now, but it looks like you're going to have to move your desk into the corner office.'

'Hogan's office?'

'That's right. Mr Lorsch thinks the best thing would be for you and Hogan to kind of . . .' He looked at Mr Newman now. '. . . shift positions.'

'Jobs?'

'Well, yes. Shift jobs. Exchange.'

Mr Newman nodded that he understood. He waited.

'I guess you know Hogan's not getting your salary, but we're not going to cut you. You'll get the same as at present.'

Mr Newman nodded.

Mr Gargan waited for him to speak. He had no words. The monstrous thing was devouring him.

'Is there anything I've done that . . . ?'

'Oh no, nothing like that. You mustn't feel it's a demotion, Lawrence . . .' Gargan smiled affectionately, his face – with the hair arching roundly from the part in the middle – taking the shape of a blanched pumpkin.

'Hogan hasn't been here more than five years . . .'

What was he saying? From what long-locked cavern in his body was so much fierce anger flowing? 'I don't know how to frame the words, Mr Gargan . . .'

'I understand, Lawrence, but . . .'

Never in his life had he cut Mr Gargan off. 'I mean to say that I wouldn't be happy in Hogan's position. He's no better than a clerk, he . . .'

'That's a mistake on your part. Hogan does important . . .'

'But why?' (And why was he so sure the thighs and perfume of Gertrude Hart had started this, had blown the lid off his fury? Good God, how dare he talk to Mr Gargan like this? The very floor seemed to be shaking!) 'Why, Mr Gargan? Haven't I done a job? I've got my glasses, I've just hired a fine girl, I . . .'

Mr Gargan was standing. He was standing at his full height which was much higher than Mr Newman's. Mr Newman stopped talking as he found himself on his feet.

'Mr Lorsch . . . and I . . .' Now he too was angry. It was dreadful. 'Mr Lorsch and I think it would be better for everybody concerned if you worked in Mr Hogan's office. There's no rush, but try to be moved by the first of the month.'

Mr Newman heard the clear bell of authority. Mr Gargan turned and walked out amid his echo.

He sat at his desk staring across the wide floor of desks and girls, staring at Hogan's closed door. A clerk now, after so many years. A clerk with no authority whatever, no appointments, no phone. He would *be* Hogan, in a sense . . .

After all these years.

He got to his feet, choking with unshed tears, took a deep breath and slowly sat down again. It couldn't be final. Not after all these years. A few words, and all the delicate parts of his life smashed to bits, his glass-enclosed office, his domain stretching out before him filled with desks and girls who depended only on him. It could not be final. . .

He opened the left-hand drawer of his desk and took out a small mirror and looked into it. His face was glistening with sweat. His nose seemed beaked, horribly. He stood up and looked down at the mirror to get a longer view. It was bad, yes, it was bad.

But it was not that bad. Not after all these years. He was moving toward Mr Gargan's office, through Miss Keller's office, and in a moment he stood before his chief.

Gargan looked at him and got to his feet. Mr Newman raised his chin as though water were rising around him.

'Mr Gargan, I can't honestly see what harm I'd be doing in my office,' he said flatly.

'That's not for you to determine, is it, Newman?'

'No, but if you want me out of the way, why not . . .?'

'Frankly, Newman, I ought to say that I didn't notice anything until Mr Lorsch made me realize. But I can see his point. We don't feel you'll make a good impression on people who might come into the outer office for the first time. We understand your situation and we're willing to pay you your old salary for doing Hogan's work. I don't know what else there is to say, fella.'

The 'fella,' to Mr Newman, was the ominous final gesture at friendship between them. It took his breath with it as it left Mr Gargan's mouth.

His first move was toward the door. But he stopped and turned to Mr Gargan and said, 'I can't see how I can accept the exchange, Mr Gargan. I wish you'd reconsider it.'

Mr Gargan's eyes stopped roving. 'I can't reconsider it, Newman.'

Mr Newman felt the pressure under which his chief was acting and sympathized, 'It's not as though you didn't know what I am. You know I'm not . . .'

'Mr Lorsch doesn't know but what he sees. And he didn't like what he saw. Neither will others, maybe, who come into

47

the office for the first time. Mr Lorsch has certain ideas about what the office ought to look like and he's got a right to those ideas. Doesn't he?'

'Well, I'll have to leave then.'

'It's up to you, Newman. I think you're being silly, but I wouldn't want you here if you're going to be unhappy about it.'

'No, I'll have to leave.'

'Why don't you sleep on it?'

'I can't. I . . .'

He choked and stood there. Waiting. Waiting for . . .

A look at Mr Gargan's tight, graven face told him he was waiting for nothing at all.

'I'll say good-bye then,' he said heavily.

'Think it over . . .'

'No, I'm afraid I'll have to say good-bye,' he said, afraid he was going to cry.

He walked out of the office without even waiting for Mr Gargan's reply. At the end of the day he stood outside the entrance of the building for a moment. The five-o'clock mobs were roaring past toward the subways. He got into step and moved with the tide. In his side pocket lay his fountain pen desk set which he had bought long ago. Its heavy base weighted his pocket awkwardly. Finally he took it out and carried it in his hand.

CHAPTER SEVEN

EMERGING from the subway he put the pen set back into his pocket, and walked toward his house a little more slowly than usual. In the subway he had taken off his glasses, but he could see Mrs Depaw spraying her lawn and he nodded to her with his accustomed reserve. Fat Mrs Bligh was sitting high on her brick porch waiting for her husband. She called down to him asking if it was as hot in the city as it was here. With a shake of his head and a chuckle, he replied that it certainly was, and went on. The small orphan boy whom the Kennedys had adopted said hello to him from the stoop of their house. Glancing blindly up toward the windows to discover whether any of the Kennedys were watching, he blinked encouragingly to the unfortunate boy, and said, 'How are you this evening?' No one else was out on the block. His eyes narrowed again as he walked, and his arm was slightly crooked over the sagging pocket. A fine dusty haze hung over the street and he felt covered with sooty perspiration. His shower beckoned like a sparkling new life.

'Aren't you going to hang your jacket up?' his mother asked, as he started up the stairs to his bedroom.

'I'm sending this suit to the cleaners,' he muttered, and went up. In his bedroom he took out the pen set and put it far in the back of the drawer that contained extra blankets. In the shower he stood with his face turned up and let the water jab at his eyes.

After he had dressed he stopped in the doorway of the bedroom and went back and took the pen set out of the drawer and stood looking around the room. Then, remembering, he got a chair and stood on it inside his closet and laid the set on the top shelf where the maid never cleaned. His mother was calling him. He went downstairs, putting on his glasses, and smelled the meatballs heating. He filled a pot with water and sat at the table, while his mother sat beside the stove ready to drop two handfuls of spaghetti into the pot.

She asked, 'Was it hot in the city today?'

'It certainly was,' he said, wiping his hand across his warm face. He took off his glasses and cleaned them with the linen napkin.

'Somebody said people were dropping dead on the streets.'

'I wouldn't doubt it,' he said.

She waited until he had his meal before him and was eating, and then she rolled her chair up behind him and sat looking through the screen door at the little backyard.

'Mr Gargan's summer place must be pleasant now,' she said.

He muttered something with a full mouth.

'You'd think he'd invite you out there once.'

He shrugged his shoulders, and tried to remember whether there was anything on the top shelf of his closet that the maid could possibly go looking for.

After supper he went out onto the porch and sat in one of the two beach chairs. Across the street the porches were filling with groups of people. Bligh called out to him from five houses up. He smiled back and waved.

'Hot enough for you today?' Bligh laughed.

Newman laughed and shook his head appropriately. Then turning in the opposite direction he quickly took his glasses off and held them. Here and there along the street the hoses started spurting, while from up on the porches people dreamily watched the cool arcs of water. A flight of girl's laughter came from somewhere and vanished. The windows were all open. A pot falling in a kitchen rang down the street. Mr Newman heard his mother behind him in the living room. She switched on the radio and a soprano sang.

'You'd better water the grass,' she warned through the window behind him. 'It'll burn up sure.'

He nodded but remained seated there. It would be bad if he came down off the porch now: everybody on the street was outside, and if someone should happen to stop and talk he knew he would get nervous. Until now it had been all right to wear the glasses on the street; yesterday or the day before he could have overridden their new stares. Yesterday he had been the man who worked for the Corporation. When talking to Carlson or Bligh or Fred next door about conditions he had always been the man who worked for the Corporation. It was who he was. Whatever they might see in his glasses would be dispelled by the sheer fact of who he was. But it was all vanished from behind him now, and he knew he would be standing before them all alone and he would blush if they noticed, like a stranger he would shift his feet before them, like one who was ashamed of how he looked.

From across the street Carlson appeared dragging out his hose. Mr Newman turned away. The skinny man playfully called across, 'Better get that water going!'

'Just resting,' Newman smiled back, and he looked down at his shoes.

Deep in his chair he sat wishing for darkness to come. Then in the dark he could make some sort of plan. It was twenty-five years since he had looked for a job. He must have one right away. Then he would stand out front watering the lawn with his glasses on. Tomorrow he would leave early, make his train, get out . . . where?

Where?

Consciously he crossed his hardening legs, leaned back further, and tried to relax.

A screen door slammed up the block, and he turned to look. On the porch of the house adjoining the candy store a man appeared. Mr Newman leaned forward to see better. Glancing around he put his glasses on. A new man on the block. A long beard, a gray beard. Good God, was that a black skull cap on his head? A black skull cap and a beard!

The old man was sitting down. He opened a newspaper. Out of his beard stuck a long cigarette holder which he held between forefinger and thumb.

Mr Newman sat gaping at the man. Probably Mrs Finkelstein's father. He vaguely remembered hearing that Finkelstein's father was dead. This must be what Fred had been talking about. A man with a long gray beard and a skull cap and a cigarette holder . . .

He took his eyes from the man and scanned the whole street. A deep awareness of change pressed upon him. The Blighs had stopped talking and were sitting motionless, staring across at the old man. The orphan boy was whispering into Mr Kennedy's ear while they watched the stranger. Across the street Carlson stood frowning with his hose in his hand. Newman's eyes moved from porch to porch. All the faces were turned the same way. Only the hissing of the hoses sounded on the street. He reached up and with a flowing motion slipped off his glasses and with wide, watchful eyes stuck them in his shirt pocket.

An exciting beat agitated his stomach. He got up from the beach chair and went down his stoop, crossed the little lawn and quietly walked down the sloping ramp to the garage doors, which he unlocked. Inside he found the coiled hose and pulled it up the ramp, unrolling it. He went back into the garage and turned on the water and hurried out to the grass and picked up the nozzle. The water spurted and spat and then came in a steady stream. He raised his head and looked toward the corner porch. Movement had begun again on the street. But it seemed quieter now. The conversations on the porches did not erupt into laughter or the raising of a voice in free argument. A stranger was present. Newman turned his head and glanced across the street at Carlson who still had not moved. He kept watching the bank man's long figure, his bony hands and white hair, and trembling, his fingers reached into his shirt pocket and drew out the glasses. He put them on. Now Carlson took a breath and turned and saw him. In the bank man's gaunt face the lips tightened and he seemed to be appealing to Newman for the answer to an alarming riddle.

Newman glanced once toward the corner, and like one who had been hurt unfairly and is ironically at the mercy of an inferior world, he brought his shoulders up in a helpless shrug and shook his head mournfully. Carlson turned and with his brows tightening as though he were in rapid thought, stared again at the old man at the end of the block. Newman faced toward the old man again. For a long time he stood there comfortably watering his lawn with his glasses on.

At nine o'clock Sunday morning he discovered himself standing in the middle of his bedroom looking around and trying to remember what he had come upstairs for. Everything was becoming hard to remember. Yesterday he had spent the whole morning trying to get himself to go to a movie but the illegitimacy of sitting in a movie house during working hours turned him away. Only last night had he realized that he had forgotten to eat lunch. Now he stood blinking at a sunbeam pouring onto the rug and at the thought of tomorrow his face began to heat. Church bells outside . . . He turned happily and went downstairs. This was something he had to do, a place he had to be. Every Sunday he went to the corner and got his paper. The world became real again.

He had hardly reached the sidewalk when an impression of strangeness slipped upon him. Something had happened on the street. He knew it. Perhaps a dog had been run over. Something had died, it seemed. All the air had been sucked off the street, nothing moved, the sun shone yellow and hot. He walked glancing. Then looked down at his denims to see if they were buttoned. Then he saw Mrs Depaw. She was not watering her lawn.

She always watered her lawn when it was this hot. There she was standing on her porch dressed in white as always, and looking like an old nurse. And in perfect stillness she was watching the corner. The pavement in front of her house was dry.

He crossed the street and continued toward the candy store, and as he mounted the curb he saw it. Three men were standing on the corner a little beyond the newsstand at which Finkelstein sat. They were looking . . . they were looking at Mr Newman as he approached. His heart squeezed painfully as he damned himself for having forgotten to take his glasses off. For it was Fred there, and Carlson and . . .

On and off – perhaps two Sundays out of five – this little sharp nosed man standing with Fred and Carlson had stationed himself on the opposite side of the street from Finkelstein's store, and sold newspapers from a pile which he kept on the sidewalk. Mr Newman had never paid any attention to him except once, several months ago, when he observed to himself that the city ought to prevent transients from competing unfairly with a storekeeper, who had to pay rent while the transient kept all his profit. He was against pushcart peddlers for the same reason.

Today, however, the sharp-nosed man had spread his papers out on Finkelstein's very corner – in fact, no more than fifteen yards from the store. Mr Finkelstein was sitting calmly in his little campchair beside his stand with his back to the three, and he was watching Newman with a peculiarly wide smile.

Newman approached Finkelstein's stand with his hand reaching into his pocket, and Finkelstein, who usually by this time had risen and folded Newman's paper ready to take away, only now got up, rather suddenly and seemingly with a thankful and relieved air, and started folding an *Eagle* for him. As the storekeeper turned to the stand to do this, Newman glanced over to the corner and waved to Fred and called, 'Morning.' The sharp-nosed little man called back instead of Fred, and he sang, 'Paper! Buy American. Paper! Buy . . . !'

Finkelstein was holding his paper out to him now. He looked into the Jew's tense face and insanely he felt his anger rising. The paper was touching his hand now. In his other hand he had the dime. His whole sense of being cut off seemed to be crackling inside of him. On the curb stood the three men. Here he stood with the Jew. He knew his face was red, wished he could buy Finkelstein's paper and then go over to the strange peddler and buy from him too. It was bad not to buy the paper from the Jew now because in the Jew's eyes he knew he looked intimidated. It was therefore not from a sense of compassion that he said to Finkelstein – as he let his own hand drop empty – 'Just a minute.'

And then he walked up to the three men and stopped in front of Fred, and smiling in embarrassment, but still angry that he had not been able to refuse the Jew without reddening, he said, 'What's going on, Fred?'

Fred glanced past him at Finkelstein and then looked intimately at him. Carlson stood there troubled, a tall gray-haired bank clerk, a very conservative kind of man.

Now with these three Newman knew an onrushing calm. It was as though he had managed to make an advantageous deal with Gargan, as though he were really an able man and belonged among able men who knew just how to conduct their lives.

Fred said, 'We're just makin' sure Billy here gets his rights, that's all. Morgenthau over there tried to push him off the block.'

As though scandalized, Newman said, 'That so!' He wanted Fred to continue talking so intimately with him – Fred and Carlson too.

'Imagine the nerve of that kike?' Carlson asked, quietly. He kept quivering as though freezing.

Newman shook his head at the outrage. It would be easier now to tell his mother that he was fired. Somehow because he had done this it would be easier to bear having no place to go tomorrow. He would be coming back each day to a block that he belonged to. Standing there on the corner he felt again like an inhabitant, and seemed quite at ease.

And then the sharp faced man held out a paper and said, 'Paper, mister?'

Newman took the paper from the man's blackened little hand and paid his dime. He knew that Fred and Carlson were looking at him and he felt that they were waiting for him to say something about Finkelstein on his own. He dropped the paper and it opened on the sidewalk. The little man helped him as he bent over to gather the sections together. Why couldn't he say something, any of the things he had so often said to himself about the Jew? His teeth grated against each other, presumably because he had dropped the paper, but he knew it was because of his inability even to mutter a curse against the man who was sitting beside the store a few yards behind him. And the only reason he could imagine for his hesitancy was that he had always been vehemently against peddlers and here he was buying from one, and Fred and Carlson were standing there waiting for him to speak and act like a man who had never had a feeling against peddlers. It was an insolent pressure upon him that he did not want and as he stood erect with the paper again under his arm he looked at Carlson whose teeth were obviously false, and a fear opened in him that they were making him into something he was not.

He laughed and patted the paper under his arm. 'Don't know why they make them so thick. By the way,' he said quickly, 'I heard your dogs barking last night. Anything wrong?'

Fred said, 'Must've been the moon,' and scratched his thigh lazily. Carlson kept studying Newman's face with a thinking expression that had suspicion in it. Fred continued, 'There was a full moon last night. Notice it, Carlson?'

Unwilling to be distracted from his intense concentration upon Newman, Carlson glanced at Fred, and, still worried, said, 'Yes.'

'You mean they really bark at the moon, eh?' Newman said with wonder, quite as though he had just learned the fact. Why was Carlson looking at him that way?

'Sure, didn't you ever hear of that?' Fred said.

'No, I never did,' Newman said. And turning to Carlson, asked, 'Is that a scientific fact?'

'Oh yes,' Carlson said, absently.

Without allowing Carlson's mind to wander from the new subject, Newman pursued, 'I was reading in the *Eagle* about this scientist who says we'll be traveling to the moon in rockets after the war.'

'Oh, that's impossible,' Carlson decided flatly. 'Anybody tries it will be smashed to pieces. Why . . .'

Newman listened with relief now that he had the searching expression wiped from the bank man's face.

For a few minutes the three stood on the corner talking about rockets. Then Newman shifted the paper under his arm, and with an easy smile, said, 'Well, I better get home. My mother's waiting for the paper.'

'See ya,' Fred said.

'Bye,' Carlson nodded.

'Thanks, mister,' the peddler smiled.

Newman turned and walked past the candy store, his eyes fixed straight ahead. A few houses past the store stood Mrs Depaw in the center of the sidewalk. As though preoccupied, Newman stepped into the gutter and started across the street. He was heading for the opposite curb and was just in the center of the macadam . . .

'You! You ought to be ashamed of yourself!' Her shrill old-woman's scream seemed to reach across to him and scratch at his neck, but he went on to his sidewalk without turning and walked steadily to his house. When he got inside he stood clenching his right hand which was trembling. Staring in thought he walked into the dining room and stood looking into the mirror that hung over a potted plant.

He watched the scene that ensued that evening from his high front porch: before the house next to the candy store on the corner a dilapidated open truck was backed up. Behind it hung the setting sun as red as a skating ball. Mr Finkelstein's head was showing above the side panels of the truck, and he was haloed by the sun as he directed the moving men who were edging a chifferobe to the truck's tailpiece. It was an old chifferobe – the father-in-law's furniture had finally arrived.

Motionless, Newman sat watching. In the back of his house his mother was settled at last at the open door of the kitchen trying to read the *Times*. He had just finished arguing with her for the fourth time today, for she could not understand why he refused to go back and make Finkelstein exchange the paper for an *Eagle*, and especially why he had taken a *Times* in the first place. He stuck to his new contention that the *Times* was better for her and had left her muttering in the kitchen.

Sitting in the heat now he wondered how he was going to pass the newsstand on the corner without taking his paper tomorrow. Of course he might simply stop and buy it as always, just as though nothing had happened. After all, he owed the poor Jew nothing, certainly not an explanation. But it was just possible that Fred or Carlson would be coming along as he was paying Finkelstein . . .

Through the corner of his eye he noticed a person stopping across the street. Carlson, he saw. The lean man, with a garden spade in his hand, was looking toward the corner at the unloading of the truck. He turned to Newman and with a jerk of his head toward the truck said, 'Invasion's on.'

Quickly, over-amiably, Newman called back across the street to him, 'So I see.'

They exchanged a mournful shake of the head and Carlson went up to his house.

Mrs Depaw stood in front of her house which was four nearer the corner than Carlson's, and watered her lawn with a fine spray. Close to her cane sat her female spaniel lightly raising its muzzle toward the cooling water. Now and then Mrs Depaw glanced across the street at Newman. She never sprayed this late in the day, he knew.

From out of the house into which the furniture was being moved came the old man with the gray beard. Following him, Morton and Shirley burst out of the house and ran screaming to Finkelstein who was standing beside the truck. He slapped Shirley, nine years old, and she ran into the house. Morton, who was eleven, stood watching the movers beside his father and grandpa.

And now – Newman nodded knowingly as he watched them – the old man will bring his chair out onto the front grass and read a Jewish paper, and in a few months another family will move in and in a year people on the block will be selling their houses. Perhaps Fred was right; they had to be gotten out of the neighborhood. And yet they did have a right to live where-ever . . .

A screen door slammed close to his ear. He turned to see Fred from next door lumbering out of his house, hitching his pants up over his hard bulging stomach. A new cigar was in his mouth; he had just finished supper. Arching his back for com-fort he stood looking toward the truck at the corner. Then he turned to Newman whose porch was separated from his by a low brick barrier. To Newman he always looked stuffed after eating, and somehow brutal with the new cigar tilted

59

upward and the teeth showing under the squinty, puffed eyes.

Facing Newman he just jerked his head once toward the truck. Newman set his lips angrily and shook his head.

Without a word Fred came to the railing and slinging his thigh onto it settled with his back against the house.

Uneasiness took hold of Newman. His palms grew slimy against the arms of the beach chair.

'Have a chair,' he said to Fred, one neighbor to another, and took off his glasses.

Fred swiveled around on the brick barrier and came over. He sat lithely on the other beach chair and leaned back looking at the sky over the flat line of roofs across the street. The sun was down now behind the truck, which cast a long shadow from the corner. Fred blew smoke which hung around his head, then turned and brought his buried eyes to bear on Newman's face. Newman felt his heart starting ahead. He had never been able to tell what Fred was feeling because his eyes showed only glints.

'Got yourself some specs, eh?' Fred suctioned a particle of food from between two teeth, eyeing the glasses.

'Yeh, just got them,' Newman replied lightly, turning them in his hands.

Fred stretched out his legs and crossed them. 'I can read signs a mile away. I eat vegetables.' He gazed over the roofs again.

'Vegetables? They never helped me,' Newman said, eagerly.

'Raw, I mean. Ever notice dogs? When they start losing sight they go and eat grass. Watch my dogs sometime.'

'I thought they ate grass for constipation.'

'Constipation always goes with bad sight,' Fred said with authority.

Newman disagreed. A month ago he would have disputed obstinately. But this was the first time that Fred had ever sat on his porch with him. 'I never knew that.'

'Sure,' Fred said, and turned his head toward the truck to their right. 'Can you read the sign on that truck?'

Newman put on his glasses. 'Ice,' he said.

'No, I mean under that.'

'Oh no, I can't read that.'

' ''Dominick Auditore, Coal & Ice. 46 Broome Street.'' ' Reading the address he seemed to have surprised himself. Both were struck by it. 'Broome Street,' he repeated. 'That's on the lower East Side.' He turned and looked at Newman. 'That's the element he's bringin' around.'

For a moment they both stared at the truck and at Finkelstein who was standing by. Fred turned and seemed about to speak, but sat looking at his neighbor's face.

Newman felt releasing words about to leap from his throat. But he was not sure they would not sound slightly false. He was not accustomed to speaking in terms of violence. And Mrs Depaw was really looking at him from across the street now that Fred had come out. He remained silent. Fred kept looking straight into his face. He felt his cheeks reddening. He took out his handkerchief and covering his face, loudly blew his nose.

'Carlson was betting me you'd buy from him this morning.'

'From *him*?' Newman heard himself starting to laugh.

'I knew you wouldn't. We're gonna have Billy on that corner every Sunday from now on.'

'Swell,' Newman said quietly. Fred nodded, and turned again toward the corner.

Newman felt as though a cool relaxing breeze were passing over him, and leaned back. Vision of a bright Monday suffused him, possibly a job with General Electric, more money too . . . Comfortably, 'How are your dogs?' he asked.

'Lazy but all right. I'm getting up a big hunt for the new season.'

'Going up to Jersey again?'

61

'Yeh.' Fred shook his head dreamily. 'Boy, what I wouldn't give to go hunting now. I could keep it up all year. Goddam.'

Never before had even such a confidence passed between them. Newman felt a timbre of friendship. He had always been irritated at the suspicion that Fred thought him a fogy. Now for some reason he had risen in Fred's eyes. It was good. 'Going to bring back any more foxes for the wife?'

'She's got two now. Don't want to go spoiling her. See my new rifle?'

'Got a new one, eh? Funny, I never saw much in hunting.' Perhaps ... perhaps he might go along next time. A good new job tomorrow, and hunting with the boys.

'Didn't you ever shoot anything?' Fred asked, incomprehensibly.

'Well, no ...'

'You were in the war, weren't you?'

'Yeh, but ...' The idea of likening the shooting of an animal with what he had done in the war confused him. 'I hardly ever talk about it, frankly. Something you like to forget.'

'Did you get any of them?'

'Well, yeh.' To end it, he admitted, 'I got a Fritz once.'

'How was it?' Fred's attention was abrupt and whole. 'How'd you get him?' His voice was breathful and his body became still.

Newman tried laughing, 'The usual way,' then looked ahead again, wondering why he should feel this fright at Fred's sudden fascination with his killing.

'Did you go up to see where you'd hit him?'

'I don't like to talk about it, Fred,' he said solemnly and with finality. It was as though the killing had consequences for him now and he did not understand what they were.

'Well, was it one shot?' Fred asked, as though it would be the last question which he insisted be answered.

Newman heard the ice truck's engine starting and turned

with relief toward the corner to see it driving away. Finkelstein and his young son were standing on the curb watching it. Mr Newman looked at Fred who had turned to observe them. Fred's cheekbones seemed swollen. He turned again to Newman and fixed upon him with his blue slit eyes.

'You know what we're planning on doing. You do, don't ya?' he said, his voice gruff and quiet.

'I . . . yeh, you've been telling me.'

'You with us?'

Newman wished they were sitting a little further apart so he would have room to move. He did not want to avoid Fred's eyes, which he would appear to be doing should he move now.

'Well, what do you want to do?'

'Drive them to hell out of the neighborhood.'

'How?'

'Put the fear a God into them.'

'You mean . . .' Newman broke off.

'Fix it so they don't like it here.'

'How you going to go about it?'

'There's an organization. You know about it.'

'Yes.'

'We're getting new people in every day. When enough gets enrolled we start moving.'

Neither of them stirred. Their voices had lowered to a whisper. Newman found himself deeply regretting having ever told Fred that he had killed a man.

'How do you mean, get moving?' he asked innocently, as though thereby to regain his old character in Fred's eyes.

'You know, so they won't want to live here,' Fred said, showing his first impatience.

Newman – leisurely, it seemed – took his eyeglasses off. Inwardly his body leaped when Fred nudged his thigh with a stony index finger.

'The thing is this. When the boys come home they're going

63

to look for an organization that gives them what they want. They ain't standing for a lotta kikes takin' up all the jobs and the businesses. You know that,' he added. Newman could not deny it and nodded. 'We're getting that meeting up pretty soon. Should I let you know? You want to come?'

'All right. Sure.' Newman said, after a breath of hesitation.

'You'll join then, heh? Everybody be glad to have you.'

'You mean . . .'

'On the block.'

'Carlson one of you?'

'Sure. Been in since the beginning. We got a big priest from Boston coming to the meeting. We work with the priests, you know,' he said, half in apology, 'as long as they stay in line. The thing is, if we all get together we can clean up the situation; knock them over'– he nodded sideways toward the corner – 'like tenpins. What do you say?'

Mr Newman raised his chin and narrowed his eyes as though deliberating. Why, he asked himself, should I assume they mean to do it violently? And yet when he turned and looked at Fred he knew that they had only been talking about violence. Before he could answer with another hesitating remark, Fred said, 'We want your class of people. This morning Carlson wanted to lay a real bet you'd buy from Finkelstein. He thought you were the type.'

Despite himself Newman's wariness fled. 'What type?' he asked quickly.

'You know what I mean,' Fred said.

Newman did not exactly know. And instantly he feared that his confusion about what Carlson had meant was showing on his face. 'I'll join you,' he said, shifting uneasily on the canvas seat of the chair.

Fred slapped him lightly on the thigh and got up, straddling the foot rest of the beach chair. Lifting one foot over, he hitched up his pants, and speaking with a grin of one letting fall a secret said, 'You're all right, Newman.' He laughed at himself, like a salesman after a sale who is admitting his humanity: 'You're one of the few on the block I was having trouble with.'

Newman laughed, 'Having trouble with *me*?'

He had not realized until now that Fred's remarks over the past year had been as earnest as all this. He had not realized how much was going on . . .

'I gotta go in, take my pups for a walk. I'm workin' on a model sailboat down the cellar,' Fred said, swinging his leg over the railing. 'Come down later if you got an hour. I'm takin' it up for a hobby. See ya.'

'Take it easy now,' Newman said, as Fred went into his house.

Staring across the street at Carlson's house, he felt a little easier about it. Carlson was no Fred. Carlson was the chief teller of a bank. A bank man. Recalling how Carlson had turned to him across the street before and said, 'Invasion's on,' Newman felt a little pride in the man's solicitude. Fred's, too . . . It would be rather pleasant being friendly with the neighbors. Perhaps through mingling with them he might meet the right kind of woman. Perhaps . . .

The thought of tomorrow again came to him. He rose from the beach chair in the pain of anxiety. Where was he to go? What would become of him? . . . From his right he heard a screen door open, and Fred came out with his two red setters sniffing wildly beside him and tangling each other in their leashes. Fred laughed across the porch barrier to Newman, laughed warmly. Then he went down the stoop to the street with the dogs, their long paw-nails ticking against the concrete walk. Talking in undertones to them he yanked roughly at their leashes whenever they strayed from his heels, and the three moved away into the gathering twilight.

Mr Newman stood for a moment listening to the vanishing

ticking of the dog's nails, and then the silence of the street filled in. Standing there he felt a deep thankfulness at the memory of Fred's warm smile. A sense of comradeship suffused him. Thank God, he nearly said aloud, not everybody is as stupid as Gargan! He would charge into the city tomorrow and get placed. A better job, even. A . . .

His eye was caught by the light switching on in the window of the corner store. Its glare poured yellow onto the dark sidewalk. On Mr Newman's face an expression of stern indignation spread. His chest expanded and his small jaw became rigid. Open on Sunday, he thought, they never let a penny get away. With sudden angry resolution he sat again in a chair. He would wait for Fred to return, and then have a real talk about this thing. Looking at the yellow light on the corner he felt a strange power flowing into him, it was as though his very body were growing larger. The vision of the bearded and skull-capped man, sitting on his block so snugly, so full of security, arose like incense before him, and he waited in the gathering darkness for the ticking of the dog's nails.

CHAPTER EIGHT

RIDING to Manhattan on the Eighth Avenue subway next morning, he urged the rocking train onward with all his might. This morning, cloudless and hot, the fabulous island at the end of the tube seemed to be awaiting him like some great fair in which he would shop among glittering wares to select the choice of his heart. He was going to look for a job.

All these years he had sniffed around the pillars of the subway feeling densely afraid and hopeful at the same time. For he had never been sure what part he could comfortably play when trouble came. But now he had faced trouble right out on the street in public, and nothing terrible had happened to him; the result, in fact, had been to join him as he had never been joined, in a new comradeship with his neighbors. He felt able, sitting there on the train. Even tough.

A better word might be dashing. After spending so many years on the same floor of one building it was an adventure to look for a job. New surroundings, new and interesting people, possibly a gigantic change in life . . . Who could tell what his talents were really worth on the open market? It was, it turned out overnight, almost fortunate to have lost the old job. They had been underpaying him frightfully. Now he would positively demand sixty-five to start. Probably he should have made the break of his own accord long ago. As a matter of fact, he thought as he stared pleasantly, he definitely should have.

The train roared on. He was dressed in his newest suit, a Palm Beach gray. His Panama hat curved quite handsomely over his erect, rather stubborn head. He wore a starched collar and a meticulously-tied blue cravat that he had been saving for some special occasion. His fingernails were roundly pared and shone baby pink. There was hardly a crease in his soul. He wore his eyeglasses.

He scanned the want-ad section of the Sunday *Times*, now that he was settled in his seat. But the paper (which he had contrived to carry out of the house as visible evidence to the corner store that he did not need a paper this morning) contained nothing of interest to his type of person. Positions such as he might accept were rarely advertised. He was a specialist. His joy kept distracting his concentration from the ads and he looked up to see a sight that quickened him – a car card mounted in the curved corner of the train's upper side.

It was a sketch of a subway interior showing a group of passengers, one of whom sat with a big cigar in his mouth. The expressions of his neighbors revealed intense disgust with him, and the caption of the picture was, 'DON'T SMOKE ON PUBLIC CONVEYANCES. YOU ANNOY OTHER PASSENGERS.' What captured Mr Newman, however, was a wobbly penciled arrow pointing at the smoker near whose head was scrawled, 'Jew.' The tinge of embarrassment that would have disturbed him once did not occur this morning. This mute 'scene'– there were several of the brethren standing right under the card – brewed within him instead a small but undeniable tension of power. Even his lifelong horror of bad taste was not called up, for the anonymous scrawler had lost some of his creeping anonymity overnight and resembled Mr Carlson more than a ruffian. He had always feared that some riot would break out and carry him into its vortex willy-nilly, and violence of any kind shook him, but that fear too he could not find this morning. For whatever happened now would find him prepared by Fred beforehand, and if he played a part it would be one that suited his temperament and respectability.

So he smiled, inwardly, at the word that was written above the selfish smoker, and merely thought it apt. And with an air of chieftaincy he turned his eyes among the passengers and found his Jew, and quite omnisciently raised his brows with the pleasing awareness of man's stupidity – man who could sit so leisurely and calm while his very doom was written on the wall above his head.

The part of the city into which he emerged from the subway was one where several giant corporations had their central administrative offices. Mr Newman, with the morning sun warm upon his back, stood a moment on a corner near Wall Street and surveyed the block. He looked then like any one of thousands of commuters who like to pause a moment on a street corner before entering the skyscrapers in which they gather their substance. He felt a lightness of heart as he strolled staidly into the cool and vaulted lobby of the building where the Akron Corporation had three floors. He rose skyward in the elevator and emerged on floor thirty-three. It surprised him how similar the layout was to that of his old company. He walked up to the young lady at the reception desk. She looked up from a newspaper she was reading and he asked for the personnel manager. He told her his name and business and after waiting some ten minutes was asked into a surprisingly sump-tuous leathered office.

He sat in a fine mahogany-backed chair some ten feet from the desk of Mr Stevens, who was not more than thirty-five and was obviously a college man.

'What can I do for you, sir?' Mr Stevens asked, and added, 'You're from the — Company, are you?'

'Why no,' Mr Newman quickly advised him, throwing his head back and smiling down his nose. 'The girl asked me what I had done and I told her that . . .'

'Oh, you're looking for a position with us.'

'I'm inquiring, yes,' he agreed with a deep forward nod.

'I see. My mistake.'

Mr Stevens, a slim man with closely-cropped tan hair the color of a boxer dog, blinked pleasantly at Mr Newman. For an instant Mr Newman had hope of possibly a really important job. The man seemed to be considering something quite important . . .

'Just what is your line, Mr Newman?' Mr Stevens swiveled around to free his legs from under his lovely desk.

'I'm personnel,' Mr Newman said, leaning forward and always smiling, to avoid looking intense. 'I hired most of the people who're working for —. I wondered whether you folks had anything open.'

'Uh-huh.' Mr Stevens uncrossed his legs and swiveled around to face forward again, studying his pencil which was very sharp. He said, 'Frankly we aren't looking for anyone at the moment, but . . .'

Mr Newman rose quite at ease, but rather rapidly. 'That's perfectly all right, Mr Stevens. I'm just kind of going over the ground for a couple of days. I stopped by because you're the kind of outfit I felt would be using my type of man. Sort of a lay-of-the-land proposition, don't y'know.'

Mr Stevens rose. He seemed happy that Mr Newman had gotten his cue so quickly. 'I hope you'll drop in again soon, if you haven't gotten anything meanwhile.'

'Be happy to,' Mr Newman assured him, his hand on the doorknob.

'And thanks for thinking of us . . . What did you say your name was?'

'Newman, Lawrence Newman.'

The pause, no longer than a second's time, brushed against Mr Newman's temples like the wing of an unseen bird. Mr Stevens looked at him thoughtfully, and then nodded.

'Newman, yes. Well, thanks a lot, sir, and I hope you'll come up again.'

'I'll try you,' Mr Newman humorously threatened, and with

the customary chuckle of departure he walked out of Mr Stevens' office.

In the elevator that took him to the street there hung a vague sweet spray of perfume. A woman had obviously been in it just a moment before. The image of . . . what was her name? Gertrude. Hart. Gertrude Hart's body seemed a presence beside him for a moment. He walked out into the lobby of the building and toward the tall street doors. What a wonderful building to work in! He would see Mr Stevens again next week. He would certainly ask sixty-five.

He opened the door of the booth a little. It was good he was through seeing people for the day. His collar was soaking wet.

'Mallon? You mean the little boy who drove the bread wagon?'

Mr Newman laughed. He loved his mother in these rare moments when he could condescend to her. 'Well, he's a man now. We're going to have dinner together. Been working a block away from me all these years and we never knew it.'

'All right, then, I'll tell the girl. What time will you be home?'

'About ten. Take care now. Did the boy deliver the paper?'

'Oh yes. Get something cool to drink.'

'I will, Mother. And sit out on the porch.'

'There's mosquitoes.'

'Then be sure the windows are open wide if you stay inside. Good-bye now.'

'Good-bye.'

He came out of the booth and walked over to the table where Willy Mallon was waiting for him. He felt happy at how well he had hidden the pen set.

'Is it all right?' Willy asked. He had a shiny washed face and what Mr Newman regarded as a typically Irish expression. His eyes were smooth-lidded and blue, and his ears stuck out.

He was only thirty-three, he said, and yet he had four children.

'Imagine,' Mr Newman said, sitting across the table from him, 'so close and we never happened into each other.'

'I don't get in till ten most mornings and I leave at four. Maybe that's why,' Willy said.

'I guess so,' Mr Newman said. He had gone into the restaurant men's room before phoning home and his hair looked as though he had just come from a swim.

'Sounds like a fine position, Willy,' he complimented unwillingly. He was slightly taken aback by Willy's hours. In fact, he was a little suspicious of Willy's truthfulness, for the man seemed too well off for his years. He had picked out a restaurant that Mr Newman would never have dared enter. It was one where many brokers ate. The service was sterling silver and the napkins were heavy linen. There were smoky beams across the ceiling and black paneling in the walls.

'Oh, I like it,' Willy said. 'Good job.'

'How long've you been with the company?'

'Since I left high school. Matter of fact it's the only job I ever had.'

'Worked right up, eh?' Mr Newman chuckled to mask his envy.

'Guess you might say that. I'm second in charge of merchandising. Actually I'm in charge. The chief's in the Navy. What about you? By the way, you know you've changed quite a lot.'

'Have I?'

'I don't think I'd have recognized you if you hadn't stopped me first.'

'Well, when you hit forty, you know . . .'

'I guess so. What'll you have?'

The waiter bent over them. Mr Newman had seven dollars in his pocket. The dinners were two dollars and up. He chose one for two dollars and was relieved at Willy's doing the same.

Although now that he had seen how well fixed the man was he regretted having insisted they dine together. He had no stomach for telling Willy Mallon, the bread driver, that he would appreciate his inquiring around for a position in his company.

The waiter gone they found words again.

'Never got married, eh?' Willy began wonderingly, as though trying to make up his mind about Newman.

'No,' Newman chuckled again, 'never really had the time for it.' Whenever he felt penetrated he chuckled, then broke off, and kept his mouth open thoughtfully and played with whatever lay near at hand. Now it was a knife. 'There's a prospect though.' He heard himself with alarm. 'She's still in the . . . well, the first stages, you might say, but she does interest me. I guess I've just been too busy to do much looking around.'

He was red in the face; he could have slapped Willy for forcing him to lie.

'How's your job holding up? Still with —?'

Mr Newman studied the glittering knife blade. A judicious sucking in of the mouth, and a moment's direct stare at Willy calculated to preface a personal statement, and he said, 'I decided to make a break, finally.'

'That so.' Willy seemed genuinely interested. He looked into Newman's glasses with deep sympathy. 'How long've you been out?'

'Just since yesterday.'

'Oh, then you've just started looking.'

'I'm not worried about it,' he assured him with what he assumed was the careless self-confidence of a man who knew his value. 'I just wondered whether you knew of anything in your place. I do personnel work, you know . . .'

'Oh, sure, I remember . . .'

'Naturally, there aren't many firms using my type of man. I mean they would have to be fairly big to need me.'

'Well, there are some, though. I don't know how we stand in our place on the personnel angle, but if you like I could find out.'

'All right, if you happen to think of it. But don't go to any trouble . . .'

'No trouble at all. I'll ask tomorrow. Who've you tried so far? I know a few people around and I could ask in other places.'

'Well, I was just coming from the Meynes Company when I met you . . .'

'Yeh, Meynes would be just right for you. Big staff . . .'

'Yes, I had quite a talk with a Mr Bellows up there. Nice fella. Kept me there nearly an hour. He said . . .'

'Say, I just remember. You know the place for you to try?'

'Where?' Newman asked, taking off his glasses.

In wavering blurs he saw the pink tip of Willy's tongue stick out slightly as the man looked up and thought, his fingers raised to snap. 'I'm trying to remember the company he's with.' The fingers snapped and he shifted impatiently, his blue eyes intent upon the glass chandelier. 'I just *saw* him on Thursday and he mentioned he was looking for a man. If I remember right it was some kind of personnel work.'

'What's his name? Maybe I could look him up.'

'*His* name is Stevens. Cole Stevens, but I don't recall the firm . . . Oh sure, the Akron Corporation. Construction stuff. They lost their man to the Army. Imagine the draft taking a man thirty-six years old and with two kids? Anyway, they can use a man . . .'

When they emerged from the restaurant, the street lamps were on and darkness was falling in the valley of the street. The giant buildings around them were already lost in the night sky. They walked together to the corner where they would part.

'Drop up when you get the chance,' Willy said, taking Newman's soft hand.

'Thanks, Willy. And my best to the family.'

'Sure thing. You want to write down Stevens' name? He's with the Akron Corporation. You got that?'

'Oh, I never forget,' Newman chuckled wearily, as though to say he was dependable and still what had he gotten for it.

'You ought to try him first thing in the morning. Because I know he's on the lookout for somebody,' Willy said with an extra note of encouragement, as though unable to understand what had caved in the man so suddenly.

'Thanks, I will. Well, good night, and don't work too hard,' Newman waved weakly.

'Take it easy yourself. And let me know how you make out.'

'I will.'

Willy waved, and walked off down a narrow street.

For a moment Mr Newman stood still on the corner. Slowly he took out his glasses and put them on.

At that hour a man can pitch a tent in the Wall Street neighborhood and sleep soundly, hardly hearing a single footfall or automobile on the streets. The buildings were locked up tight, like tall vaults. The stores were dark. As far as the eye could see the city was dead, and the green smell of the sea hovered along the sidewalks. Mr Newman felt forced to walk; the mute height of the buildings moved him. He walked slowly, like a man who has used up his strength rushing to a sale, only to find all the goods sold. No other living thing breathed with him on those streets, no dogs or cats marauded, for there were none there. Even the pigeons were huddling high against the churches, quiet and still and unseen. He walked, staring passionlessly at the low stars which hung between the buildings at the far end of the avenue where it was cut off by the bay. At last he felt very tired, and he sat on the high stone curb bounding the lawn of Trinity Church. Above his head and behind him he heard the flurry of pigeon's wings, and then they grew used to him and it was quiet again. His hollow loneliness descended upon him once more and he sat very still with his back against the iron railing of the churchyard, and listened to the silence.

He could not think because there was nothing to decide. Instinctively he knew there was nothing he could do about it. It was such an outrageous farce that it required a much wilder laughter than he could ever generate, and all he could do was look at it, shocked and paralyzed. A total stranger looking for a man with just his experience had taken him for a Jew and therefore he had not gotten a job that was rightfully – almost fatefully – waiting for him. But what shocked him into this dulled stupor was that he could not go back and explain to the man. This was what made him stare so dumbly now.

With all the words in the English language there were none that could explain to Mr Stevens . . .

What was there, exactly, that ought to be explained? He tried to fathom it now. Very well, he thought, I could convince him I am not a Jew. I could even go so far, let us say, as to bring him my baptismal certificate. Very well. He would believe then that I am what I really am.

Mr Newman's thoughts became lost. For he knew that whatever the proof, Mr Stevens still would not hire him, nor would he like him any better than he did now. It was dreamlike and fugitive and yet he knew it was so. For he knew that in the old days in the glass cubicle no proof, no documents, no words could have changed the shape of a face he himself suspected.

A face . . . The monstrous mockery of the thing started tears to his eyes. He got up and started walking again as though to find ahead of him in the dark the clue to this confusion. Was it possible, he wondered, that Mr Stevens looked at me and thought me untrustworthy, or grasping, or loud because of my face? It could not be possible, he thought. It simply could not be. Because I am not untrustworthy and I am a quiet person. And yet it would be absolutely impossible to convince the man.

76

Alarm began digging like a point into his flesh and he walked faster. There must be something he could do that would henceforth indicate to an employer that he was what he was, a man of great fidelity and good manners. What could he do, what new manner was there that he could adopt? Had he changed his old manner? God almighty, had something about his way of walking or talking changed these past days? He carefully reviewed himself and decided that he was the same outwardly as he had always been. Then what in the world could he do to show these people that he was still Lawrence Newman?

His face. Beside a lamppost on a corner he came to a halt. *He* was not this face. Nobody had a right to dismiss him like that because of his face. Nobody! He was *him*, a human being with a certain definite history and he was not this face which looked like it had grown out of another alien and dirty history. They were trying to make two people out of him! They were looking at him as though he were guilty of something, as though he would hurt them! They could not do that! They dare not do that to him because he was no one else but Lawrence Newman . . . !

The sound of his own voice shattered his vision and the empty public street appeared around him and he stood stiff.

Trembling, he looked ahead and saw the lights of a subway entrance and hurried toward it. It was two blocks away, long blocks. He passed the churchyard, and the tombstones now swept him with their cold meaning; the dark itself seemed to have cavernous form, and he strode toward the entrance lights and when he got there he was almost running.

When he got home he went directly to Fred, whom he found in the chicken-wired backyard kennel. When he opened the gate the two red setters paced toward him sniffing wildly and stood there delicately lifting their paws and looking up at him. With Fred he talked quietly of the weather and the moon which hung low behind their heads, throwing their shadows long across the dirt kennel floor.

'Pity they have to be cooped up here all year just for two weeks' hunting,' Newman said quietly, staring into the dogs' eyes.

Fred reached over and stroked one dog's head and then stood looking down at them with his hands on his hips. 'Don't you worry, I'll have a place in the country some day,' he said, as certain as if he were actually negotiating the purchase but was merely being businesslike and reticent.

'Saving for it?' Newman asked, smiling.

'You can't save for the kind of place I want. But I'll have it.' He kept looking down at the dogs.

'You really mean that?' Newman whispered, impressed.

'Certnee I mean it.' Fred looked into Newman's glasses now. 'I ain't bein' a sucker all my life. We bust the Jews open and it'll all come out like from a cracked slot machine. They got so much they're washing their dishes in hot seltzer.'

Newman laughed softly and Fred did too as he bent over and picked up a broom and swept droppings over to one side. Newman stood there motionless, watching him.

After a while he went down in the cellar with Fred and watched him sandpapering the model boat. He had his glasses on and a strange pleasure of accomplishment flowed through him as he sat there so wordlessly welcome. And while Fred's chafed hands rubbed the sandpaper back and forth, back and forth, Mr Newman began talking of the war and how he had killed the German. The sandpaper stopped and the cellar was quiet when he described the wound, for he had gone up to the dead man and had seen the bullet hole. It ran through the neck and out the top of the head.

CHAPTER NINE

LATE Sunday afternoon. A little suburban street lined with young trees. The dry leaves hang motionless. In the window pots the geraniums droop under the weight of dust. An old woman carefully soaks the plot of yellow grass before her house, an aged spaniel nodding in the heat beside her. Two sunburned boys kick a stone along the gutter as they head home from the beach, their bathing trunks slung on their red shoulders. A girl in shorts hoses her car, watched from a front porch by a party of men trying to play cards. Atop a tall ladder set against a house in the middle of the block, a middle-aged man stands painting the shutters of his bedroom windows. Heavy horseflies find the geraniums, the old woman, the spaniel, the girl, and strike against the neck of the man on the ladder.

In such detail the block impressed itself on Mr Newman as he slowly spread green paint over the hot-smelling wood. For although intent upon the wet brush in his hand, he was not on the ladder because his shutters needed painting. He had been driven up there like a cat that sometimes leaps to the branch of a tree for no discernible reason, and sits carefully surveying what seems about to transpire below.

Only on the ladder could he accomplish his end. Sitting on the porch he would have to face Fred and Carlson directly when they returned from Paradise Gardens. In the back yard he might seem to be hiding from their view, while way up here he could be seen but at the same time be facing away from the street, so that if they chose to say hello to him they could, and if not they could ignore him again and he could pretend that he did not even notice their return.

Very slowly he spread the green paint, rested for long protracted moments, and then worked for just a little while and stopped again to listen for Fred's car. The heat pouring out of the bricks threatened to sicken him, but he would not come down. He must know.

The horror of a nightmare, the ruthless but undefined force of an hallucination was upon him and he was striving to break out of it and understand what was happening to him. Brushing the paint in carefully, he strove to recall what had brought him to this.

Looking back over the past job-seeking days he could not clearly remember whether something had happened on Wednesday, Friday, or Monday. The days had passed, their shapes and colors were now merged in a single gray.

Only Friday was clear. A terrible thing had happened on Friday.

Leaving a building the first inkling of the terror came with the wind. Although it was still midsummer the weather for a moment suddenly seemed to have turned to fall. He imagined snow falling soon. The change in the air brought the fear that he might actually go through the whole summer without a job. In winter one could not pretend to oneself a sort of vacation. On cold days a man did not wander through the streets like this.

As though to escape the vision he turned into a cafeteria and took a piece of cake, a cup of coffee, and a glass of water, and sat at a table. Chewing the pasty cake he reached for the glass of water. The back of his hand clipped it and it fell off the table.

After a single glance he pulled out his clean handkerchief and smiling politely, offered it to the matronly woman next to him, whose stocking was drenched. Her eyes rose to his – two eyes turning to metal an instant after she saw. His apology froze in his throat before the curse that curled on her lips. As though a sudden icy wind were rushing at him from her he felt he would have to shout through to reach the human being behind her button eyes. He turned back to eating and left the glass on the floor, and her to her mumbling.

Rising to go he saw the young man at another table who had been watching him but whose gaze he had dared not meet until he was ready to leave. The same lordly sheen was glassing the young man's eyes and Newman, as though on business, hurried out, his heart pounding.

Walking along the street that afternoon he could not stop his body's quivering as the presence of animosity began to keep pace with him. Neither wholly here nor there, not on that corner nor on this, but a shadow of it on one passing face, and a peculiar glance from a man coming out of a store. A truck driver cursing at a flat tire was, strangely, cursing at him. Ridiculous ... and there. Always there beside him. Utterly ridiculous and utterly there.

The subway that night rocked him home. Strangely, these nights he liked the subway crowded. He would catch the train at two minutes before five and get a seat, and then at succeeding stops people would rush in and he would be buried there in his seat surrounded by those standing. And sitting there this night he let his mind get lost in the patterns of a woman's dress which was no more than a foot from his face, and in this privacy he saw the truth. In the offices he had called on there must have been jobs open. There was a war on. Personnel men were at a premium because the companies were hiring thousands of workers. But for him there was nothing but the polite smile of refusal. Because he was talking to other personnel men, men who had the same instructions he had had when he worked for Gargan. And they were as sharp at classifying people as he had been. The fact was that he would never again be a personnel man. It had been his one pride in life, the thing that had made it possible for him to go on without a wife, and he would never have it again; that thrill of hiring and being responsible would never again be his. What in God's name could he be now, at his age? He thought of taking a factory job of some kind. Or simply a clerk's job, or something in an office, or anything . . . He could not, he simply could not. He was a personnel man, a . . .

With the sixth sense of a subway traveler he knew his station was approaching, and he managed to rise to his feet. In former times when passengers had refused to let him through to the door he had shouldered his way with some play at indignation. Now he rather gently drew the attention of the person in his path by a tap on the arm – and the action itself broke his heart. The train slowed and the crowd pressed him from behind. The train stopped. The doors slid open. His face was pushed into the back of the man ahead. For an instant he could not inhale and deep within him a weeping threatened to break open and he had to get out. The mass began to move now, impelled by their hunger and their need to get home and change clothes, and suddenly he was pushed out of the train and flung against a fat man who was standing directly in front of the doorway. In falling he threw his foot forward to stop himself and it pounded down on the fat man's toes, and to right himself completely he had to grab onto the man's lapel for an instant. The fat man struck his hand away as sharply as the crowd surged past. Mr Newman stood panting into the face of the fat man who stepped to the doors and, holding them back while he spoke, shouted between his teeth, 'You people! When are you going to learn your manners!'

Mr Newman started to laugh and instead heard a sob of rage in his throat. The train took the man away.

That night after supper he felt again a driving need to be with Fred. The fence dividing their back yards was only two feet high and he stepped over it and descended the concrete steps and entered Fred's basement. Fred was there at the workbench and beside him stood Carlson. Mr Newman went over to them and stood watching Fred's hands which were setting the tiny gasoline engine in place in the bottom of the boat. The two men did not seem to notice his arrival. He understood, they were intent on the boat.

The engine in place, Fred went to a chair and sat and Carlson went to the rocker and they talked about the engine and Fred explained how much gas was needed to drive it fifty yards across water. Newman stood there at the bench. They had not even said hello. Ten minutes passed. He felt himself blushing and put in a word. Fred glanced up and acknowledged his presence and then continued talking with Carlson who stubbornly kept his hard eyes only on Fred.

After a few minutes more Newman suddenly raised his head. 'Is that my telephone?' he said. The three listened, and he hurried out of the cellar.

Up in his room he stood at the window looking down at the darkness over the back yard. His brows were drawn together. His breath kept coming short. Then he lay down, dumb, senseless. And eventually he slept.

Atop the ladder now he realized that he had finished painting the shutters. And still Fred and Carlson had not returned from Paradise Gardens, where they had gone for a beer two hours earlier without inviting him, although he had been sitting within earshot on the porch. Newman inspected and re-inspected the shutters to find a spot that he had missed. But the wood was all newly green, every inch of it, and the same color, this time, as Fred's and the rest of the block's.

He could not stand up here any longer. The rung of the ladder was hurting his arches. Carefully, he took the paint can off the metal hook and rung by rung, descended. As he reached the floor of the porch he heard the engine of a car turning the corner.

At a glance he recognized Fred's car, and busied himself with lowering the upper extension of the ladder. The car pulled to a stop at the curb.

Now he heard the squeaking of the springs and the slam of the car door as both men got out. Lowering the upper extension of the ladder by releasing the rope that held it up, Newman never turned his head. He had painted his shutters. It would be unheard of for Carlson who noticed everything to pass without commenting on the job he had done. Too, now that they were seeing him again it was impossible to believe that they would go – Fred into his house and Carlson across the street to his – without uttering a greeting, let alone an excuse for not having invited him to go along.

The ladder came down as he let the rope slide slowly through his hands. He heard Carlson's heels as the man crossed over to his house. He heard Fred coming up the cement walk, heard him mounting his porch, heard his screen door open . . .

Unable to restrain his voice, Newman turned his head and said, 'Hya.'

Fred had the screen door open, and looked through the screen at Newman, his foot on the threshold. His puffed eyes were reddened, his cheeks relaxed by the beer. Newman watched with alarm as he slowly moved his head forward until his nose was bent against the screen. Then smiling idiotically and without focus, he muttered hoarsely, 'Had a couple . . .' With a swaying attempt at entering his house erectly he struck the doorjamb with his shoulder and disappeared inside.

That night, lying in bed beside his open window, Mr Newman looked at the moon, for he could not sleep. Fred's nose bent down against the screen hung in his mind. Had that meant something, the way he had done it so methodically? A bent nose . . . And yet he had said a rather friendly thing immediately after. And too, he had been drunk. But why was he acting so peculiarly?

The hours moved by quietly and they left him silent and

alone. After a while he got up and went into the bathroom, turned on the light, and stood a long time looking at his face in the mirror. There were no thoughts, no plans, not even fear. He seemed unable to feel anything any more.

In the morning he opened his front door and stepped out on his porch, and his right foot hesitated a moment before coming down to the brick floor. His garbage pail was lying on its side in the middle of the gutter. On his lawn its contents were carefully spread out. He looked up and down the street. All the other cans, with the burlap bags full of paper, were standing at the curb, covered.

CHAPTER TEN

MR FINKELSTEIN was still a young man, but as a Jew he was very old. He knew what was going on. He could hardly help knowing. Twice in the past three weeks, when he had come out of his house at six in the morning to open his store he had found his garbage can turned on its side, its contents kicked all over his sidewalk.

So when, on this Monday morning, he came out of his house at six o'clock and found his garbage can again turned over, with grapefruit rinds thrown up to his very front porch, he hesitated hardly a moment, and proceeded to gather the garbage together again with two stiff pieces of cardboard and dumped it back into the pail. He was smiling all the while. Whenever he was frightened and angry in this particular way, he smiled. It was like an old joke that had been repeated and repeated to him all his life, and all he could do now was to smile at the idiocy of the teller. He smiled too, however, because he had an instinctive feeling that from one of the houses across the street somebody was watching him gathering up this garbage.

It was only when he straightened up after setting the can in its rightful place and looked up the street at the cans set in their proper places before every house – only then did he grow confused. For he noticed with a start that garbage was speckling the lawn of Mr Newman's house, too, and Mr Newman's garbage can was also lying on its side.

Mr Finkelstein observed this carefully, studied the facts. Could it be, he wondered, that his wife had always been right when she claimed that Newman was strictly a Jewish name? That he did not believe, although he did not know why. He simply had always taken it for granted that Mr Newman who worked for that big company was not a Jew, although lately . . .

Anyhow he had work to do, so he opened his store, pulled down the transom over the door, moved his wooden stand outside, and opened the package of papers that the truck always left on the sidewalk. He had hardly begun to cut the twine when he noticed a little edge of yellow paper sticking out from under the top *Times*. He drew it out. It had writing on it. His easily aroused temper banged against his temples as he read. Then folding the yellow sheet carefully he tucked it into his shirt pocket. But he put it so that a little of it stuck out.

After distributing the newspapers neatly over his stand, he put the stopper under the door of the store, brought out his little camp chair, and sat beside the stand, ready for the morning trade. After a few minutes and a few paper sales, he adjusted the yellow sheet so that it stuck out of his pocket a little more.

Sitting there he looked Buddha-like. His wife cooked too well for his own good. He was only forty-two, but already his jowls were heavy. He had just reached the time of his life when he realized the uselessness of trying to keep his belt from sliding under his belly. But he had very broad shoulders and thick arms and wrists and he walked lightly on his tiny feet. Even at this early hour, and before breakfast, he smoked a cigar which never left his mouth. This morning was cool and the sky wonderfully blue and the clouds were fair and white, and he let his soft underchin rest on his chest, folded his arms, and allowed the early sun to rise upon the back of his warm neck.

He always sat still. He had the ability. The garbage on Mr Newman's lawn glistened in the sun as he watched. And at eight o'clock, as usual, Mr Newman came out of his house to go to work. Mr Finkelstein observed how he stopped when he saw the garbage. He watched him start back into his house and hesitate again on the porch steps. He saw him turn toward the garbage again and after a moment's pause start picking up some of it. Then he saw Mr Newman drop the garbage and wipe his hands on the empty burlap bag, and take the pail from the gutter onto the curb.

Now Mr Newman was coming down the street in his direction. He saw him slowing before his neighbor – the hunter's – house and look at it. Then Mr Newman turned and looked across the street at Mr Carlson's house. After a moment he came on down the street toward Mr Finkelstein, his eyes scanning the garbage cans as he passed them.

He had never seen Mr Newman so upset. The man's right hand was half raised as he walked, and it shook visibly. Mr Finkelstein watched as he drew nearer. His distraction was so terrible that Finkelstein could not help but feel sympathy. When Newman came to within ten yards of the stand, Finkelstein assumed the blank stare which he had lately learned to cultivate, and waited for Newman to pass him by. But the man halted beside him.

Leisurely, Mr Finkelstein looked up. Newman's lower lip, he saw, was quivering like a live clam. His eyes were blinking rapidly as though to clear away a dream.

'They kicked mine around too,' he said, and motioned toward his own garbage pail which stood twenty feet away.

Mr Newman looked at Finkelstein's garbage pail and then turned back to him. He started to speak but his throat clogged. He cleared it and whispered huskily, 'Who did it?'

Finkelstein laughed. 'Who? Who always does it? The Christian Front.'

He studied the jerky squirming of Mr Newman's lower lip.

'You think they did, eh?' Mr Newman said, absently.

'Who goes around kicking over garbage pails but those bums? Decent people don't do that.'

'It could have been some children,' Mr Newman said, his voice deadened.

'It could have been but it wasn't,' Mr Finkelstein laughed.

88

'I didn't go to sleep till one o'clock last night and I got up before five . . . I shaved this morning. Between one and five you don't find children going around the streets. Don't worry, it was the Front.'

Mr Newman's face started getting red. And Mr Finkelstein could not tell whether it was anger or fear pumping up his blood. He decided to risk the question.

'But you got nothing to worry about, Mr Newman. By you it was probably a mistake.'

Mr Newman turned to him quickly. But he saw that Mr Finkelstein's little black eyes were filled only with curiosity and no conviction at all that it was a mistake; he, too, was merely asking. Newman stood there, absently smoothing down his vest, and then walked on toward the subway.

Finkelstein watched him go. A very neat and tidy man, he thought, as he watched Newman in his immaculate blue suit disappearing around the corner – a clean man. It probably only bothers him because they dirtied his yard.

He smiled to himself again and sat on his camp chair. After the morning rush was over he took the yellow paper out of his shirt pocket, unfolded it carefully, and adjusting his horn-rimmed glasses to midway down his nose, read it again.

'Jew, if you don't get out of this neighborhood in five days you'll wish you never was born.'

Five days, he thought, and laughed a little, soundlessly. Nice of them to give me five days. He laughed again and slipped the warning halfway into his shirt pocket, fixing it so that it stuck out. He sat again and scanned the street, ready to break out in a smile.

CHAPTER ELEVEN

THE shock of the garbage pail seemed to have sharpened New-man's sense of the practical. Instead of stupidly returning to the big resounding names of the business world he studied the help-wanted ads from a new angle and fastened upon those calling for hundreds of mechanics, tinsmiths, tool and die men. Any company, he figured, which required so many new workers was likely to need a man to hire them. And it was by this logic that he decided to go to the administrative offices of the Meyers-Peterson Corporation, a company he had never heard of before.

The main plant was in Paterson, New Jersey, but here on the tenth floor of a Twenty-ninth Street building in Manhattan was an air-conditioned layout which began to heat his deep-grown admiration for bigness and stability. The company in peacetime made fans and other electrical equipment. The offices – at least this waiting room, which was all he had so far seen of the place – were modern but respectably worn. He was pleased, too, at the executive-type gentlemen who were waiting on the other chairs and couches for appointments within. If he could get set here, he felt, he had a good chance for a job that would last into the postwar period.

Sitting on the leather chair as an outsider waiting to see a Mr Ardell, he feared this coming disastrous era. But when he permitted himself to believe that he would be hired today he rather enjoyed the prospect of having a job in the midst of the coming unemployment. For he had never gotten over re-senting the wages that were being paid to nearly any man who could lift a hammer. In fact, as a man of so many private dis-tinctions he could not help longing secretly for the old days of the other depression, when he was so certain of his job while others were being let out all around him. There was less pleasure in earning when it was easy to earn.

And somehow, as he studied the waiting room and the girl at the reception desk, he got the strong impression that he would be working for this firm. He tried the name of the company on his lips. 'I work for the Meyers-Peterson Corporation, electrical stuff,' he said, as though to an inquiring friend. And it almost sounded all right.

In all his calculations this day, the image of a garbage pail lying on its side never rose before his eyes. Because it rested deep down in him by now. For three days he had been wandering around the city with the overturned can in his mind. He had gone to the city that morning and returned at night. After dinner he had gone down to Fred's cellar and told him about the incident. Fred had seemed surprised and assured him it was a mistake. Either a mistake or the result of some of the boys getting out of hand. And he had been relieved then. It was only after he had gone to bed that he began to wonder. Surely Fred must have noticed the garbage when he walked his dogs before going to work that morning. Why had he wanted to seem ignorant of it? Fred always walked his dogs at seven in the morning.

The receptionist beckoned two of the waiting men and they went out of the room through a wide archway beyond which Mr Newman could see a corridor of office doors. She was kind enough to tell Mr Newman that he would only have to wait a few more minutes for Mr Ardell. He felt well disposed toward her then. It was the first time since he had arrived that he had felt well disposed toward her, since she was a Jewess. It was this fact – although he would not for a moment take it consciously into account – that had led him to believe he would find a position here. On stepping out of the elevator he had seen and instantly registered her face on his mind, but his mind had a way of blurring what it did not want to see clearly. From the moment he set eyes on her he felt he had a chance here. But not because they hired Jews, for he was no more a Jew than Herbert Hoover was. He simply had a chance here because he had a chance here. As Mr Lawrence Newman, a man of great business experience, he had a chance here. At the moment, no other reason existed on the earth.

The receptionist called to him now. He got up and went to her. She rose from her chair and walked him to the archway and pointed down the corridor and told him how many turns to make and in which directions.

He walked away from her and made his way down the corridor to Mr Ardell's office. He knocked on the glass pane and heard a voice within. He opened the door and entered, his hat in his hand.

At first the office seemed to be empty because the chair behind the broad desk was vacant. He had stopped just over the threshold when he heard a woman's voice to his left. He turned his head.

'Won't you sit down?'

In his excitement he saw her but his eyes seemed to be leaping around in his head, so he sat quickly in a chair beside the big desk. His back was toward her, for he would never presume to turn the chair around to face her. All he knew was that something had exploded in his life, and he was blind until the debris settled back to earth.

As she passed his elbow and sat before him at the desk her perfume hit him like a stick. He sensed her thighs flexing as she sat, and the sound of her dress crackled in his ears.

He looked at her and had no idea what expression was on his face. He was trying to smile, however. Her extraordinary right eyebrow, raised as it was, appraised him as it had that other time, but now he could not get up and walk away from it. The curve of her incredibly living lips changed momentarily, as though to conform with the differing opinions of him that were revolving in her mind.

'Mr Ardell's gone out. I'm taking over till he gets back. If you want to wait for him you can. Some men don't like to be interviewed by women,' she said, official and cold.

He floundered uncertainly among the timbres of her voice. 'I . . . it's all right with me.' He laughed. Idiotically, he instantly thought.

'You want to work here?' she asked flatly.

He nodded. 'I wondered if there was anything here for me.'

'What kind of work do you want?'

There was a contralto deadliness in her tone, as though she were about to trap him mercilessly. She never once moved. A woman restraining fury might sit so erectly, with the eyebrow raised and the eyes so fixed. Still, it might be her usual business manner, he thought hopefully.

'I'd like to use my kind of experience if I can.'

'You don't need your experience for this place. They hire anybody in this place. All they do is ask if you're a citizen. Jews, niggers, wops, anybody.'

Air rushed into his mouth and dissolved his words.

'You thought I was a Jew,' she said vengefully.

She was asking him. He nodded infinitesimally, his eyes wide and fixed upon her.

'So you were cockeyed. You see that now, I guess.'

It was hard for him to grasp. It was dreamlike to him. It was like seeing a face in a movie change and dissolve, taking on a new character and yet remaining the same face. She had not changed since the interview in his office. But her features had a new effect upon him. Her eyes in which he had detected that mocking secretiveness were now simply the darkened eyes of a woman who had done a lot of crying. And yet they were the same eyes. Her nose . . . it occurred to him that the Irish often had a dip to their noses, and he thought now that it became her well. And yet it was the same nose. Her loud way of talking no longer seemed offensive. He felt rather that it was forthright, and where it had then indicated crudeness now it bespoke a contempt for evasions. As a Jewess she had seemed dressed in cheap taste, too gaudily. But as a gentile he found her merely colorful in the same dress, a woman who expressed her spirited nature in her clothes. It was as though she now had a right to her faults; as though her flair, her style, her abruptness no longer sprang from bad breeding and an ignorant aping of genteel manners, but from a rebellious mind, an angry mind, a mind that dared to override the smaller rules of behavior. As a Jewess she had seemed vitriolic and pushy and he had hated himself even as he was drawn fearfully to her, but now he no longer feared her for now his love could flow unstained by the guilt of loving what his dignity had always demanded he look down upon. He swallowed as his eyes lowered to the desk top.

He could not understand how he had ever mistaken her. There was nothing about her that was Jewish. Nothing.

His face softening with remorse he met her gaze again. 'I want to apologize, Miss Hart. I was under a tension that day.'

She blinked ironically and raised her brows as though bored. 'I can imagine,' she said.

He did not understand. His head stuck forward an inch, as he asked, 'What can you imagine?'

Her eyes opened upon him. His skin began to burn. If she did not make herself clear in a moment he would drown in the condescending playfulness of her stare. But she said nothing, and merely sucked in the corners of her lips.

'I had orders, Miss Hart,' he said, picking his words. 'I couldn't take a chance.'

She forgot about her lips and her face relaxed and she was listening.

With an air of the confidential he continued, and he was

94

leaning toward the desk. 'That company doesn't hire them. Under any circumstances. They never hired any since the day they opened their doors. You understand? None. Under any circumstances.'

He saw her attitudes dropping away from her, and felt hope in the drawing together of her confused brows. Her blinking stopped, her hands lay motionless on the edge of the desk. He gave her his full-face, and by the thickness of a penny raised his head. He could almost see what was happening to him in the chamber of her mind. And then her brows smoothed and she moved, and looked away running her tongue once over her lower lip.

'Well,' she said, softly and troubled, 'it don't matter anyway. I can't hire you myself . . .'

'I don't care about that. I . . .' He was leaning over the edge of the desk; his cheeks were puffed unnaturally and his flat, fine hair slid out of place. 'I have thought a great deal about you since that day. Please believe what I say. I really have.'

She seemed flattered despite herself. One soft arm slid out slowly along her chair arm.

'Yeh?' she said without committing herself.

'I've been having a hard time since . . . as a matter of fact since the day you saw me.'

It seemed to interest her. He continued.

'You see, I . . . well, frankly, I had to quit that position. They were going to transfer me to a clerk's job.'

'Why?' she asked, fascinated.

'Well, they seemed to feel that since I got my glasses I didn't make the kind of appearance they wanted in the front office.'

'You know what I mean then,' she said. For the first time her voice softened. It contained some compassion for him, he felt, and he was strengthened by it in his quest.

'I know just what you mean.' He felt a flood rising in him

and it poured out. 'I've been trying to get placed and it's the same thing everywhere I go.'

'Sure, they're all morons. You'll never get anywhere with them.'

'I decided that too. That's why I came here.'

'How'd you know this place was Jewish?' she inquired.

'Why . . . is it?'

'Didn't you know?'

'Well, the name . . .'

'Meyers is a Jew.'

He pretended to consider the fact, and did not speak. What Meyers was did not matter at all now.

'You don't want to work here, heh?' she smiled, as one in the jaws of suffering, to another about to enter.

He raised his eyes to hers, sadly, and inwardly happy that she had identified her plight with his.

'Well, you better want to.'

He blinked as though helpless and hurt.

'You're in a bad way yourself, Mr Newman. I can see it now myself.'

'Can you?'

'Oh yeh, it's there all right.' Her eyes moved over his face.

'I'm really sorry I mistook you . . .' he began, getting to his point and helping her to hers.

'It's all right. God, it wasn't the first time. The only reason I blew up at you was I thought . . . well, you know.'

'You really did?'

'Well . . . not exactly. You know how a person does. If you get mad enough at somebody you almost wish they were one of them. It depends on how you look at a person. I mean like now, for instance.' She looked at him as if he were someone who had asked for a comment on a new way of combing his hair. 'Right now it wouldn't ever come into my mind. You know what I mean?'

'Oh, certainly,' he said.

Never had he spoken so fluently with a woman he considered beautiful. And looking into her face now he knew somehow that he was her first confidant too. A moment of calm seemed to have arrived, a moment of contented silence. For the first time there was nothing to make them tense and Newman examined the pause with gratitude and expectation. And when she spoke he felt he was hearing her private voice, as surely as he was seeing the relaxation of her shining eyelids for the first time.

'I can't hire you,' she said quietly, looking down, 'but if you come back in about an hour Ardell will be here and I'll tell him about you.'

'Fine. Is there a position open?'

'Well, it ain't exactly your old line but it's a decent kind of a job. They want a man who could interview people coming here to sell the company things. You'd send them to the right department. You'll have to learn something about the kind of things they make but they'll teach you. It's kind of a sales-traffic-control thing . . . I think they call it that. The company's bigger than it looks. They're taking two more floors in this building in October. What you do is keep salesmen from cluttering up the wrong offices. I got an idea it's going to be an after-the-war job unless the whole country closes down when peace comes.'

'What is this Ardell?'

'Oh he's all right. He's Catholic. Don't get the idea they only hire foreigners from that receptionist out there. Peterson's a Swede or something, you know. There's all kinds here. They got a nigger for a bookkeeper, even.'

She got up and he did too.

'I got some typing to finish. You going to come back?'

He thrilled at the suggestion of interest in her tone.

'Oh yes,' he said quickly, 'you say about an hour?'

She looked at her watch. 'Yeh, make it an hour. I'll tell him about you.'

Their eyes met. 'Thanks a lot,' he said, drawing in his stomach.

'Chalk it up.' She denied the fractional advance listlessly, went over to her typewriter and, ignoring him, began typing rapidly.

He sidled to the door smiling, but she did not look up, so he went out. When he got to the street he was surprised that he had forgotten to ask what salary they would be paying. It hardly mattered, naturally. Nothing — nothing else in the world seemed to matter. As he walked he felt needed, almost necessary again. She had practically implored him to come back, which at the moment was equivalent to Fred and Carlson and Gargan and Mr Lorsch giving a party in his honor; at any rate, the invisible presence of danger was nowhere on the street that day.

CHAPTER TWELVE

HE was not happy. After two weeks he saw that he was a glorified usher to salesmen, none of whom had come to see *him*. He was not happy but he had never been quite so eager to get to his place of business every morning. She was making him feel so alive that his whole existence before knowing her began to look like a desert and a stupid waste of years.

They were walking along Fifth Avenue one night for the breeze. His feeling for her sometimes rose so high within him that he wanted to hug and kiss her on the street. Especially at times like this when pássing men gave her a second glance – he knowing all the time that all he had to do was lean over to her ear and ask her, and she would marry him. It was a rare thing in his life to be able to reach out and get something he wanted.

The clean broad avenue was so nearly deserted that she could talk freely. She had gulped down two glasses of straight Scotch, which unnerved him a little, for he had always had a definite notion about women who *enjoyed* drinking. Besides, she kept talking very loud.

'Yeh,' she was saying, pronouncing it *yaih*, 'I'm not just what you might call a choir girl.' She glanced at him, ready to burst out laughing. 'That embarrasses you, don't it?'

'Oh, go on,' he laughed, as though it would take more than that. She made him thirst for her when she spoke this way, and she frightened him.

'I was going to marry an actor. Never marry an actor.' She laughed and pulled his arm. He laughed with her, but not so loudly. Every time she had a drink this actor seemed to creep into the conversation. 'He was younger than me, but he was beautiful. Real cute, you know?'

Her eyelids seemed to thicken. She had never revealed so much about him. 'I kissed him good-bye one morning and he never come back.'

She seemed ready to talk it out about this person.

'Do you still ... I suppose you still care for him,' Newman ventured.

'Me?' She laughed scoffingly. 'I'm a very hard woman these days, Signor.' It was a curious sentence she repeated now and then. 'I keep wondering about you. Weren't you really ever married?'

'Oh no. I've always been an old batch,' he smiled.

'How do you keep looking so neat?'

'Oh, I'm careful, that's all.'

'You are,' she said, inspecting him with some wonder, 'you're a careful type of man.'

'I have my moments,' he said uneasily. He realized that for the first time they were really talking about each other.

They had reached the park and they sat on a bench from which they could watch the big hotels facing Park Plaza. A line of horse-drawn carriages stood at the curb near them, beside each carriage an old driver with a silk hat. Behind them a marble fountain bubbled and a boy sat on its rim with his feet in the water.

She never let go of his arm, even as they sat. They were silent for a while, watching limousines pull up to the glittering doorways of the elegant hotels.

Softly she said, 'What kind of car do you have?'

'Plymouth.'

'What kind? I mean the body.'

'Oh. A sedan,' he said, as a gray roadster passed.

'Uh huh.'

She stared at the traffic again. 'What do you do for excitement usually?'

'Not much. Been pretty busy all my life, just working.'

'Some have it all and some got nothing.' Her sudden philosophical moments pleased him. She seemed poetic at times.

'That's the truth, I guess. Although I've had my share of things,' he sighed.

'Yeh? Like what?' she asked idly.

'Oh, a nice home, and . . . well, a good job.'

'But didn't you ever have a good time?'

'Well, sure, I . . .' He started to say that he used to bowl with Fred and had great times taking drives in his car. He turned to her. 'I guess I've never had what you mean,' he said.

'That's the trouble with you, Lawrence.'

He felt he was shrinking and there was nothing for him to say except something foolish. 'I've been what they call repressed, Gertrude.'

'That's why I always picked actors.' He did not know quite what she meant by picked, but he shed it from his mind. 'Actors got style sometimes. They make a dollar and spend seventy-five cents. Everybody else is saving to pay insurance.'

She seemed to be telling him that she knew how hard he had found it to pay the two dollars and forty cents for their seats at Radio City two nights before.

'Well, actors make a lot more money than . . .'

'No they don't. You'd be surprised.'

'Would you like to go to a night club sometime?' he asked.

She looked at him and smiled. 'You ever been to a night club?'

'Not the ones in New York. I used to go to one in Queens with Fred. He's my neighbor I was telling you about.'

'A Queens night club,' she said.

'There's some pretty fast places in Queens.'

'What'd you do there?'

'Oh, we'd have a drink and dance.'

'You have a girl with you?'

'Not usually. Usually I'd dance with Fred's wife. But I don't enjoy dancing very much. I find most women are pretty dumb. I mean they're not serious,' he added quickly.

'Do you drink a lot?'

'Not much. Just on occasion.'

They said nothing for a few moments. She kept staring across the avenue at the hotels.

'A penny for your thoughts,' he said, pretending to chuckle.

She turned deliberately to him. The drinks had worn off. 'You going to keep taking me out?' she asked, weightily.

'Would you like me to?' he fumbled.

'Say yes or no. I'm not the harpooning type,' she said with a strange tinge of annoyance.

'Well, of course I'd like to. I was just wondering how you felt.'

She held his gaze relentlessly. 'Why do you take me out?'

'I like your company. That's the truth.'

'Nothing more?'

'Sometimes you're . . .' he started to reprimand her gently.

'I know all the answers, don't I?' She turned her head away as though worried about herself.

'That's all right,' he managed. But she kept her head turned away.

After a moment he said, 'Tell me more about yourself, Gertrude.'

'Why?'

'I guess I want to know you better. You mentioned you'd been in Hollywood. How'd you like it there?'

'Oh, it's all right.'

'Were you trying to get in the movies?'

'Uh huh.'

'As an actress?'

'I'm a singer.'

'Really? Professionally?'

'Sure. I've had over two hundred engagements.'

'What kind of singing?'

'Any kind. Hot, blue, or for weddings.'

'What happened? Lose your voice.'

'Unfortunately, no.'

'Why do you say that?'

'I still want to sing. I still can.'

'Why don't you?'

'You don't make the same mistake twice if you can help it.'

'Like what?'

'I don't want to just go around with a band. I want to be seen. Like in the movies.'

'Why didn't they take you? I'll bet you sing beautifully.'

'I got the wrong type of beauty.'

'Oh.'

'I got the test but I looked too tragic for a singer.'

'Oh,' he repeated quietly.

'Then where'd you go? You stay in Hollywood?'

'Stayed there for the weather.'

'You were out of work long?'

'I didn't feel well . . . You want to hear about it?'

'I do. Really, Gertrude.'

'All right. I got this test and they didn't take me. Then I got to realize that it wasn't any use, you know? So I quit the profession. I'd made some contacts, though, and I thought maybe I could pick up some parts. But my contacts were all after the same thing and I got so I couldn't even stand to have a bus driver touch my hand to put the change in. So I stayed there two years working for a man who had a dog-manicuring place. You know, washing and clipping . . .'

'Yes, I've heard of them.'

'He was all right to me, for a man. I came around to myself. And I began to go out again. Well . . .' She thought. He watched her inward stare as the passing headlights smoothed their glow across her relaxed face, which held a majesty for him now. 'I

103

fell in love with this actor. I brought my mother out for the wedding.'

'Where is your home?'

'Rochester. Seven sisters. I'm the oldest. My mother came and he went.'

'He didn't marry you?'

'Not even maybe. He just lit out.'

'Is that when you were ill?'

'Yeh. That's when I was ill. I went back to Rochester and sat around. That's when I realized what was wrong.'

'How do you mean?'

She turned to him and thought for a moment. 'You ever listen to Father Coughlin?'

'Oh, sure. Many times.'

'It felt like he was talking to me. I could tell listening to him that he was on the level. That's all I want with people, is for them to be on the level, and he was. He just put me in a sweat listening to his voice. And the things he said were so true, you know? He's the only priest I ever heard who had the nerve to come out with things. He really knows what God is about . . . Or don't you think so.'

'I do. I think he was very forceful making his points. Are you Catholic?'

'No, but I go to church most Sundays. But you don't have to be Catholic to believe in him.'

'I know. I just asked.'

'He made me believe in God again. He really did. I'm not kidding, he gave me hope. I mean that there were still some honest people left.'

A quietness, an exalted calm fell over them. He was sure she was referring to him then, and to the kind and straightforward way he had treated her the past week. In the moments of their silence he thought to himself that she was spiritual. A woman who had been roughly handled. He wanted to cradle her head

104

in his arms and protect her, then. And yet he could not help wondering how she had gotten that Brooklyn way of talking when she came from Rochester where the speech was so different.

'Did you go to school in Rochester?' he asked, his tone inconsequential.

She looked at him. 'Don't you believe I come from Rochester?'

'Certainly I do. I just wondered . . .'

'You believe everything I say?' she asked in deadly earnest.

If he said no, she would get up and walk away. He knew she would. So he said he believed her. And without warning she took his face in her hands and brought her lips up to his, held him so he could not move and looked into his eyes as though she would cry. And then she kissed him hard and let him go. He sat there blind. In a moment she took out a handkerchief and held it to her nose with her head tipped forward and he saw she was crying.

'Don't cry,' he said, grasping her hand.

She got up and started walking away. He caught up with her. She said nothing. They strolled along the edge of the park. Thank God, he felt, that it was so dark.

After a moment he got the feeling that she was waiting for him to lead her somewhere. Until now they always had a destination when walking together. The entrance of the park was a quarter of a block ahead.

He took hold of her arm with his hand, awkwardly, as though to help her up a step. But there were no steps around and he did not know whether he should say something before slipping his whole arm inside hers. The entrance to the park was only a few yards ahead and she seemed to respond to the slightest pressure of his hand. Holding his breath he drew her slightly to the right, toward the entrance, and she obeyed. They turned into the dark path that wound down toward the little lake.

On both sides of them lay the rolling swells of earth and the still trees. The path descended between hillocks and there was no air moving at all. Passing a bench he kept his eyes straight ahead when he saw a sailor and a girl lying stretched out on it. It occurred to him that he had not been in the park at night since his boyhood. In those days there were men who wandered about among the dark bushes with flashlights, and when they found a couple in the grass they would demand money from them.

'It's cool in here,' she said quietly.

'It is, yes,' he agreed.

Was it time, he wondered, to ask her to take him to her room, or would she be insulted? Off to the side, from out of the blackness among tall lilac bushes he heard a movement and a hastily whispered word. Gertrude seemed to change the rhythm of her breathing. He could not do it. Whatever she expected of him he knew he could not do. In the dark he saw an empty bench under an overhanging tree.

'Want to sit down?' he asked, thinly.

'Sure,' she said.

A girl ran up to them as they came to the bench. She was breathless and the glow of a distant light caught her face; her mouth was soft and small, like a baby's, her hair was a mass of little ringlets, and a brown comb clung precariously to a loose strand.

'Gee whiz!' she panted, right into Newman's face. She was in terror, he saw. She jerked her head to look behind her and her curls shuddered.

'Gee . . .' she said, gulping for breath.

'What's the matter with you?' Gertrude asked, calmly.

'My girl friend. Did you see a girl in a blue dirndl and sandals?' she asked desperately.

'No, we didn't see anybody.'

'Gee whiz.' She started to cry.

'Cut it out,' Gertrude said annoyed. 'Where'd you leave her?'

'I think a sailor's got her,' the girl said, looking behind into the darkness again.

'What'd he do, grab her?' Gertrude asked, angry at the sailor.

Newman glanced at Gertrude, puzzled. He would have walked away by this time.

'No, we went out. My sailor went away and then I looked for her and she wasn't there,' the girl explained.

'What, did you get picked up?' Gertrude frowned at the girl's stupidity.

'Yeh,' the girl admitted. But Newman saw that she knew she was not being condemned.

'You know their names?' Gertrude asked.

'Yeh, but not their right names.'

'Well, you better call a cop, that's what you better do.'

'I don't want to. Please, they'll take her to jail.'

'You're drunk, aren't you?' Gertrude asked with knowing detachment.

'No, I was drinking but I'm not drunk any more. Please, her mother'll murder me. It's her first time out. She's just a kid. Please, I promised to take her home by nine o'clock.'

Gertrude thought a moment. Newman still had her arm, and he sensed disaster should Gertrude decide to follow the girl.

'Where'd you leave her. Come on,' Gertrude said at last.

Thankfully, the girl gave Gertrude one glance and with a child's hand gestured for her to follow. The three hurried along. Newman tried to think of something to say; he could not bear merely following.

Down the dark path they walked intently and rapidly. Newman's skin began to tingle; he felt proud and afraid of Gertrude. Who was she? Who was this girl? What was he doing here? In Heaven's name . . . !

They came to a drinking fountain and the girl halted and looked around trying to remember her direction. She pointed at a low hill that rose from the left of the path. The hill was covered with bushy trees and there were no lights shining out of it which meant that there was no path into it and no police.

Pointing, the girl said quietly, 'I think I left her up there. Could you go up there with me?' she pleaded.

Gertrude peered through the darkness at the hill. Newman pretended to study it too. A fear of the dark that he had always had now flowed down upon him from the hill. His kneecap twitched.

'How drunk was this sailor?' he asked the girl, formally.

'I don't know. I don't remember. I got to find her; please, Mister.'

Gertrude looked at him. 'You want to go up there?'

Her voice was whiney with excitement. He wanted to go away. She was a stranger now. 'All right,' he whispered.

'Come on,' she said.

With the girl in the lead they moved off the path and started up the little hill. Once off the path they could see nothing whatever. In the darkness he heard the girl sniffling up ahead of them. In a moment they could make her out, bent over slightly as though to see the ground under the low branches of the trees as she climbed. Newman clung to Gertrude's arm. His body was radiating heat and his collar was choking him. He felt bigger somehow, a little brave, unusual. It was as though he had always wanted to follow things through this way and now he was doing it, as though Gertrude had discovered this yearning in him and had taken it for granted. And he loved her for her confidence in him as they climbed through the darkness behind the crouched and sniffling girl. There was a rustling among the twigs of a bush. The three halted. Newman started in shock as he felt Gertrude's fingers digging into his forearm. She was pressing his arm against her body at the same time. The girl got down on her hands and knees and looked into the bush.

After lowering her head way down to see beneath the thick upper leaves she got up and came to Gertrude and whispered into her ear, 'It's not them.' Then she turned and continued climbing. Newman felt Gertrude's fingers relaxing. The girl was moving a little way from them now, for they had slackened their pace. Ahead and above them they saw the top of the hill and the outline of a giant black tree against the sky. As they approached something white showed at the foot of the tree. They saw the girl halt beside the tree, and in a moment they came up to her and stared at the flattened bed of newspapers on the ground. The girl leaned over and picked up something and walked away from the tree and stopped where the tree's shadow ended in moonlight. Newman saw she had a small whiskey bottle in her hand. Gertrude made no move to go to her and they stood that way for a while watching the girl who was reading the label. Gertrude was looking around, not at the girl any more. The girl dropped the bottle and came over to them. She took a thoughtful breath, and said quietly, 'They were here.'

She turned her head surveying the dark slopes below them. 'Would you come with me? There's a place they might have gone for a drink. Please, I gotta get her home. I just gotta. Please, Missis,' she said, threatening to cry.

'Go ahead,' Gertrude whispered. Newman quivered at the low languor of her voice. The girl started down the way they had come. Gertrude and Newman turned and followed. In a moment the deep blackness of the hillside swallowed them again. They could not see the girl now. Newman waited for Gertrude to hurry a little, or to call out for the girl. Their steps slowed. And then they stopped and Newman felt Gertrude's body relaxing and he moved and stood in front of her. She was a foot downhill and he above her and taller now. He managed to take hold of her arm and instantly she slipped her other arm about him and he was kissing her lips and her perfume streamed into him as though the mouth of the bottle had opened under his nose.

Staring up through the leaves of the tree he could see the faint glow of light that the city surrounding the park threw up against the sky. His body felt disconnected from him, numb, like his jaw at the dentist's.

'God!' she exhaled softly. She was shaking her head from side to side. It was the first word either of them had spoken in half an hour.

He turned and looking at the side of her face tried to compose a few words. His sense of pity was so intense that it stifled him.

'God,' she exhaled again, and turned her head to him. 'Where'd you ever learn your ways?'

'I . . .'

Before he could begin his apology her face moved up to his and she kissed his lips and he shivered. Then she let her head rest on the grass again. 'God, we shouldna done it. You just swept me off my feet, y'know? You just swept me away.' She laid the back of her hand over her eyes.

His pity fled as he realized how much she loved him. He came up on one elbow. 'Do you . . . you feel all right?' he asked falteringly.

'Yeh,' she breathed softly, 'I'm fine. God,' she erupted again with a sigh, 'I'd of never expected it of you. You just swept me away.'

Astonished, he tried to remember how it had happened, and wondered if this was what was meant by sweeping a girl off her feet. 'I couldn't help myself, dear,' he said, with less apology.

Suddenly she sat up and grasped his face and kissed him, forcing his head deep into the grass. Then resting her cheek upon his chest, she whispered wondrously, 'God.'

He stared up through the tree. After a moment he expanded his chest and kept it that way, breathing with his stomach. Sensation was beginning to flow back into his body. His limbs seemed to be growing longer and thicker. For an instant he felt six feet tall.

'Gertrude,' he said. They ought to be moving on. He kept glancing into the dark, ready for the twinkle of a flashlight.

She raised her head and looked down at him. 'You look like Claude Rains now,' she said.

'That's because you can't see my face,' he smiled.

'I can just imagine what you look like now, though. You got the same little bags under your eyes. You're about his size too. You really are. I saw him in Hollywood. You're a lot like each other.'

'Oh, go on.'

'I'm not kidding. You could make a fortune in pictures.'

'Oh, stop now.' It embarrassed him, and drew him.

'You're wasting yourself; you are, really.'

'I'm not an actor. Never could be.'

'Not necessarily an actor. You could be an executive. You're an executive type.'

'You really think so?'

'I do. You know most executives don't get there till their forties. I read it in an article when I was having my hair done.'

'I've heard that said, but . . .'

'You ought to look around sharper. There's probably a lot laying dormant in you. I looked up your month on the zodiac, home.'

'Oh, did you? I meant to ask you.'

'You're the executive type, all right.'

'Well, I don't put much stock in those . . .'

'Don't kid yourself. Some of the biggest stars in Hollywood don't make a move until they see what the charts have to say about what's in store for them.'

'I've read that.'

'It's true. For all you know you could have the possibilities of a big man. I mean it. Sometimes I look around in the office at some of those executives and then I look at you . . .'

'Well, I can only try. I do my work and . . .'

'Nobody gets anywhere just doing his work. You got to make contacts. You're hiding yourself under a bushel so the light can't come out. I've been wanting to tell you this. Really,' she said. 'What you ought to do is think of some business to go into. Something that would give you a chance to spread out and show your abilities.'

He listened for footsteps. If he could only get walking again without seeming prudish . . .

'What sort of business do you mean?' he asked.

'Oh, there's hundreds of different kinds. I can just see you in charge, though.'

'I *am* used to being in charge,' he agreed partially. 'But it takes money to start a business.'

'Not if you got the right contacts. You take that Mr Galway in the sales department?'

'Yes?'

'You think that boy is going to keep working for a salary once the war is over?'

'I don't know him hardly.'

'Well, I talk to him now and then. The armistice whistles ain't hardly going to stop blowing before that boy is out of the office looking for his own business to start. You ought to get to know him. Or even Mr McIntire. Although Mac'll probably get drunk after the war's over and stay drunk till the next one starts. But he's got ideas, Mac has. The thing is, you get to know some of those boys, Lawrence. I can see it. Really. Get into their crowd a little. Pick up some pointers.'

'I don't know if I could do that, Gertrude . . .'

'I don't mean that you . . .'

'No, I mean I'm not the type, I don't think. You have to weasel people in business. I . . .'

'But there's businesses where you can act very nice.'

'That's true but . . .'

'That's the kind I mean,' she said. She was on her elbow, her face close to his. He kept looking up past her at the tree, trying to see the truth of what she said. 'Galway's going to open a plastics factory. You get places if you start with the boss. You might even work into a partner after a while.'

She lay back in the grass and he looked at her face. 'You should go to the Coast sometime,' she said. 'The houses they live in! God . . .' she sighed wondrously again. 'That's what I dream about,' she said softly, 'it's all I ever dream of.'

'Well, we can't all be rich.'

'You could,' she said, stroking his cheek. 'You've got that way about you. I've got instincts about people. I'm psychic that way.'

'I don't know. I doubt that I'll ever be really rich.'

'Wouldn't you even want to be?' she asked playfully.

'Oh certainly. You wouldn't find me turning down money.'

'But you don't think about it,' she asked.

'Well I do, yes. I just . . . well, I don't know how a man goes about getting rich.' He laughed at how mechanically he had pictured the process. With his left hand he stroked the grass, then thought of dogs and raised his hand to his stomach.

'It's what I said. Contacts. Connections. That's why I advise you to get next to some of the people at the office.'

He looked at her a long time. No one had ever seen the character of a leader in him. He knew he could never be boss, but what captured him was the simple possibility. She saw in him what no one ever had, and he wanted to know her and so discover himself. For a long time he lay beside her turning this exciting idea. And then he realized fully for the first time what he was doing. He was lying on his back beside a woman in the middle of the park at night. And there was nothing frightening about it. It was a young thing to be doing. Already, he thought, she was leading him into new paths. Who knew to what stimulating life she might draw him?

He studied her profile. An air of concentration flowed from her. 'A penny for your thoughts,' he said.

She laughed quietly. Above them the tree stirred in a little wind that quickly died. 'I was just thinking something silly. As usual.' She rubbed her lips lightly over his and for an instant he could not breathe.

'What were you thinking silly?'

She hesitated a moment. 'What I would say if you asked me to marry you.'

'What I would . . .'?

'No, what I would say if you asked *me*,' she laughed shrilly and gay.

His laugh accompanied hers. And she lay there smiling. It took a minute before he realized she was waiting.

'What would you say?' he asked, striving to make it all a joke.

'I probably would say no,' she said.

Dumbfounded, he lay there with his tongue stuck to the roof of his mouth. It seemed impossible. He did not know her again. If he lost her . . .

'Why . . . why would you say no?' he asked, anxiously.

'Because I'd probably ruin your life.' Her smile went.

'Oh no . . .' He would be dreaming her again . . .

'I probably would. You'd have to go dancing with me. I got to have a dance once in a while.'

'I'd love to go dancing with you. I didn't say I wouldn't want to go dancing with you.' And at the dream's end she would not be there.

'Would you, really?'

'Sure,' he laughed, as though she were a child, 'I'd do any-

114

thing you liked. I just never went out much because I
didn't have the kind of woman who appealed to me. Really,
Gertrude, I never stop thinking about you. It even seems sometimes that I had been thinking about you for years before I met
you.'

He was thrilling her a little now, just a little. And he had
grasped her hand where it lay on his chest.

'I always had an idea of a certain kind of woman. I can't remember when it started but I've had it a long time. And she
carried herself just like you. That's why you struck me so the
first time I saw you.'

He could see her eyes glistening in the semidarkness. She
was waiting for him to do something extraordinary, he felt,
and he did not know what to do. So he moved his face toward
hers and she kissed him lightly and then looked at him again.
And they both began to breathe in longer draughts.

'Marry me, Gertrude,' he pleaded. It sounded theoretical
to him.

'All right,' she said.

He could not hold his awkward position after a moment and
he let go of her hand and lay back.

After a while she said, 'When will we do it?'

'When would you like?' he asked, turning to her. He could
not get over how theoretical it was. It did not seem to be
inevitable, suddenly.

'The first of the month?'

'All right. I'd like you to come home and meet my mother,'
he said, wondering if he would still know her by the first of the
month.

'OK. You think she'll like me?'

'Oh I'm sure she will. She's been wanting me to get married
a long time.'

'Is she very religious?'

'Well, not fanatic. Since she got so she can't walk I take her to church in a taxi once in a while. About once a month. We'd have to get married in the church,' he said, half asking.

'It's the only place,' she assured him.

'Are you religious?'

'I go every Sunday,' she said.

'Really? What church?'

'I go to different ones. You mean the denomination?'

'Well yes.'

'Don't you remember what it said on my application?'

'Episcopalian?'

'That's right.' She seemed a little hurt, and somewhat belligerent.

'That's good,' he said, as though it were of great importance to him, 'I'm glad you are.' She softened, he thought. 'Because that's what I am and it'll make it easier with Mother.'

'Then give me a kiss,' she said, 'a real one.'

He kissed her and she held him a long time. 'We'd better go,' he said in a whisper.

They got up and he walked her to her rooming-house, wondering about grass stains. An hour later he was coming down his own dark block and he felt a yearning, an indefinite need for something; it was as though he had lost something in the grass perhaps ... a coin, or his watch. A sense of having dreamed it all pervaded his mind. Who was she? He really didn't know her. He knew she tended to make things up. It even occurred to him that she had never been in Hollywood at all. And now he would be coming into his house and telling his mother about her and he did not quite know what to say about her character. She was religious, anyway, and that was good. He would simply say he had picked out a nice, Episcopalian girl and dwell on that. Then again, maybe he ought not to mention it yet. Maybe tomorrow he would want to call it all off. And yet ... she was so amazingly like the woman in his dream. The same softness on her hips.

Climbing the high stoop he decided that probably it always happened in this casual, almost accidental way. Probably tomorrow he would feel positively in love, and not at all afraid. Probably, he thought as he softly opened the door, he would start being happy tomorrow.

CHAPTER THIRTEEN

'You make a pretty picture with that thing on,' he said. The blue bandana over her hair and tied under her chin made her look madonna-like, he thought.

'Just to keep my hair straight,' she replied, pleased.

He drove with both hands clasping the wheel, his head raised so that he could see better over the hood. The warm summer air smelled of the woods that lay on both sides of the highway and he opened the second button of his sports shirt to feel the breeze on his chest.

'Isn't it beautiful?' he said.

'I'd like to pick some flowers,' she said, watching the colors of the blooms beside the road.

'Better not. I noticed a sign a way back forbidding it.'

She breathed in deeply, and exhaled, and then shook her head in wonder at a grove of exceptionally perfect pines, the smell of which had filled her lungs. 'The things God makes,' she said.

'It's beautiful,' he agreed, and quickly returned his gaze to the road, smiling softly.

Looking ahead she said, 'You sure they'll have a room for us?'

'Oh, sure. Especially now with gas rationing.'

'There's still cars on the road, though.'

'But not enough in volume to crowd the places. Anyway they don't cater to the usual mob in this place.'

'I hope the lake is clean.'

'Like silver. Of course I haven't been there for five years, but it was clean then.'

'And they dance?' she asked, as though for confirmation.

He laughed, and patted her knee. 'I'm not taking you to a

fogy place. Matter of fact, I went there for kind of romantic reasons.'

'You did!' she scoffed, interested.

'Really.' He looked at her and they both laughed.

'Did you find anything?'

'Well,' he blushed a little, cocking his head as though he were not telling all, 'I had some very interesting conversations.'

'You.'

'You think I'm a regular fogy, don't you!' He burst out laughing.

'Sure you are.'

'Supposing I told you that half the time I'm thinking of you.'

'I wouldn't believe it.'

'Well it's so. And before you came I was thinking of women in general.'

'You.'

'I always had an idea of a certain kind of woman. Really. And you're it.' He glanced seriously at her, then back to the road. 'I'm serious.'

'I believe you, Lully,' she admitted quietly.

They rode on for a while. 'This is what I always dreamed of,' he said. 'I mean being married and taking a drive for a weekend. I always had to go alone.'

'How many times did you go to this place?'

'Only once to this place. But I went to others.'

'And never found anybody at all?'

'Nobody.' A thought struck him. 'None of them looked like you.'

She leaned over and kissed his cheek and waited for him to turn his head to her.

'Better not while I'm driving,' he said, for as she kissed him they had passed a man waiting to cross the road.

'Let him see,' she taunted.

'I don't care about anybody seeing, I just . . .'

'You're embarrassed for him.'

'No,' he laughingly complained, 'I just drive when I drive and that's all I can do.' A car sped past them and then moved over into their lane and disappeared around a curve ahead.

'Darned fool,' he said. 'People don't care whether they live or die.'

All of a sudden she jumped a little, ecstatically, and gripped his arm and pressed her leg against his. He blushed and reached down and squeezed her thigh, making a mock-angry face. They rode that way for a while. Through the corners of his eyes he saw the forests and the hills and noted the hidden sensuous nooks. She did not move her thigh away. He thought, then dared say it.

'If they give me my old room it'll be great for us.'

'Off by itself?' she asked.

'That's what I mean.'

There were moments when he dared say these things and hold her thigh in broad daylight. As in the nights – he had come to live only for the nights – he felt willing to die for her at these times. Now he glanced at the sun and gauged its distance to the horizon.

'Tonight we go out in the woods,' she said, 'all right? I love the woods.'

'We can go near the lake,' he said, remembering a certain spot he had picked out for a girl who had never arrived. Now the girl would come, she was his wife, she could not run away or be coy and make things difficult for him, and it was all respectable and honorable and still there was this incredible sting in it that he hoped would never go away.

They drove, and he thought of the garbage can and swore with the passion of a knight's resolve that she must never know of it and be made unhappy. He returned his hand to the wheel.

'Wouldn't it be wonderful if we had a place of our own in the country?' she mused carefully.

'The kind you'd like would have to have forty-six rooms.'

'Well there's nothing wrong with having expensive tastes. You know what you never did?' she said in that same half-relaxed tone.

'What did I never did?' he said.

'You never had a talk with Mac.'

'Now look,' he said conclusively. 'Mac is a man who drinks a great deal and has a number of very good business ideas. And none of them takes less than a million dollars to put into operation.'

'Then you talked to him?' she asked with a quick sharpening of interest.

'I always talk to him.'

'I mean about maybe getting together with him.'

'Even if I had anything to offer him I wouldn't. He's a terrible drunk, dear. You know that.'

'That's true,' she said, thinking.

'Let's try to get along with what we have.'

'Yeh, but don't you want me to make a home for you?'

This, he understood, was another way of asking when she could quit her job. It distressed him. She seemed more beautiful every day and he could not understand why she had given herself to him so freely and after such a short courtship.

'I told you dear,' he said kindly, 'you can quit any time you feel like.'

'But I can't on the money you're making now. I really can't understand you.'

'I've got two thousand dollars, Gert, Now what kind of a business can you open with two thousand dollars?'

'Well, think about it. Let's think,' she asked as a minimum.

She turned and looked out her window, reflectively. After he had carefully negotiated a sharp turn and was settling back for a straight run, he glanced at her. Where was her mind now? Like last Sunday when they were driving around Sheepshead

Bay to watch the boats. In the midst of a simple conversation she had suddenly announced that she was not from Rochester, had never even been in Rochester. She had been born and brought up on Staten Island. The Rochester disguise was for the benefit of employers who might take her for a Jewess if they knew she was a New Yorker. Which was all right. He could understand it. But riding with her now he felt as he always did when she fell into a prolonged silence; a dread came over him that she was thinking about places and people, and things she had done of which she had never told him. Again he took his eyes from the road and glanced at her. She was smoking now, slowly drawing on the cigarette, her eyes narrowed thoughtfully. She shifted and he noticed the full curve of her hip.

'It would be nice,' he said, controlling his voice, 'to have a place in the country. You're right. It would be a nice thing to . . .'

With a single movement she slid across the seat and gripping his arm with both hands, pressed her lips against his ear. 'You're not mad at me, are you, Lully?' she whispered.

His spine chilled because of the closeness of her mouth, and he laughed, 'No.'

'Are you mad about Wanamaker's?'

'Why should I be?' he asked.

'You looked mad.'

'I just didn't think you ought to send hundred-dollar dresses from stores when you know we'll just have to send them back.'

'But everybody does it. I just wanted to try them on at home.'

'It's all right,' he assured her unconvincingly. 'It just seemed a little silly. You did look nice in that red dress, though.'

'It was rose,' she said, pleased. 'God,' she nearly shouted, 'you got no idea what I could look like!'

He laughed with sharp joy and fright, for it was nearly a thousand dollars worth of merchandise she had sent home.

And two days later he had had to face the same truck-driver who had delivered them. She simply paraded around the house looking glorious in hundred-dollar dresses and then he had to help her pack them all away in their boxes, and when he lowered the top of the box over them it was like burying something.

They drove on. 'You've got very good taste, Gert. I never thought you could look like that. Really, like an actress. Exceptional taste.'

'It's what I pride myself on,' she reminded him.

The road had climbed continuously and now the trees dipped away from the right side and there lay the Hudson far below them, the sun exploding in flares in the hollows of the water.

'This is it, I think,' he said. He slowed down and both leaned forward to read an approaching billboard on the left side of the road.

'Can you see the river from the hotel?' she asked excitedly.

'No, but it's a short walk. This is it,' he said, stopping the car on the road shoulder. She turned in her seat as he had been training her to do, and looked down the road through the back window while he studied the mirror. Then with a roar of the engine he swung the car across the highway, pulling to a rocking stop on a narrow dirt road in front of the sign.

He could not read the sign without getting out, so he said, 'See if there's a diagram on it. I seem to remember.'

She stuck her head out the window and read the sign aloud: 'Riverview Village.' To him she said. 'This is a homes development.'

'I know, but there used to be a diagram telling how to get to the hotel . . .'

'Oh yes. '' Riverview Hotel. Stay on dirt road keeping right.'' ' She pulled her head in. 'Just keep right, I guess.'

He drove the car up the dirt road and into a wood through which it led. She set her hair in order. It was combed down from a part in the center now, and her forehead seemed to protrude less than it had with her hair upswept. He thought her more freshly countrified, more Rochester this way, and encouraged it. She ran a finger over her lipstick and pulled up her stockings.

'You know who I wish was with us?' she said. The excitement of having arrived at a strange place made her voice sharp and quick and he had to smile at the laughter in it.

'Who?' he asked.

'Fred from next door.'

They hit a bump and flew up off the seat. The road tilted upward suddenly and he shifted to low. Ahead of them the sky hung like a blue cloth at the end of an alley of pines.

'Why Fred?'

'He's nice. We ought to get to know them better.'

The car whined slowly up the grade. He wondered if he ought to mention the garbage pail to her. He had hardly spoken to Fred lately and never again with any intimacy. He saw the blue sky ahead and the garbage pail moved across his horizon, hung there a moment . . .

The nose of the car tilted forward, and ahead of them, surrounded by an acre of lawn, stood the hotel.

'Oh, it's beautiful!' she said, clutching his arm.

He felt proud. Apparently they had painted the place, for it looked better cared for than five years ago, and a little country clubbish. Across the road from the front porch a large parking-space was marked off. Only a dozen or so cars were parked there. He pulled up beside them.

Buttoning up his shirt, he let her have a moment to do more eagerly what she had done before – pull her stockings tight and fix her hair. She carefully folded up the silk handkerchief which had been tied over her head and then threw it into the back seat anyway. She got out, he behind her.

Outside the car, he reached into the back seat and took out his Panama hat. He unpinned the tissue paper he had it wrapped

124

in, then folded the paper neatly and tucked it into the pocket of his jacket, sticking the two pins in the door upholstery.

'Hurry up; hurry,' she whispered as he put on his hat.

Laughing quietly, he chided, 'Hotel won't run away.' Then he leaned inside the car again and pulled out two valises, set them on the ground beside the running board, and stood locking the car.

'They're all watching us,' she whispered gleefully from behind his back.

He picked up the valises and, turning toward the hotel, saw some people sitting on the porch in rockers. She took his arm and they walked across the road and mounted the wide steps of the hotel. He kept a shy smile on his face, a proper smile as the guests looked through them in the usual way. One old man was carving a piece of wood, with a little boy watching close by his knee, and he looked up and nodded pleasantly to them as they crossed the porch and entered the lobby.

'Very nice crowd here,' Newman said quietly as she crossed the empty lobby at his side.

They stood before the registering desk and he put the valises down and rubbed his hands together to get the sweat off. His back was wet with it.

'Some of them looked pretty young,' she said hopefully. Through the white-curtained windows the backs of heads were showing from the porch.

He looked around at the silent lobby which smelled of the pines. To their left were three open French doors through which they could hear the tinkle of silverware. Now and then a waiter passed beyond the doorways, carrying clean dishes or tablecloths. How often he had sat here waiting, waiting desolately . . .

'Setting up for lunch,' he said with experience. She had let go of his arm and was leaning against the desk looking taller than usual, he thought, for she was stretching and standing on her toes with her back a little arched as she surveyed the lobby with comfortable appreciation.

'I'd better let them know we're here,' he said, and touched a little bell that was on the desk.

They waited several moments, looking out toward the porch. Low conversational voices rose and died momentarily out there. He felt the embarrassment of being ignored, and turned to her.

'Always find somebody interesting to talk to here. Nice lively crowd.'

'You recognize any of them?' She indicated the porch.

'No, there's always new people. But they don't stand for any of this summer-hotel rowdyism.' He talked with relish, enjoying the unique privilege of opening a little bit of the world to her.

'I'd like to take a swim before lunch,' she said, glancing at the suitcases to recall where her suit was.

'You can swim all day if you want to . . .'

They heard the loud creak of the rocker on the porch, and looked toward the door as a man entered the lobby. He was the small old man who had been carving the wood. Mr Newman did not recall him from his previous stay. The old man crossed the lobby toward them, smiling tiredly with his head cocked to one side. As he walked he was wiping off the long blade of his knife and snapping it shut and knocking it against his palm as though it were a pipe.

Ignoring Gertrude altogether he stopped before Mr Newman. His head was bent forward a little. He had a thick head of white hair through which he ran his fingers now that the knife was settled in his pocket.

'Yes, sir,' he said quietly and with a soft smile.

'I'm Lawrence Newman, and this is Mrs Newman . . .'

The old man nodded to her saying, 'How do you do,' and closing his eyes, which opened again only when he was facing Mr Newman an instant later. The introduction did not seem to

126

make much difference to him, for he stood smiling kindly at Mr Newman just as though they had not gotten beyond his initial 'Yes, sir.'

Mr Newman started again. 'I had a very good room here five summers ago. I wondered whether we could get it again.'

'You can't get anything here. Full up,' the old man said, closing his eyes once and opening them to stare all blue into Newman's face.

'Oh,' Mr Newman said. Somehow he could not meet the blue gaze of the old man. Looking down and then glancing at him, he said, 'Is Mr Sullivan around? He'd remem . . .'

'He's swimming,' the old man said, his head unmoving, 'but he couldn't help you. He's my son. I own the hotel.'

Mr Newman met the old man's adamantly kind gaze. 'I see,' he said, quietly. He took a breath. 'I thought he'd remember me. I was here for two weeks . . .'

The old man's eyes closed as he shook his head with the smile still soft. 'Full up, mister. Couldn't help you if I wanted to.'

'We'll go on to the other one then, Lawrence,' Gertrude said, coming to them from the desk. Newman turned to her quickly. She was looking at the old man. Her eyelids were heavy and low and the little red splotches were showing on her face. 'We wanted to save gas, that's why we tried you.'

The old man's smile came down. 'I'd be glad to help you if we weren't so full up,' he said, with deeper baritone.

'Yeh, I know. You must be mobbed with twelve cars out there. What, did the rest of your guests get here by yacht?'

'I said what I have to say, lady.'

'Jump in with your son and drown, will ya?' She turned now to Newman who was standing between the valises gaping at her. 'Let's go, Lawrence,' she said huskily.

Newman could not bend his back. He felt as though turned to iron. 'Come on,' she said angrily, 'before I get squeezed to

127

death in the mob here.' With which she turned and strode across the empty lobby to the door and went out across the porch. Newman picked up the valises and hurried after her without turning back to the old man.

They bumped along the dirt road through the woods. He did not look at her, but instead involved himself in the details of driving. He rolled up his window when dust rose from the road, then rolled it down an inch, then down three inches more; held the wheel tightly in both hands, moved way over to the forested edge of the road to avoid a tiny bump, wiped a film of auto dust from the dashboard with his fingertips, pulled up his trouser legs a little more to keep them from creasing. And he drove at a crawl in low, as though they were not running away at all. She sat drawn away from him against the door, and he knew her body was stiff.

At the highway he pulled to a stop and looking left to see if any cars were coming he noticed the billboard sign. He had remembered it all through the five years since he was last here, like the washstand in the room he had, and a certain tree by the lake at which he tied his canoe. The sign was something he clearly remembered about the place – the English-type scroll of the lettering and the red and white border. And he was stilled and surprised now at the words, in smaller letters, set under 'Riverview Hotel.' 'Restricted clientele,' it said. In the ten seconds it took for him to glance up the road and at the sign he wondered whether they had had that on the sign the last time. He drove onto the highway thinking about it. It couldn't have been on there before . . . and yet somehow he knew that it had been there. But in those days it simply meant that anybody was welcome who was nice, and wasn't loud. It meant there would be your kind of people there, not that they would absolutely refuse a room to a person if he looked a little . . . Strangely, as he drove on slowly, he saw himself standing in front of that Mr Stevens of the Akron Corporation. And for a moment he felt hot with anger again that they should lie to his very face that way, as though they could tell by glancing at him that he was loud and unmannerly and a low person, and his hands hardened on the wheel and he said, aloud but in a whisper, 'The idea!'

'You'd think he'd at least of thought up a good excuse. Crowded! I wanted to choke him, I wanted to choke him, I swear I would have choked him!' she cursed, gritting her teeth.

'Don't . . . don't take it to heart, dear,' he pleaded, feeling his own failure to come off with dignity. 'Please, try to forget about it.'

'Why don't they do something about it?' She was on edge and he speeded up as though to ward off her imminent explosion into tears. 'Why don't they take everybody and find out who's who and put the damned kikes off to themselves and settle it once and for all!' She breathed in a quick sob.

'Now, dear . . .' he said helplessly.

'I can't stand it, I can't stand any more. You can't go out of the house any more without something happening. Go to another place, Lu. Where are you going? Go to another place,' she demanded, as though she would grab the wheel momentarily.

'We're going home,' he said.

'I want to go to another place. You hear me? I want to go to another place!' she shouted.

'Now stop that!'

'No, let me out, I'm not going home! Stop the car!'

'Let go of my arm. Now let go!' He flung one arm out and she let go of it.

'I want you to stop the car. I'm not going home.'

He pulled over to the road shoulder and drew to a stop. She sat looking rigidly ahead. With a nod back, she said, 'Turn around and find another place.' She turned quickly in the seat and looked through the rear window. 'Go ahead, there's no cars coming.'

'Gertrude . . .'

'I want you to turn around,' she said, implacably watching for cars through the rear window.

'Now just calm down a minute,' he said with warning in his tone, and drew her shoulders around until she was facing front. But she would not relent in her demand and merely sat waiting to repeat it. 'I'm not going through that again today,' he said. 'I don't want you insulted and myself either.'

'Turn around,' she said.

'They're all restricted hotels along here. I'd forgotten about it, but the sign reminded me. It'll be the same everywhere else around here.'

She looked at him with her eyes sizing him up. He could feel her probing him. 'Listen,' she said, abruptly, 'why do you always let them make a Jew out of you?'

'I don't always do anything,' he replied.

'Why didn't you tell him what you are? *Tell* him.'

'What? What am I going to tell him? If a man takes that attitude you know you can't tell him anything.'

'What do you mean, you can't tell them anything? When they pull that on me I let them know what I am. Nobody makes a Jew out of me and gets away with it.'

He started to speak and cut himself short. The garbage can . . .

Facing the wheel, he laid his hand on the gear shift and pressed down on the clutch pedal.

'Where are you going?' she asked.

He stopped moving. He could feel the waves of her anger. Without turning to her he said, 'There's a little state park down the road. We can have lunch there and sit by the river.'

'But I don't *want* to sit by the river! I want . . .'

His head jerked around and his words clipped out, 'I can't go through that again! Now stop it!' he commanded angrily.

Rolling along the highway, they sat silent and apart. Momentarily words rose to his lips, and then slid down again. He could not bring himself to tell her what had been happening to him on the block. It would soil all their days. It would crawl in between them during the nights. He had wanted to make a new life with her and now this thing was making it bad again. Nevertheless he could tell her that much. What confused him into this silence was the way she had taken the hotel man's side, despite her anger. To her it was simply a matter of straightening out their identities, and then they could go on and enjoy the hotel for the weekend. He did not know how to say that he could never feel at peace in that hotel any more now. He did not know how to tell her that they never ought to try to convince a hotel man or anyone else that they were Gentiles. He could not understand this feeling of his. But it would be like begging, like being admitted on trial, and if they made a gesture or said a word the air around them would grow cold, and all weekend he would have to be showing what a nice fellow he really was.

He turned off the highway where the log buildings of the little state park lay, and pulled to a stop at the edge of the river. A few yards ahead of the front tires the river lapped at the stony shore. He shut the motor off and they sat listening to the water gurgling among the rocks. He turned to her, knowing she was still angry. She was sitting with both hands clasped demurely in her lap. Maybe he ought to tell her about the block, and about his feeling.

'Gert,' he said.

With a hurt blinking of her eyes she turned to him.

No, he could not tell her. She would simply criticize him for not having gone in to Fred and raised hell the minute he had seen the garbage pail turned over. She would never understand why he had gone to Finkelstein then, and talked with the man about it. And he could not explain, because he knew that he himself no longer understood what kept him from making an honest plea for Fred's recognition. But it was like begging the hotel man to let him in and he could not do it: he was not what his face meant to people, he simply was not.

'Let's see if they have clams. Come on,' he said. He knew how she loved clams.

'You can't stand clams,' she said.

'I'll watch you eat them.'

She managed a smile of forgiveness and touched his hand as they got out of the car. They strolled along the river in the sunshine and sat at a round table with a hole in the middle from which a big umbrella stuck out. She stared at the speckled river. He reached out and turned the umbrella.

A waiter came with a pad.

'She'll have some clams,' Newman said.

The waiter asked him what he would have.

He opened his mouth to say he wasn't eating, and then he saw the waiter's face. A gray memory unfolded in his mind, and he realized that Jews did not eat clams.

'I tell you . . . I believe I'll have some too,' he said.

The waiter went away. She was looking at him and he reached over again and picked at the thick wooden stem of the umbrella, digging his nails into the soft wood.

'We'll turn around and try up the road a few miles. There must be a place,' he said quietly.

She nodded in complete agreement.

CHAPTER FOURTEEN

HOURS come when the familiar seems about to change its shape, verging on the strange and unexplored. He kept scanning the old factory streets of Long Island City through which they were driving on their way home early the next evening. He had never before noticed how many houses were boarded up as condemned, how much smoke hung in the air and how the setting sun made it sparkle like dew on the windshield. The forge shops and the gray slime dried on their sidewalks, the block-long factories and their slate-colored windows, the Negroes sitting on the broken steps of their wooden houses — the ghastly stillness of Sunday twilight and its sense of pause caught him and he saw it like a scene lifted up out of the world.

On both sides of the street they were traveling two-family houses began to appear, and then trees, and then a few open lots, and they were nearing their neighborhood. He stopped for a light and stretched his sunburned legs and only now noticed that the sky was darkening. His eyes felt gritty and tired.

'I guess the day's over,' he said quietly.

She glanced skyward through her window and remained silent. He started ahead again with the green light.

Darkness was falling very fast. A fine need to get home pressed his foot down on the accelerator ... home and the lights on, he thought, and all quiet and known. Uneasily he noticed the happenings outside the car. Two fellows hurrying across the street all dressed up, a small group of old people waddling home from church, a tall man pushing a baby carriage and dragging a puppy which skidded unwillingly on its haunches, two ice cream vendors jangling the little bells over their white refrigerator boxes ...

He frowned, remembering the carousel, the white and colored swans, the yellow swans jerking ahead and then back, and underneath them in the ground that terrible rumbling . . .

The street lights burst into glow. Night. Now it was night. He switched on his headlights.

He turned right into a sidestreet. Three blocks straight ahead was home. His lights swept the deserted sidewalks on each side.

She stirred. He heard her stockings whisper as she uncrossed her legs. 'When Fred goes hunting he takes Elsie to a place in Jersey somewhere. Why don't you find out where it is? Maybe we can go there. Although that hotel wasn't too bad.'

He nodded, 'All right.'

'You won't do it.'

'I will,' he lied.

He was crossing over into his block when he saw Mrs Depaw in her starched white dress standing in front of the candy store, whose windows were dark. The store always kept open Sunday nights. The old lady was talking to a man who kept shifting as he listened, while she leaned forward and spoke excitedly into his face. Passing, Mr Newman glanced beyond her at the store, wondering why it was closed, when the flash of his lights crossed the large window and he saw the long strips of adhesive tape stretched the length of the pane.

Gertrude seemed to awaken, and turned around to look at the tape. He swung wide, approaching his house, and turned into the sloping runway and stopped the car before the open doors of the garage beneath the porch.

He switched off the engine. She turned to him. 'Something must've happened,' she said worriedly.

He got out of the car and opened the rear door and took the valises out. She went up onto the porch and stood looking toward the corner. He passed her and carried the valises into the house without turning at all. His mother was sitting on the

134

back porch and he called hello to her and carried the valises upstairs. He opened them and put the clothes away in exact order, then neatly set the bags up on the closet shelf. He got under the shower before turning the water on, to save hot water and the gas that heated it. It was half an hour before he came downstairs, his face shiny and his hair combed flat across his head. As he reached the livingroom he saw Gertrude going out onto the porch. He went out and found her standing at the railing, looking toward the corner. She turned as he came up to her.

'He had a fight with that man who comes around selling papers every Sunday.'

'Did he get hurt?'

'No. They fell against the window and it cracked. Your mother saw it from here. Everybody on the block was watching,' she said.

He felt dulled; a hum seemed to be sounding behind his head. When he spoke he heard his own voice as though he himself were a little distance away from it. 'Take a shower,' he said. 'I'll put the car away.'

It was completely dark on the street now. Mrs Depaw was gone from the corner. Lights shone in the houses. From down the block somewhere a radio came on loudly and then was tuned down. Gertrude had turned back to watch the corner. He could sense a decision in her, for when she thought intently she hardly breathed. 'Go up, go on,' he said, and started to go down the stoop to the car.

She stopped him by turning. He waited for her and she came over to him and spoke softly on the top step. In the dark the whites of her eyes seemed luminous and wide.

'What are we going to do?' she asked.

'Don't be silly.'

'Your mother says Fred's in the Christian Front,' she explained.

'I know that,' he replied evenly.

'Suppose he . . .'

'Don't be silly.'

'But suppose . . .'

'Don't be silly now.'

'But that man in the hotel yesterday . . .'

Angrily he blurted out, 'Now stop being silly. This has nothing to do with us.'

He started to turn on the step and descend when she grabbed his wrist. He looked up at her quickly.

For a moment she stood that way holding onto him. Then she said, 'Come over here, I want to talk to you.'

She would not let go of his wrist and he came back onto the porch and they sat on the beach chairs in the dark. She glanced toward Fred's porch and then turned around to him.

Speaking quietly she said, 'Your mother just told me about the garbage can.'

He kept his silence. A stone was forming in his stomach.

'Why didn't you tell me about it?' she questioned. She spoke precisely, like an interviewer.

'I want to forget about it. I want you to be happy here.'

'You shouldn't've done that to me,' she said.

Now he heard her fright. 'What do you mean, do that to you?'

'Fred's in the Christian Front. You should have told me.'

'What's the difference?'

'It's a lot of difference.'

'Why?' he asked, trying to see her more clearly. The light in the parlor threw a glare across her cheek. He became tense at the look of alarm and indignation on her face. 'What are you talking about Gertrude? I don't understand what you're talking about.'

She started to lean toward him over the arm of her chair when they saw it. A sedan was pulling to a stop in front of the house

. . . no, it was rolling a little. It stopped before Fred's house. Three men got out, and without speaking walked up to Fred's stoop and went up and into his house.

Gertrude listened for sounds from Fred's house. After a moment she asked, 'Who were they?'

'I don't know, I never saw them before.'

'What's he having, a party?'

'I don't know, Gert,' he repeated, irritated.

'You're not really on speaking terms with him, are you?' she accused.

'We say hello.'

'You used to be more friendly though, didn't you?'

'Not much more, no,' he said, trying to calm her.

'Your mother says you used to go down his cellar all the time.'

'That's true.'

'Why don't you any more?'

'I don't know what good all this is, Gert.'

'I want to know. What'd he say when you told him about the garbage can being turned?'

'He said he didn't know anything about it.'

'That's a laugh. You know it's a laugh, don't you?'

'Yes, I know.'

'That's their favorite trick, you know. That's what they call a tactic. You know that, don't you?'

'I didn't think of it just that way, but I guess it is.'

'First the garbage pail, then they bust a window or two.'

'Not on my house they're not.'

'What are you going to do, stand out all night to see they don't do it?'

'They're not doing it on my house.'

He saw the second car turning the corner, saw it heading down the street and prayed against its slowing down. But it slowed and swerved, stopping with precision behind the other car that stood before Fred's house. It was a big coupé. The door opened and a very fat man squeezed out and stood on the sidewalk looking at the houses. From around the other side of the car another man came and halted beside the fat man. They were trying to see the number of Newman's house. Newman did not move. The fat man said something to the other and walked onto Newman's lawn and came up to the foot of the porch. Newman actually turned as he sensed Gertrude drawing back into her chair. Then he looked down at the fat man who was calling to him.

'Beg your pardon. Which one is 41 dash 39?'

'Right next door,' Newman said, pointing at Fred's house.

'Thanks a lot,' the fat man said. With the other he crossed the lawn and mounted the porch heavily, and they went together into Fred's house.

Newman felt that if he touched Gertrude she would scream out. He looked at her in the vague light from the parlor.

'What's . . .?'

'Sssh!'

The minutes passed. He could hear nothing from Fred's house. They must have gone down into the cellar. She moved her foot on the brick porch.

'That's no party,' she whispered, with awful accusation. 'They got no women. That's a meeting.'

'I guess so.' His heart was pumping rapidly and he moved in his chair to stop it. 'What about it?' he said carelessly.

She did not answer. He listened with her. There was no sound from Fred's house.

'What about it, Gertrude?' he demanded.

After a moment she looked toward the corner, then glanced down toward the other corner and out at the two cars. She got up, and without waiting for his assent, started for the door to the house.

'Come upstairs,' she said quietly, and went into the house.

He got to his feet and gravely followed her in.

He sat on the small satin-covered armchair a few feet from the bed, watching her as she half sat against the headboard, one leg dangling over the bed's edge. Only the little night lamp was on near her face. She sat that way a long time, her breast rising and falling with the remorseless rhythm of her thoughts. He watched her narrowed eyes and saw her coldly as through a window.

'Lully,' she began quietly, 'this is what I got to say. Maybe I shoulda said it to you in the beginning, and maybe not. But you didn't tell me something either, so maybe it's just tit for tat.'

'What didn't I tell you?'

'About the garbage can. About the Front being alive around here.'

'It didn't seem important. I don't see why it is now.'

'All right, let me go on. First of all.' She stopped, glanced over at him as though to see if he were angry, then continued staring ahead with thoughtful, narrowed eyes. 'First of all, you got to stop fooling around. Either you get in with Fred and join the Front or we get out of here and get out fast.'

He felt he was sinking. 'What . . . what?' he stuttered.

'I said it and you heard it.' She would not look at him. 'There's a big rally next Tuesday night. You're going to go.'

'How do you know there's a rally Tuesday night?'

'I shop in the stores here. There's been handbills flooding the stores. You've seen them yourself.'

He admitted it by his silence.

'Are you going?'

'I don't know.'

'Why don't you know?'

'Fred told me a long time ago about a meeting of some kind.'

'Yes?' she prompted.

'But he never mentioned it again. I don't know if I'm welcome, I mean.'

'Well, you go and you'll be welcome.'

'I don't know.'

'You're going to go, Lully. They're drawrin' a ring around us. You'll break out now or you'll never get out.'

He looked at her a long time. 'How do you know so much about the Front?' he asked, and did not want to ask it.

She thought. 'Never mind,' she said, tossing her head. 'You go.'

'Why were you afraid of that fat man?'

'I wasn't afraid of anybody.'

'You know him, don't you?'

'No.'

He got up. 'You do. Please tell me the truth now, Gert.' He came to the bed and sat on the edge facing her.

She gazed past him. He could not tell whether she was about to weep or break out in wrath, but there was something running powerfully inside her and she was holding it down.

'There's no use, Gert, if you don't tell me the truth.' He lifted her hand and stroked it. 'Please. Please tell me.'

A little sigh escaped her. And she looked into his eyes as though to gauge him. 'I'll tell you,' she said.

He waited and she wet her lips and looked down at her dress. 'Before the war I lived with a man.'

'Lived with him?'

'Yeh. You'd guessed there was something like that, didn't you?'

'I did, yes.'

'Well, I did. It was in California.'

'Hollywood?'

'On the outskirts.'

'Was he an actor?'

'No, there was never any actors. I made it up about the actor.

'Why?'

'I don't know. I'm always making something up.'

'Don't cry. Go on. Please, Gert, don't cry.'

'I'm not.'

'What happened? Who was he?'

'He was that dog manicurist I told you about.'

'The one who was so nice to you?'

'Yeh.'

'How long did you live together?'

'About three years. A little less.'

'After you tried to sing in the movies.'

'I was never a singer. Not really.'

'What then?'

'I was a typist in a studio. Typist-secretary. I took singing lessons on the side, but I couldn't make it.'

'I was wondering why you never sing for me.'

'I can't. I'm no good. But I tried to. I wanted to be a singer all my life. It was the only way to get into pictures. Me not being a knockout facially, I mean.'

'Yes, you told me about the test.'

'They never gave me a test.'

'Oh.'

'I tried for one but I was a typist and that's what those Jews out there decided I was going to be.'

'Oh.'

'So I couldn't stand it any more. Then I met this man and we got to be friends and I quit the job and we lived together.'

'Then what happened?'

'Well, he was all right for a while.'

He changed his hold on her hand. 'Then what happened?' he asked.

She glanced up at him, gauged him again, and looked at her dress once more. 'He was all right. I mean he knew how to entertain. Good at a party, you know. I don't make a secret of it, he was very nice and he had a good business. Then he got mixed up in the organization. They had another name for it out there but it was on the same order. There's a million organizations like that out there. Against the Jews. You know.'

'Yes. Like the Front here.'

'That's right. Naturally I didn't pay much attention at first, although it was a good organization. They had a lot of good ideas which anybody would agree with.'

'How do you mean.'

'Well you know, like the Front. They wanted to make Hollywood gentile again. Get the Jews out.'

'Oh,' he said softly.

'But after a while it got so he couldn't talk about anything else so I had to get interested. He started bringing these people to the house and they would stay up all night talking.'

'What'd they talk about?'

'Ways and means. They would get together after Coughlin broadcast and go over what he said. Things like that.'

'Then what happened?'

'Well, when he first started going into it serious I didn't think much about it, but after a couple of months I began to see that they meant business. He got to be a very big shot amongst them. When we'd go out to certain places where that crowd hangs out they'd all turn around when we came in. I started going to these meetings with him and typed letters for him and turned into his secretary, kind of. He sometimes had a hundred and fifty letters a week from all over the country to answer. We got another new car and . . .'

'He was getting paid out of it?'

'Oh sure, there was a lot of good money in it. I got a house-maid. But no cook. I always like to eat my own cooking. We were doing all right for a while. But then the others started horning in on us. I mean the other outfits. He tried and tried but the others wouldn't get together and amalgamate. Some of them out there are crazy as coots. All they know is Jew, Jew, Jew, and no business sense. You know?'

'Uh huh.'

'Naturally the membership started getting all mixed up about which outfit was better and after a while it got so that one meeting we'd have two thousand people and the next meeting maybe fifty would come and the next there'd be three thousand. Like that. We never knew where we was any more. Naturally dues fell off because the membership didn't know from one week to the next whether we would be in existence. Anyway, the wind-up was that he decided his outfit was going to be different. He started up a new thing, an action corps. It was just for young guys who had plenty of what it takes. They'd go to work on a neighborhood and lay for some Jew and beat up on him. They modeled themselves after the Front. They got results too. For a while there I really began to think they'd scare every Jew out of Los Angeles. Naturally though, the cops began coming around because of the complaints. So it got to a pass where we would stay out late just to make sure we wouldn't be paid a visit. I got very nervous and disgusted with the whole thing because it wasn't getting anywhere really. Everything would be fine for a month, but as soon as he would lay off the beatings the corps would start fading away. They wanted action and he couldn't hardly have them going out every night. You know. And all the time he was fighting the other outfits and arguing and making plans to disgrace them and things like that. And the wind-up was I got a big headache out of it and I finally put it up to him.'

'Oh, you wanted him to keep clear of it.'

'That's right. I said, either pull out or I'm going. It wasn't any fun with him any more, you know? I could see where it was all headed. Straight for the jailhouse for us. And I'm not the type. Well, he wouldn't give it up, and we had a big argument and I left.'

143

She reached over to the night table and got a cigarette and lit it. He got up and brought her an ash tray from the bureau and held it for her. She put the match in and exhaled the smoke.

'That's how I happened to come back to New York,' she went on.

'Why didn't you just stay there?'

'Well. Because of this.' She thought, turning the cigarette slowly. 'I made up my mind to make a new start in life. I just wanted to have a nice house and nice things and live like other people do. See, he paid so much attention to his outfit that his business started going to pot. And it was getting to the point where I'd be going out to work again to support him. I could see it coming.'

'Oh.'

'Well I wasn't going to do that. You don't blame me, do you?'

'No, I just wondered why you came here.'

'Well really, it was that. I just wanted a nice home and everything nice. Then I came here.'

Now she looked at him. He knew from the premeditation of her gaze that she was about to appeal to him. 'I came here, Lully, and I tell you this. I never saw such Jew hate as there is here. New York is crawling with it. It's every place you go. You know that. I don't have to tell you that.'

'Yes, I know.'

'Well, I said to myself, forget about it. Live your own life. See, in California, even all the time I was with the organization I tried to keep my own point of view. I figured, maybe it looks like everybody is ready to get going on the Jews, but I kept in mind that I only knew that kind of people, and probably most people never gave it a thought, and that we'd never get any place actually. You know? But when I came here I was bowled over. I was wrong. There's a time coming, Lully, and it's not far away. Once all these organizations get together and join up into one outfit they're going to have enough people to swing this country. Now wait a minute, don't cock your head that way, listen to me. You know as well as me that everybody, pretty near, has no use for the Jews. That's true, isn't it? All right. A depression comes along, and you know as well as me that it's coming. All right. A depression comes, there's people out on the street, an organization comes along that can get them going and it's the end of the Hebrews. Wait a minute, before you answer . . . You saw that fat man.'

'Yes.'

'His name is Mel. He's from California. I don't know his real name but he calls himself Mel. I happen to know that in Detroit his name is Hennessy.'

'You know him, then.'

'I met him once at our house. He came with money to keep the organization going when it started going downhill. I don't know who's giving it to him but he's got money. From the very beginning he had one idea, to get all the organizations together into one outfit. He said that one year after there is one big organization in this country there won't be a Jew standing up in America. He's right. I know he's right. And now he's here. And that means one thing. They're getting together. When the war's over they're going to be working hand in glove and you're going to see fireworks. In California I didn't think it would amount to anything, but after I see what's going on here I tell you it's going to happen, and when it does I'm going to be on the right side and so are you. So you're going to that meeting, you hear?'

He set the ash tray in her lap and got up. 'Now let's not . . . let's not rush things,' he said, turning toward the windows at the front of the room.

'I know what I'm talking about. You don't know what they can do. Lully, look at me!'

At the window he turned around.

145

'Before the war they caught some of them with rifles and bombs, did you know that? Fred's got rifles, hasn't he?'

'He's a hunter, he uses them for hunting.'

'When are you going to wake up? He's got two revolvers, hasn't he? Who hunts with revolvers?'

'He just goes in for target practice sometimes.'

'Not sometimes, all the time. I wouldn't be surprised if they all get together up in Jersey and practice.'

'But he brought home foxes. He hunts, dear, he hunts.'

'I'm telling you what I know, Lully, and you're going to listen to me!' She got up quickly. 'You're not going to be able to argue with them once they make up their mind they don't like you. If any one of those stew brains that hang around them gets the idea we're a couple of Hebes . . .'

'Well, in California they didn't think that of you, did they?'

'No, because I was in at the beginning. I talked up about the Jews. Not like you. You never say anything.'

'What is there to say? You want me to go out and make speeches?'

'You don't have to go out and make speeches. But take yesterday, for instance. You should've told that hotel man what you think. You should've spoke up instead of standing there like that. I was never so humiliated in my life. That's probably why Fred got sick of you. You never say anything. I notice it myself.'

'Well I used to, but I . . .' He broke off, perplexed, and looked down at the rug. 'I don't know what's happening to me.'

'Why, what's happening to you?'

'I don't know,' he said honestly. Then he went to the chair at the vanity table and sat, his face worried and reddened. 'I just can't seem to bring myself to say anything about them any more. I feel it. Sometimes I feel like I could almost murder them. But I can't seem to say it any more.'

146

Quietly, mystified, she went closer to him, and looking down at him, asked, 'Why?'

Seeking his reply he sat motionless and silent. What had seemed like one thing had turned into another. He had gone along all his life bearing this revulsion toward the Jews and it had never been anything of importance to him. It was much the same as a dislike for certain kinds of food. And then he had come to see how many others shared his feeling, and he had found stimulation around the subway pillars and all the time he had felt no great personal fear about what was looming up ahead. In those earlier impressions of the violence to come, the attackers were ... well, if not gentlemen, certainly amenable to the guidance of gentlemen much like himself. They would clean up the city overnight, as it were, and then the city would belong exclusively to people like himself, and the riffraff who had accomplished the change would somehow disappear into the anonymity from which they had sprung. But hearing her tell it, they were not anonymous people to begin with and they could hardly be expected to disappear just when they had succeeded in taking the city.

She was standing over him and her very position inflicted a pressure of decision upon him, and he got up and walked to the bed and sat down. She came over and sat beside him, waiting for him to speak. He looked at her, then at his hands.

'I guess the truth is that I wish the whole thing would blow over.'

'They turned over your garbage can. Somebody's got you marked for a Jew.'

He saw it now. What he wanted was to go back to the old days when his hate had no consequences. It used to be a comfortable thing and there were no rifles and fat men involved in it then.

'I'm not the type to go around beating up people,' he said, although she knew it.

'You don't see Fred going around beating up people. He's got a spot in the outfit. That's what you've got to do. Get yourself a spot. You're an executive type, Lully.'

His body seemed to pause. *You're an executive type, Lully.* He looked up into her anxious eyes.

He knew there was a hurt expression on his face. But he was beyond hurt, wandering toward a memory that seemed suggested by this moment. He was sitting like this, and she . . .

Her office. The day he had found her again. The way her face, her whole meaning had changed.

He studied her now, not knowing what he was trying to realize. She was talking. He could not focus on her words. This was the same woman he had so despised in the glass cubicle. How amazing it was, how strange. He kept watching the living flesh of her face, her moving lips, and played upon her features with the hands of his mind, changing them back to what they seemed to have been in the glass cubicle. She was still talking . . . talking . . . her face changing. There she was in the cubicle . . . the heavy purse . . . the pin . . . the furpiece . . . overdressed, overpainted, Jewish. Now he changed her back, began hearing her words. Here she was, Gertrude, his wife, gentile, as easily understandable as his own mother.

'. . . the best thing,' she was saying. 'So you go to that meeting, Lully.'

A strange flush was on his face. He kept looking at her and beyond her. And he found his arm moving around her back and his hand clasping her waist. His head moved closer to hers . . .

She put her hand on his shoulder. 'Now, before the war's over,' she was saying. 'When the depression comes everybody'll be getting in and then it won't do you one bit of good. They're liable to figure you're a scared Jew trying to cuddle in for protection. That's why I say . . .'

Talking, she let herself be pressed back on the bed. Her hands kept a pressure against his shoulders and as she talked he leaned harder against them until they gave way and he broke in to her lips. Kissing her a great sadness surged over him, and even while she laughed as though it were all silly she was trying to free her lips and hold him away from her to see him, for she knew something was wrong. But he pressed and held her so she could hardly breathe. And then she stopped struggling and he rested his head close to hers on the bed. If she talked again he would kiss her again. No more, in God's name, no more talk! Why did everyone know what to do except him? Fred, she, even Finkelstein . . . only him. It was not the danger; he had always known that only hoodlums would do the dirty work. Why was he acting so proper suddenly? He had always known it. Every morning on the subway, every night coming home. Why suddenly was it such a horror to him? What was Finkelstein to him? What right had the man here in the first place? Why was he acting as though the man . . . ?

Hearing her swallowing as though to speak, he opened his eyes. And in that moment she was as she had been in the cubicle the first time, he could smell the office in his nostrils and he saw her there so overdressed, so . . . A silent cry started in his chest. No, she had not been overdressed, she was beautiful. He liked her that way, had always liked women that way. A shout clamored against his throat and he knew that he would have taken her whatever she was. In Ardell's office that second time he would have taken her Jewish or not Jewish. And that was why. He knew it, he knew that was why she mustn't talk any more about meetings and this murder that was gathering itself . . .

'See, Lully, the . . .'

With a high laugh that sounded boyish although strained, he moved his lips against hers and in the silence knew that this would be his life.

With a start and a stiff raising of his head he awoke. Listened.

Then lowered his head to the pillow, his eyes wide open. It was dark outside and he saw the stars through his window. He tried to remember if he had been dreaming, the agony of confusion upon him. Something had awakened him, he knew. But if it was a dream that had done it, the dream was closed off now. Breathing minutely, he turned his head to train his hearing in all directions. The silence was whole. And yet there had been a sound that did not belong in the night. He looked at the sleeping face of Gertrude. Perhaps she had spoken from a dream. No, it was not that kind of sound. An idea struck him; he looked at the crucifix which Gertrude had hung on the wall, thinking it might have fallen and made the sound, but it hung there in the shadow. The vision of a merry-go-round ... *'Aleese . . . !'* No, that was long ago ...

Suddenly remembering, he turned his head toward the bedroom door – toward the street. All at once it was quite clear that it had come from the street. He lay still, fighting to recall the kind of sound it had been, the web of sleep folding away from his mind. Maybe they had come for Finkelstein ... *'Aleese! Police!'* ... maybe it was later than he thought and Finkelstein had come out to open the store and they had jumped him and he was lying out there in the street, or was still fighting them on the corner ... He reached out for the clock. Ten after four. Relieved, he knew Finkelstein would not be out at this hour and they would certainly not break into his house for him. Relieved, because he did not know what he would do if he saw the man being beaten up out there ... or rather, because he did know he would do nothing, but that it would bother him for a long time. No, he would call the police. That was it. Simply call the police and not have to leave his house ...

Simply call the police ...

It came sharp and quiet, and he knew it for the sound that had awakened him. Sliding his legs off the bed he found his slippers and then his glasses and tiptoed out of the room, along the corridor, and down the stairs. There ... again. He took long tiptoed strides past his mother who was snoring in the living room, and stopped at the windows and peered through the slats of the blinds.

They were finishing. Two men ... they moved athletically like boys. One of them was shaking out a paper bag onto the lawn, the other quietly kicking the garbage about. In the middle of the street the big coupé stood without lights. The garbage can lay overturned right in the middle of the sidewalk.

Damning the street lamp for being on the other side of the street he peered to catch a glimpse of their faces. They both wore sweaters. He planted the sweaters in his memory, and breathlessly searched for their faces. The taller boy threw the empty bag down and wiped his hands and loped toward the coupé. The other boy gave something on the grass one final kick and followed. As he passed under Newman's tree he reached up and ripped a twig from a low branch and flung it toward the house as if it were a stone.

Newman discovered himself with his hand on the knob of the door. What was required? He could not be expected to fight two of them – perhaps a third was sitting behind the wheel of the car, waiting. And yet they were spitting in his face. They were spitting at him. What was dignified, what in God's name was dignified!

Outside the motor was turning over with the grinding of the starter. He turned the knob and walked out on the porch, having timed his appearance with the speeding away of the car.

He stood watching it roar down the street, then saw the tail light flash on as it swung around the corner and disappeared, leaving the night's hum of silence upon the air. White and clean in his pajamas on the porch, he stared down the stoop at the glistening of some wet food leavings that were scattered in the grass. Descending the steps he pulled up his sleeves and bent over a clump of chop bones, touched them and withdrew his hands, for the bones were cold and revolted him. He stood erect.

For an instant he saw himself standing on the public street in his pajamas, surrounded by garbage. It was like a dream's continuation and he felt the torpor of one watching his own dream. The torn, three-leafed twig caught his attention and he went to it and took it from the lawn to the curb where he dropped it. Then coming erect he looked left and right along the street and stopped moving as his eye held on a form in white near the corner. Finkelstein was standing watching him from under the street lamp there. In his hand Mr Newman could make out a garbage-pail cover. A hot sense of embarrassment pressed him toward his house and yet he could not get himself moving. It was as though to move away would confirm his demonstrated cowardice. Mr Finkelstein had set the cover down and was coming toward him, walking measuredly along the center of the street. Newman stood still. I am not afraid of him, he said to himself. For a moment it was as though the Jew had been the one to spread the garbage, for it was the Jew approaching now, and Newman had only to cope with him. He stood motionless, watching the man bearing down on him along the middle of the cambered asphalt, heard his slippers hissing, saw his belly outlined under the pajamas, and felt as though the world had stopped and left him pajamaed in the night in the open air alone with this Jew.

He turned toward his house and walked rapidly up to his stoop, and without hesitating hurried up on the porch and went inside. As he climbed the stairs to the bedroom he could see the scorn on Finkelstein's face and he damned it out of his mind.

He slid in between the sheets. Gertrude moved and he knew she had been awake all the time.

'What happened?' she whispered.

'They turned it over again.'

'Did you get out and talk to them?'

She would have gone out and talked to them, he realized. And he resolved to gain that kind of understanding of them so that he could go up to them and say, 'Now look, boys ...' and carry it off as though he were utterly ruthless and quite one with them.

'They got away before I could get outside,' he said.

'You better go to that rally then,' she decided definitely. 'Are you going?'

'Yes ... sure,' he said, and rolled onto his side and closed his eyes, quite as if there had never been any doubt.

CHAPTER FIFTEEN

IN more peaceful times it took the form of a desire to go fishing.
When his wife and two children and his old father-in-law got
too much for him, he had his wife pack his lunch, settled her
in the store, and took the subway to Sheepshead Bay. There
he avoided the big fishing boats that took out dozens of people,
and rented a rowboat. The ocean is wide and he need only row
a half mile out of the bay, drop his line, and enjoy 'solitude,
the golden graile of the city man.'

Lately, however, he did not like the idea of spending a day
out of reach of his family. Even though they might not be able
to get in touch with him as he wandered about the city, he
would still be on land – the same land they lived on – and it
would make him feel they were safer. So he left his wife on
this Wednesday morning and took the subway out to Bushwick,
where a big toy firm was located. There he made some purchases which he carried away with him in a long cardboard
carton.

It had taken most of the morning to complete the trip and
make the purchases and he was about to call it a day and take
the subway home when he remembered something. It was the
anniversary of his father's burial.

Mr Finkelstein was not a religious man. Furthermore, he
had buried his father some seventeen years ago and was not
particularly attached to his memory any more. Despite the
Law which requires the son to do homage at the elder's grave
at least once each year, Mr Finkelstein had not been to the
grave in three, maybe four years – he did not remember exactly.
This negligence was due chiefly to his lack of awe for the dead,
rare among the Jews, and his intense preoccupation with the

events of this world and the news of the day. To the dead he wished all good luck, but he saw no reason for standing before a stone in the cemetery and pretending that he was sorry. He despised all hypocrisy, and this weeping over people who had been dead for years was to him a travesty and he refused to have anything to do with it.

So it was strange for him to be halted at the very turnstile of the subway, recalling that his father had been buried on this day and wondering whether he really oughtn't go and see the old man. But wondering is a false word for his mental state at this moment. All he knew was that something was drawing him to the cemetery. A true solemnity of soul had somehow descended upon him, and he obeyed it and went back to the street, walked some seven blocks to the trolley, and took it out to the populous graveyards at the northern edge of Brooklyn.

The Jewish dead lie in the earth much as they lived on it — crowded together, one headstone touching its neighbor. Mr Finkelstein entered the cemetery and walked along a winding concrete road which meandered through all parts of the grounds in great loops. To a man of Mr Finkelstein's speculative propensity, this roundabout way of arriving at a grave presented interesting possibilities. He noted, as he walked, how most of the expensive mausoleums were congregated within easy view of the gates of the cemetery, lending the place a staid and upper-class atmosphere. But once past them the long acres of headstones told the real story, to Mr Finkelstein's mind. Here were the people, the mass of them. And for every broad and well cared-for stone there were hundreds, thousands, of cheap slates tilting to leeward, their graves sunken or flattened out like so many deflated chests. Off to the right a small funeral procession was making its way and he listened for a moment to the faint sound of the wailing. Another one for Moses, he mused, and went on down the curving road.

His father's grave was hard to find, but his sharp memory led him surely. He turned off the main road into a little gravel path, then left it and stepped gingerly among the graves of a plot, and squeezed himself up to the resting place he sought.

Looking at the inscription on the stone transfixed him. It always did, despite his cold views on death. But today it was worse, somehow, worse than ever. He looked at the gnarled slab of rock and at the lumpy grass grave, and there was speech forming in him. It distressed him, for he did not like to be affected by this kind of thing. Despite himself he set the carton of toys with one end on the ground and the other resting against his leg, and placed his hands on his hips.

What am I doing here? he wondered. Underneath is probably not even bones left. Maybe one bone. What can I say to a bone? What am I doing here?

He could not leave yet, however, for it was as though he knew he had come for some reason and nothing had happened yet.

And then he knew. Standing like this before the old stone he could remember what he had to remember, what he needed now. An old story. He had come to recall the story, the one story his father had been able to tell time after time from start to finish without changing it. Mr Finkelstein had always believed this story, as he had disbelieved the others the old man told, because this one had come out the same every time. And he stood staring at the stone recalling it.

In the old country, the part of Poland that belonged to Austria in those days, there was a great baron who lived on an estate to which there was no end. No man in the nearby village had ever walked completely around it and nobody really knew where its boundaries lay. But there was one part of it that was surrounded by a high iron fence which had taken many years to build. Behind this fence were high trees and thick bushes and no one in the village could tell what lay beyond them. But it was assumed that the baron's house was inside there somewhere. Who would build such a fine fence except around a fine house?

It was always quiet, however, beyond this fence; no people were ever heard talking beyond it, and no sounds of wagon wheels or scythes ever came over it. And then one day there was heard a great shouting and roaring inside the fenced acreage. The people of the village ran to the fence and some of them hoisted themselves over it and climbed the trees and looked inside. They saw peasants running toward a mired wagon, and they saw men with pikes and whips fighting them off. They saw a kind of battle going on, and the battle ended only when the men with the weapons were beaten to the ground. Then the peasants took the pikes from them and killed them all.

The whole story only came out later. What had happened was this. Inside the fence the baron kept several hundreds of serfs. The emancipation had been proclaimed generations before, but it had not penetrated many estates. The serfs were never let out of the estate and lived and died there never knowing the world outside. Then one day they were dragging this wagon along when its wheels sunk into the mud and refused to be pulled out. The overseer ordered them to pull harder, and finally raised his whip. As they pulled on the straps he brought the whip down on several of their backs. This was not unusual but it happened once too often, for this time the peasants dropped the straps and turned and looked at the overseer. Then they surrounded him and as he struck at them again and again with the whip, they took hold of his throat and broke his neck as he stood there. They let him go when he stopped flinging the whip and when they stepped away from him he fell to the ground and they saw he was dead.

There he was, dead, with the whip still in his hand. They did not know what to do, so they stood there waiting. For now their anger had cooled and they were waiting for someone to come and take the overseer's place so that they could go on with the day's work. After a few hours of waiting they saw another official and they called him over to tell him that they needed another overseer, because this one had fallen and broken his neck. The official looked at the dead man and saw, and he went back to the house. Then it was that this gang of overseers came charging down on the peasants with apparent intent to kill them.

But they were against being killed, so they screamed for help and sent men running, and while they fought off the attackers they made contact with other peasants working in other fields and pretty soon there were about two hundred of them beating up the overseers. And finally they killed them all. Then they started to move, and they went to the baron's house. He was away at the time and they knew it. So they went into the house and tore it apart. They broke the furniture and pulled the strings out of the piano – which they had never seen before – and they ripped the stuffings out of the sofas and tore the pictures out of their frames on the walls. They went into the kitchen and spilled salt all over everything edible and they ran up the big stone staircase and tore the bedrooms apart. And then they found the box.

In the master's bedroom they found this strongbox, and because it had a big lock on it they ripped the lock out and opened the box. And inside they found many beautiful pictures of the king. They knew it was the king because in their huts the baron had ordered that they hang the king's picture beside the crucifix. But their pictures of the king were not as beautiful as these in the trunk. These were surrounded with golden curlicues and there were words written along the borders. They loved their king so they took the bundles of pictures out of the box and distributed them among themselves. It was very strange that all the pictures were exactly alike, and they could not get over the fact. After this they left the house and went back to their fields and continued their work, each man with at least ten or twelve of the pictures carefully folded in his pocket. They were going to replace their old pictures of the king with these new ones. A few of them had enough to cover all the walls of their huts and could not wait for the sun to set so they could get home and do it.

But that evening the baron returned. When he found his house that way and all his overseers murdered, he dispatched a rider to the city which lay a few miles to the east where the king's soldiers were kept in barracks. Then he walked among the huts of his peasants and saw these pictures on the walls. He said nothing, however, and went back to his house.

But he did not stay there long. He got on his horse and rode out of his estate and into the little village that lay nearby. There were many Jewish families in this village and one of them was that of Itzik, a peddler, who was at home after a season of traveling the countryside with pots and pans which he sold to the country folk. The baron called this Itzik out of his house and said, 'I have changed my policy. The gate of the manor will be open to you tonight. Go there with your wares and if any of my serfs wish to buy, you may sell them whatever they can pay for. I am not going to supply them myself any longer.'

Itzik thought about this and calculated the face of the baron. Squinting up at the setting sun, Itzik said, 'I would be very happy and honored to do this, Excellency, but you know I must pay in money for my pots and pans and your serfs do not have any money.'

'Go and they will pay you.'

'But, Excellency, already my house is filled with sour cream and many hides which I have had to take in exchange for my goods. The people even outside the estate have very little money. I have no way of disposing of these things, Excellency. I can't buy pots with sour cream, I must have money to buy.'

The baron looked down at him and said, 'Go into my estate and take your business with you. Go now.'

Itzik realized it was a command and bowed low and the baron rode away. He hitched his horse to his wagon and drove behind the baron and when he reached the gate of the estate he found it open for him and he drove in. He rode through some woods and then he came to the huts of the peasants. It was the first time that a stranger had entered their compound and they all came out to see. Sadly, Itzik got down from his seat and they crowded around him and his shining pots and pans. In Polish he told them that they could buy anything on the wagon. Then he fell silent. It was the worst sales talk he had ever given. He hoped, too, that they would not understand about buying, for he knew they had never bought anything in their lives. But some instinct led them to understand that he was trying to exchange these pots and pans, and several of them gingerly pointed to certain of the articles on the wagon and asked Itzik how they could have them for their own.

'Well,' he said, 'if you have in your houses anything of value, show it to me and I will tell you how you can have these pots and pans.'

Several of them went into their huts and brought out what they thought might have value. One woman brought him a shoe which she said a priest had worn, but Itzik shook his head. Another showed him a little bag of broken buttons, and he shook his head. Then a man came to him and said.

'I have a picture of the king. I have twenty of them.'

'How big is this picture?' Itzik asked.

'Here, I have a few of them in my pocket,' the man said. With which he drew out a handful of the carefully folded pictures.

Itzik looked at the pictures and noted well the numbers printed in the corners. '1,000 Kroner' was printed there. He took a breath.

'Have any of you others got such pictures?'

A babble of replies greeted his question. Before he knew it they pulled him into a hut and there on the walls he saw pasted up hundreds of 1,000 Kroner notes. He went into the next hut and the next and finally stood in the middle of the rutted road and realized that he had walked into a gold mine.

What could he do? He saw now why the baron had commanded him to sell to the peasants ... they certainly did have money. He had been one of those who had climbed the fence and seen the peasants murdering their overseers. He added one and one and knew that this fortune of money had been stolen from the baron's house. He added still another digit and concluded that the baron would like nothing better than that he, Itzik the Jew, should fleece these ignorant people out of their fortune and later be found at home with the piles of money on his person. In short, he saw a pogrom in the making.

His first desire was to flee. Leave his wagon, pans and all, and streak for the fence and get away. But he had a family in the village outside and he could not bear to desert them at a time like this. And there was another reason why he did not simply run away. He was not a fool, this Itzik. He knew what was going on in Europe for he had, in his travels on his wagon, seen many sections of the country, an opportunity denied to most people in those days. And in his travels he had been often degraded and spat upon for being a Jew, and he had come to a time in his life when he was sick with it all. And this predicament now seemed to him to be the final indignity in a life of indignities.

So with the great bitterness that comes when a man must display his rebellion, he went about among the huts and took down the king's pictures wherever he could find them, and in return gave his wares to the peasants until his wagon was empty and in his pouch lay more than a million Kroner. Then he got onto the wagon, took his seat, and drove out of the estate. On the way he saw no one and arrived at home unmolested.

Night fell. He ate his supper, said long and special prayers, and lay down to sleep. Around him slept his children, and beside him his wife. He waited for the sound of horses' hoofs and the smell of burning.

And when it was very dark he heard the hoofs coming. He ran out of his house and warned his neighbors, who bolted their doors and shuttered their windows. Then he ran back into his house and did the same. In a few minutes the cavalry pounded into the town and started smashing the houses of the Jews. First one house and then another, with the women screaming, and two of them being raped on their doorsteps.

Then they came to Itzik's house and smashed down his door. His roof started to burn. He tried to hold his family around him but the soldiers ripped away his children and spitted them like little pigs, and they raped his wife three times, and him they clouted on the head with bayonets and left for dead.

When morning came Itzik awoke in great pain. He looked around at his dead family and got to his feet. To his surprise, in the middle of the room lay his pouch. He opened it. The hundreds of notes rested snug and untouched.

Like Job he sat on his floor staring at the sunshine outside. Later in the morning the baron came with two soldiers, walked into his house, bent over and took the pouch. Without even looking at Itzik he went out again, got on his horse and rode away.

From that day onward Itzik the peddler was insane. Others had to bury his dead, and for many years after he said not one word to anyone. And one day he walked out of the village in the direction he had taken in years past when setting out on his journeys. It is still told in that region that he walked the whole route, which covered hundreds of miles, and when he had finished he came back to the village and after a few days he died.

Mr Finkelstein stood looking not at the gravestone which was before him, but at the face of his father which floated in his mind. And within himself he framed the old question that he had always asked his father when the story was done.

'So? What does it mean?'

'What it means? It means nothing. What could this Itzik do? Only what he had to do. And what he had to do would end up the way he knew it would end up, and there was nothing else he could do, and there was no other end possible. That's what it means.'

Mr Finkelstein turned away from the grave and started to return to the gravel path when an old man with a curly gray beard came toward him. He recognized the man as one of those who make their living saying prayers for visitors to the graves. He did not like these characters, just as he did not like anything that was formalized and insincere. The man, dressed entirely in black, met Mr Finkelstein as he stepped over a grave onto the gravel path. He asked whether he might not say a prayer for whomever it was that Mr Finkelstein was visiting this day.

'No thanks, I'm all right,' Mr Finkelstein said.

Apparently the old man had been watching Mr Finkelstein before, since he pointed at his father's headstone and said, 'You didn't leave anything.'

Mr Finkelstein looked at the headstone and recalled that he ought to have placed a little pebble on it to signify his having paused there and paid his respects. Here and there on other headstones were pebbles of all sizes, like calling cards that would survive the rains. He turned to the old man and said in Yiddish, 'If he saw me he knows I was here. If he didn't see me he won't notice a pebble either. Let be.'

He started to turn to go when the old man said, 'You saw the broken grave?'

Mr Finkelstein turned back and looked in the old man's tiny eyes. Now with the business behind him the old man had a moment to waste. Pointing behind Mr Finkelstein he said, 'They came in and they broke it, the *momseirem.*'

Turning around, Mr Finkelstein saw a headstone lying on its face. He walked over to it with the old man and stared down. Upon the smooth back of the stone which now looked up at the sky a yellow swastika was painted.

It turned something in his stomach. For the stone in falling had dug a hole in the soft earth of the grave. Tears threatened his eyes and he turned away and looked at the old man.

'Did they catch them?'

'They did it at night. Nobody knew till this morning.'

'They shouldn't leave that mark on it that way.'

'They're getting something to wash it away with. What will be, mister? In America *noch*.'

Mr Finkelstein looked into the old man's watery blue eyes. The mystification he saw there, the sadness and the death of hope that this had happened 'in America *noch*'– the face and the slumped attitude of the old man somehow recalled his father to him. He shrugged his shoulders and hoisting up his carton of toys walked up the winding road to the gate.

On the trolley home he sat in a quiet mood as does one whose life is approaching a verge, an unwanted climax, a moment that need never have come and yet, despite all planning and all illusory hope, was coming closer and would soon arrive. He felt within him that peculiarly philosophical brooding that is the cemetery's souvenir to its visitors. And he saw again, as he had seen it many times before in his life, how terribly wrong his father had been and so many other fathers who lay beside him there. That Itzik, that peddler – there was a meaning to his story. And it was not that the Jew was fated to a bloody end. (Mr Finkelstein did not intend to die that way, nor would he allow his children to die that way, nor his tall wife.) The meaning, he saw again as he rode the trolley through Bushwick, was that this Itzik should never have allowed himself to accept a role that was not his, a role that the baron had created for him. When he saw that the baron was bent on diverting the peasants' wrath from himself, he should have allowed his indignation to carry him away and gotten on his wagon and driven directly home. And then when the pogrom came, as it would have no matter what he did, he could have found strength to fight. It was the pogrom that was inevitable, but not its outcome. Its outcome only seemed inevitable because that money was in his house as the horses' hoofs came pounding into the village. That money in his house had weakened him, it was the blindfold they had put upon his face and he had no right to let them put it on him. Without that blindfold he would have been ready to fight; with it he was only ready to die.

To Mr Finkelstein rocking homeward on the trolley the moral was clearer than it had ever been. I am entirely innocent, he said to himself. I have nothing to hide and nothing to be ashamed of. If there are others who have something to be ashamed of, let them hide and wait for this thing that is happening, let them play the part they have been given and let them wait as though they are actually guilty of wrong. I have nothing to be ashamed of and I will not hide as though there were something stolen in my house. I am a citizen of this country. I am an honest man, he thought as he got off the trolley and went down into the subway that would take him home, I am no Itzik. God dammit to hell, he said to himself as he pushed through the turnstile, they are not going to make an Itzik out of me.

A clattering on the floor of the platform brought him back to his surroundings. In going through the turnstile his cardboard box had broken open. At his feet lay two baseball bats. A third was starting to slip through a hole in the box. He set the box on the concrete and gathered the two bats together and pushed them back through the hole. Then he went on to the front part of the platform and waited. Next time he would see that they wrapped bats in heavier boxes. It was the first time he had ever bought bats, having decided only in the last few days that they were a good thing to have in the store.

CHAPTER SIXTEEN

FOR nearly forty days the city had had no rain. It is an insidious pacifier, rain; the people stay at home and the pages of the precinct blotters do not turn so often. But when the sky stays as blue as it did this summer, day after sweltering day, and the humid air chokes a man out of his sleep, it is the streets and stoops of the city that become populated and the authority of the family disintegrates for a time. The ice cream parlors crowd up, and the saloons; the beaches are flattened down by more people than they were meant to hold – the city empties out into its own swelling arteries. In this summer the city had had no rain and no real cool weather for nearly forty days and the people were rubbing against each other in their irritated quest for a draft and just one moment of easy breathing. Some took their alarm clocks and slept all night in Central Park, others, braving the sandflies, stretched out on the Coney Island beach. And many of them were robbed there and others were pilfered on the tar roofs of the tenements where they had closed their eyes to rest. People lay out on fire escapes which collapsed in the small hours of the morning. Others, out late, came home to find their apartments robbed, for they would not lock their windows and keep out the air. There were all sorts of accidents, some gloomy and others only expensive. Now and then an overworked refrigerator exploded right in the kitchen. Two boys trying to get an extra breeze stuck their heads out of the windows of the Culver Line and were decapitated by a stanchion. Several pregnant women dropped their babies before time in the monoxide-filled buses. One man on Sixth Avenue was so aggravated by the heat that he took a shotgun and fired twice into a crowd which was waiting for the traffic light to change.

He said, later, that he could not stand the sight of so many people. A woman, nearly seventy, was caught trying to climb over the fence around Central Park reservoir. In the station house they allowed her to take a shower and sent her home with a wet handkerchief. In the Bronx there were many dogs running loose infected with rabies. Hundreds of people were contracting infantile paralysis, and it was rumored that the waters off Coney Island were polluted. But the people kept coming to Coney Island, and many of them stirred up the water around where they stood to make it look foamy and fresh and ward off the paralysis; the life guards noticed this. In the cafeterias the smell of souring milk turned everything the customers ate into something sour. They could not enjoy a meal and they had had no sleep. In Brooklyn there was an exceptionally heavy invasion of stinging flies and it was difficult to buy screens because of the war. Two enormous amusement parks burned down and several piers caught fire. People were afraid to go to the amusement parks after this and afraid to go to Coney Island, but they had to go, and they went, and they were always worried. Even the subways started acting peculiarly. In one week alone three trains were discovered speeding along on absolutely the wrong tracks. For nearly forty days the city had had no rain.

And in Queens it was the same as everywhere else in the city, except that there were more mosquitoes. There are very few trees in Queens and the land is board flat, and as in all flat places the heat seems more relentless, especially in the sections built upon filled-in swamps. There, in the empty lots, the earth is cinders which need hardly more than the movement of the sun to stir them into a fine ground haze of dust.

It was through one of these empty lots that Mr Newman made his way at a quarter to eight that summer night, after the city had been so long without rain. His shoes split black cinders as he crunched along and little puffs of dry smoke billowed under his trouser legs every time he put a foot down. He was cutting across this lot to save steps, but he regretted having done it now. He was a very clean man and he could feel soot on his sticky calves. The clean shirt he had just put on at home was already gummy against his spine. Despite the heat he still wore his jacket and a tie; the meeting, after all, would have a certain degree of formality, he thought, and he might be making acquaintances tonight who would be important to him. He believed in the strength of first impressions.

When he reached the sidewalk again the hard concrete relieved him, and he recalled the good news he had gotten during the day. The firm was going to keep him on after the war was over. He thought of how it would be, earning sixty-two a week during the coming depression, and pleasantly recalled how much sixty-two could buy when things were down to normal once more. In all, he felt the approach of a rather pleasant time of his life.

Turning a corner he saw the crowd moving into the hall at the end of the block. He slowed down. He would wait and then enter and find a single seat. As he approached the hall, he saw that a police car was parked at the curb opposite it. Near the car six or eight policemen were standing idly by. There were a surprising number of young boys charging around the edges of the moving mob. Some sailors were standing away from the crowd, watching in silence. Then they turned and walked away, talking among themselves. Mr Newman arrived at the entrance and stood to one side watching the people enter, trying to spot Fred.

The sun was down now but there was still some orange light around the rim of the sky, and he could see the faces quite clearly as they moved through the heavily columned facade. Most of them seemed middle-aged. To Mr Newman it began to look like one out of three, at least, was old. But quite a few soldiers. Quite a few. One hobbling in on crutches with an old man and a sailor breaking a path for him. A hand touched Newman's arm and he turned to look into the face of a humpbacked man in a Panama hat, selling papers. The man held one up to his eyes. It was the *Gaelic-American*. He shook his head. Never read the paper. The man in the Panama went away, moving in little circles as he covered the mob.

The crowd on the street was thinning now. Mr Newman moved into the remnants of the stream, keeping an eye out for Fred, and made his way through the doors of the old stone building which once had been a bank. He knew the interior, for he had attended a meeting here before the war. He had not stayed very long that time, because the people around him had been so obviously ragged and edged with queerness. But tonight as he sat down he was surprised. In the light of the hall the audience appeared more middle class. There were several people present with their families. Two ministers were sitting together . . . another pair on the right. Something was peculiar about the audience, their expressions. In no other mass of people had Mr Newman noticed such nervous concentration upon what was happening up front. Whenever anyone walked onto the low stage all heads craned and there were unintelligible whispers all about him. He studied the stage, trying to pick out Fred.

High over it hung a fifteen-foot photograph of a painting of George Washington. Mr Newman stared into the President's face and felt a funeral mood spreading over him. The cheeks in the picture were colored so brilliant a pink that the face seemed to be gazing out over the audience like one embalmed. Draped about the portrait were at least fifty American flags of all sizes descending in folds to a row of tall urns filled with cut flowers. He began to smile at the woman seated on a folding chair among the urns. She was stout and heavy-busted and her nose was flattened severely, and across her chest she wore a broad red satin band with gold letters on it reading 'MOTHER.' The other half dozen on the stage with her were men who sat a foot apart, saying nothing to each other with the intensity of men sworn to a system of silence. Probably officials of some sort. It mystified him that Fred and Mr Carlson were not among them. He scanned the faces in the rows around him. No one he knew. He felt disappointed and foolish . . .

The terrible heat of the people was beginning to fold upon him like wool. The man on his left had deep creases in his red face and a watery beard of sweat was dripping out of the creases and down his chin. On his right a very tall blond man sat quietly staring ahead, from one moment to the next folding and unfolding the jacket on his lap. People were standing up to pull their buttocks free of clothing and then sitting down again. There were sighs all around, as though people were making one effort after another to start anew and breathe normally. A heaving movement was suddenly sweeping the hall . . . *Father!*

Mr Newman turned in his seat with his neighbors and saw the priest. The man was built like an athlete and was striding up the aisle in the direction of the stage. Flanking him were two men in shirtsleeves who looked like brothers. They had the identical frown of watchfulness on their faces. Behind them marched half a dozen other men, rapidly, as though they were bringing some sort of dispatch to the assembly. The crowd was leaning, waving, everybody telling his neighbor what his neighbor was trying to tell him – that this was the priest from Boston, that this was the important priest from Boston. '*Father!*' He kept laughing and saluting people all over the hall. He had a very thick neck that was hard to turn. Reaching the steps of the stage he bounded up two at a time and started shaking hands with the people seated there behind the thin podium. The men who had come in with him took seemingly prearranged places at the extreme edges of the stage, and although there were chairs for them they preferred to stand facing the audience. Mr Newman forgot the priest for a moment and watched these men.

He could not get over the fact that they were all scanning the audience and frowning. Who were they looking for? He could not quell his growing uneasiness. He had a job that would last, what was he doing here? But looking at the sharp, excited eyes around him, he remembered the burly youths shaking out the garbage on his lawn and finally felt wise at having come tonight. It was definitely a wise thing for him to be doing. But this heat . . .

Silence. The silence of a stopped wind held the audience. The priest had suddenly turned from a man with whom he had been speaking and stepped up to the podium. His smile was gone. His broad jaw, shaven to a shine, set itself in his heavy head. He had no notes and simply rested his arms upon the podium and slowly, ever so slowly, moved his eyes across the faces before him. For moments the silence held. A situation seemed to have formed. Already something seemed to have happened and this man in black had stepped forward to destroy the situation. The crowd leaned toward him mentally as toward a street accident. Mr Newman forgot all his calculations. His mouth had fallen open a little. He forgot to blink his eyes. He was breathing quietly.

'I need no introduction,' snapped the priest. It was as though he were continuing a speech instead of beginning one, his tone was so startling and fiery. It seemed he was already angry and Mr Newman wondered why.

The priest, after this pronouncement, appeared to turn his eyes toward each listener individually. He rolled his gaze around all the far peripheries of the crowd and seemed to gather them toward him. Then he smiled, modestly, intimately, and picked at the wooden podium.

'No, I need no introduction,' he said, quite softly.

The crowd tittered in mystification and with some love. Mr Newman laughed too, a little. It was a strange kind of a speech. He understood nothing of what had made him laugh but he was intent on finding the clue, and he listened, and the crowd listened.

With a great breath the priest threw his resonance into the hall. 'I need no introduction because you know me. I wear the cloth and by that you know me!'

Applause started. The priest raised his hand.

'I have come to you tonight, good people, in the terrible heat of this day, to bring you a message from a city. A city beautiful to my eyes but a city reviled and crucified by some who breed hate and feed upon that hate. A city which has stood fast upon its independence, just as it stood fast in another era when America was dumping the tea of the worst — I say the worst tyranny of all time, bar none!'

Applause burst from the audience like a thousand arrows sprung at the same instant and with it rose the roar of voices.

'I bring you this message from *Boston*!'

Before the roar could subside it lapped over itself.

'Boston is cleansing herself, ladies and gentlemen, Boston is standing fast!'

Now the roar was a wave gathering its force over Mr Newman's head. He understood now. He had read how they had been beating up Jews in Boston. A sudden movement at his side . . . the man on his left was standing and thrusting his fist into the air and down again as though pulling a bell cord and shouting, 'The Jews! The Jews!' Mr Newman looked up at the face of the man, the creased and sweating face, and he saw the eyes and he looked away. In a moment the man sat down and Mr Newman could feel his glance. He turned slightly to the man and nodded. But the man was already looking at the priest.

Once more the priest stood picking at the splinter in the podium. He seemed to have forgotten entirely the crowd which was settling back to silence again. Suddenly he looked straight at them and held them in an angry stare. Mr Newman felt he was a man who said things as they occurred to him and he was curious as to what would come out next because he was afraid that anything in the world could come out.

'But before I go on with this message, my dear brethren and co-patriots, before I continue I should like to inform, nay, warn you that there are amongst us tonight certain representatives of the press – how shall I say it? – the international press.'

All around Mr Newman people were turning to look at their neighbors. Mr Newman looked at the man with the creases in his face just in time to meet the man's full gaze. He smiled at the man but got no reply. He studied the faces around him and did not notice anyone who might be Jewish. To aid those who might be somewhat backward in understanding him, the priest continued, 'I think we all know how to tell an internationalist from a nationalist.'

There were guffaws and a little more looking around at faces. Again Mr Newman turned to look at the man beside him with the creases in his face, and again he discovered the man looking at him. He felt anger growing in him and faced forward, but the stare of the man's eyes was like a hot light on his cheeks.

'The reason I inform you thuswise,' said the priest whose hands were now upon his hips, 'is that we may expect, as in the past, that these gentlemen will give us due attention in their newspapers and that since their sympathies inevitably interfere with their jobs as reporters we must be prepared for exclamations of dissent upon their part. Should any such outbursts take place, I trust you will restrain yourselves and deal with the gentlemen as befits your good sense and qualities of leadership . . .'

Mr Newman's mind floundered in anxiety. How were they to deal with them? Supposing this person on his right, the calm man with the jacket in his lap, should suddenly erupt against the speaker? Was he to assist in throwing the man out? Was that what the priest meant by leadership? Or was he simply to abide the man? He did not want to be caught without a prearranged plan of action, for he knew that somewhere in the hall Fred was sitting, and in it too the people who had turned over his garbage can, and he would prefer to be seen doing the right thing vigorously. He wanted to be known as one of these people, as in fact he was, and he had no faith in his reactions in emergencies. The voice of the priest cut through his thoughts.

'. . . close to the end of the most brutal war in all history. Many of us in this very gathering have lost blood brothers and husbands and friends . . .'

Newman's eyes wandered over the heads around him. In an aisle to his right a soldier was sitting bareheaded, a steel brace supporting his neck and chin. His mouth hung slightly open as he listened, and he seemed to be blushing. Mr Newman wondered anxiously whether it was embarrassment or anger at . . . What did they think about, these soldiers? He wondered if they blamed the Jews for the war. His eye caught another soldier sitting behind the wounded one. He was writing in a pad. Was he for or against? He scanned the audience avidly for more soldiers. Suddenly he realized the hall was crackling with applause. He looked up at the priest quickly, and raised his hands from his lap when the applause stopped. As he lowered his hands the man on the left with creased face glanced at him. The man's face was without life, without expression, like the face of a sun-bather. Mr Newman lowered his hands and looked ahead.

'How can we in all honesty . . . victimizing . . . money . . . brethren . . .'

An icy coolness was rising up the back of Mr Newman's neck. He raised himself an inch off his chair to relax himself, and noticed an old lady down the row whose shoes came up to her calves, and were laced with white string. She clasped a bundle of newspapers to her bony chest. A stench flowed into Newman's nostrils, the smell of feet and the aged. He rubbed his neck. It was freezing. Under his chin the skin was hot. On his left a new agitation ... the crease-faced man was grunting. Sitting there with his eyes on the stage, and grunting and pulling at his knee, his eyebrows working up and down as he held a repressed conversation with the priest. Newman edged away and his shoulder touched the blond man on the right who unconsciously pressed him aside with his big hand and folded his jacket again on his lap. Newman saw a heavy gold ring on his hand and stared at it for a moment ...

'... War! Why! Why, in God's name, why!'

From behind a bellow of hoarse voices ... 'Jews! J ...!'

Newman leaped in terror ... the man on his left had shot up with his right fist in the air, and he roared out a great, 'Ohhhh!' and panting for breath, sat down. His grunts were rhythmical now, in time with the priest's compelling stanzas, and he kept rocking forward in the rhythm and rocking back, pulling on his knee over which his pants were drawn up in a knot of wet creases. Mr Newman drew his elbows in and his knees together and tried to blot out the people from his mind, and then he felt the wave starting again.

'... long, oh God, how long!'

It rolled like a living beast over his head; it was something that could almost be touched, it had weight as it displaced the stinking air overhead and rushed the length of the hall up to the podium. People were on their feet, roaring and applauding. He tried to remember what the priest had said. The old lady with the high shoes had dropped her papers on the floor and stood prayerfully facing the priest, her yellow hands clasped to her chest. Where was Fred? Something fell to the floor behind him, something heavy. Someone faint, he wondered? Where was Fred, he pleaded, where was someone he knew?

'... byword from now on. Action! Action! Action!'

The floor was shaking with the stamping of the people. The priest's face was wine red as he called over their heads, his arms stretched out stiff, his fists clenched. The crease-faced man on the left was standing, his arm pumping up and down in the air, calling 'Ohhh!' They were on their feet all around him now and the odor of their bodies choked him, and he started to get up when something heavy fell upon his shoulder and he turned in horror and saw the crease-faced man, wild and pouring sweat, staring into his face. And he realized the man was holding onto his collar. 'Say!' he complained, and struck the man's forearm modestly and feared that his suit would tear. The man just kept working his jaws with his lips extended, and shook Mr Newman and grunted at him. Mr Newman grabbed onto the man's arm with both hands and tried to loosen his grip, but he feared for his coat. So he turned his head around for help in time to notice people looking at him, while on the stage the priest stood on tiptoe trying to see into the circle which had formed around him. Catching sight of the priest, Mr Newman started to call to him but a new face moved up very close to his face. This new man was one of those who had been standing to one side of the stage.

'Get his hand off me,' Mr Newman said to him.

The man from the stage looked at the crease-faced man and said, 'What's the matter?'

'He didn't clap once!'

Mr Newman felt a laugh idiotically bubbling up in his throat, but the faces around him were not laughing. 'Well for pete's sake,' he said to the faces around him, 'I never clap. I just don't, that's all. Even at the show . . .'

'He's a Jew, for Christ's sake!'

The owner of the voice was beyond the circle of faces. Mr Newman instantly stood on tiptoe as best he could – for the fist was still clamped to his collar. 'Now you cut that out!' he demanded.

'Christ Almighty, can't you see he's a Sammy?' The voice broke through the ring around Mr Newman, and its owner grabbed him by the lapels and pushed him against the seat. His horror shot into his back like a needle and he shouted, 'I'm not!' The vision of himself as a baby being baptized somehow passed before his mind as he felt a thrust against his neck and heard his jacket ripping down. Quickly he pulled off his glasses and turned his face for all to see. He met a hand slapping his face – a woman's hand – and he was being pushed from behind. Faces rushed past him and he was struggling to reach the ground with his feet but they tread air. Not since long ago in the army had he been touched, purposely pushed, wrenched; he had never played football or done heavy work and this thing blazed his horror and his dignity and he kept shouting, although he did not know he was shouting, until something solid struck his shoulder and he spun around and almost fell, but gained his balance with his arms outstretched. And in that instant he saw the pavement under him and realized he was out on the street. For an instant he stood there hearing, seeing nothing, and then he heard his shout and felt the soreness in his throat, 'I'm not, you damned fools, I'm not!' and realized he had the glasses raised in one hand and was pointing at them with the other. Around him the faces clustered, but strangely he did not know whether these were the ones who had been mistreating him or whether they were curious passersby. But he no longer cared what scene he made – it never occurred to him that he was making a scene – and in his confused fury and with the driving indignation that was eating into him he started through the faces toward the lighted doorway of the hall, and he was stopped again by hands on his shoulders and on his arms. 'Don't be a damned fool!' he shouted into the eyes of the faces, and the echo came back, 'Sammy, God damn! Sammy ya, Sammy ya Sammy!'

'But I'm not, you damned . . . !'

'That's what they all say when you got them against the wall!'

This he heard. This he heard normally and loud, and it cut

him to a halt. He looked to his right and saw a face, and he looked to his left. He turned completely around and saw still another face, remembering, madly, the frustration of arguing with Gargan about his eyes ... There were only three men standing around him now. The others, he realized, had gone back inside. Now these three turned and walked past him toward the hall entrance. He did not want to be left alone by them. He did not want to be alone at all. They had to understand that he was Lawrence Newman of a family named Newman which had come from Aldwich, England, in the year 1861, and that he had pictures at home showing his baptism and if they would stop just there on the steps for one moment only he could explain how he had been employed for more than twenty years by one of the most anti-Semitic corporations in America and that he . . .

The push in his chest felt like a rock had hit him and he sat down on the sidewalk. Looking up he saw the three men going into the hall. An arm, firm but seemingly inoffensive, lifted him to his feet and he looked up and saw a cop.

'I'm not,' he said hoarsely, and stopped talking.

'You better go home, mister,' the cop said.

'But I . . .'

'How do you feel? You hurt?'

'No, I'm not hurt. But they're crazy, they're out of their minds. Can't they see I . . .?'

'You better go home now,' the cop said. 'Don't bother with them nuts.' His voice was very deep and its cajoling tone told Mr Newman that he was not being believed. A weeping, a sobbing started in his chest and he walked past the cop. Down the street he walked, his mouth open, his hands unmoving at his sides. The sidewalk kept tilting him off his straight course, and when he felt the knowledge of his body again he was sitting amid tall grass. He got up and saw that he was in the middle of a lot and a mosquito was biting into his neck. He slapped it and kept staring around. For a long time he could not concentrate on the neighborhood, and then he saw the El and got his direction. He had walked half the way home.

It was only after he had gone on a few yards that he understood why it had taken so long to find out where he was. His glasses were hanging from one ear. When had he put them on? Or had someone stuck them on his face as a jibe? He stopped and examined them. The lenses were intact but the right bow was bent. He stood there trying to bend it back to shape and finally gave up because the mosquitoes were at his face again. And he put the glasses on and continued walking through the lot. His nose felt uncomfortable because the glasses were twisted a little and were edging into his nose bone and he had to walk, after a few moments, holding them so that they would stop cutting in that way. And all at once he could not bring his feet forward and his sobbing caught him. He stood in the dark with the wild grass around him, crying into one hand while with the other he held the glasses in place. He heard himself wheezing and coughing little coughs, sounding just like a child with a cold, and something insane was laughing in screeches inside him at the same time and all he could do was shake his head and keep crying.

When it was over he found his handkerchief and blew his nose and wiped his face. He threw the handkerchief away because it was soaked, and then he walked on toward his corner and toward his house. Reaching the sidewalk he was relieved a little, for he was still minutely concerned with the cinder dust on the lot, and he walked a little faster. As he took his first speedier step he heard another pair of steps behind him; they were leaving the cinders and coming onto the sidewalk. If they are coming after me, he said to himself, I will smash them. He stopped and turned. A man his height was walking toward him in the darkness. The man, in shirtsleeves, stopped before him and hoisted his pants over his belly.

'Good evening, Mr Newman,' said the man.

Mr Newman's tensed body unwound. It was Mr Finkelstein.

'Could I help you?' he asked.

'I'm all right.'

They stood there.

'I think you want to take off your jacket. It don't look nice,' Mr Finkelstein said after a moment.

Mr Newman started to deny it when he noticed that half his jacket was hanging loose from his shoulder. He drew down on the edge of his sleeve and half of his jacket slipped off and hung from his hand. He took off the other half and rolled them both up.

'You going home? I would like to walk with you, if you don't mind company,' Mr Finkelstein said, and fell into a slow stroll with him. They walked a whole block in silence. Finally Mr Finkelstein spoke. 'I seen there what happened.'

Mr Newman looking straight ahead, made no reply. In the lot behind them crickets were chewing noisily at the night. After waiting a few moments, Finkelstein spoke again.

'I figure,' he said, 'that they'll come to me anyway, so first I'll go to them. I stood outside. I seen what they done to you.'

Mr Newman made no sign of so much as hearing what the other said. They walked a block in silence.

Had it been daylight he would have made an effort to get away from Finkelstein; even now in the darkness of night a stain of resentment was spreading through him at the way the man had managed to impose himself, when it should have been obvious that he wanted to be unseen.

And yet as they walked along the dark street Mr Newman felt a sharp curiosity. What had Mr Finkelstein to say to him now? Despite himself he felt drawn to this man. It was not that he thought of himself as being in the same situation as the Jew walking leisurely beside him, for consciously he did not think of himself that way. It was only that he saw the man in possession of a secret that left him controlled and fortified, while he himself was circling in confusion in search of a formula through which he could again find his dignity.

He glanced at Mr Finkelstein's protruding jaw and bulbous nose. Mr Finkelstein turned to him, and spoke with some embarrassment.

'The reason I stopped you just now is this,' he said. Then he looked down at the sidewalk and thought. 'First I'm asking you to understand me; to you I ain't pleading for anything. I'm out for information. What'll happen is going to happen and I myself can't stop it. I am a man what reads every day several newspapers. All kinds, from the Communist to the utmost reactionary. It's my nature I shouldn't be happy unless I shall understand what is going on. This I can't understand.'

Mr Newman found himself listening. For beneath Mr Finkelstein's deep voice a quavering betrayed itself. It drew him. It was something he instinctively believed he might comprehend. The man beside him was feeling some intense emotion. They kept walking. He wanted something tonight that he could understand. He listened to the deep, nervous voice.

'The other day,' Mr Finkelstein began carefully, 'a colored man – I never seen him before – he comes into the store for Camels. I ain't got Camels and I tell him I ain't got them. "Who you savin' them for?" he says, "the Goldbergs?" If we was outside the store I would have hit him with a box. On times like that I get a certain feeling about those people. To me they ain't regular. But I try to stop my thoughts about them. I say to myself; after all, how many colored people do I know? Better I should be saying, this colored person and that one I don't like. But I got no right I shall condemn the whole people because I don't know the whole people, you understand me? If I never seen California redwood trees what right I got to say they ain't so big? You understand me? – I got no right.'

They crossed a street, and Mr Finkelstein went on. 'So what I don't understand is this – mind you this is information I'm asking, not favors from you. You understand?'

'Yes,' said Mr Newman. He realized that the man was still taking him as one of the Front. It relieved him, for he had a lurking fear that Mr Finkelstein was about to embrace him as a brother. And now he found he was more at ease with this Jew, for he was not imposing after all. 'I understand what you mean,' he said.

'What I don't understand is how so many people can get worked up to such a pitch about Jews when in that whole hall there ain't a person who knows – himself personally – more than three Jews to speak to. Before you answer me – I understand how a person can hate a whole people because I myself slip into the same thing when I forget myself. But I don't understand how they can get excited enough to go sit in a meeting on such a hot night for the purpose they shall get rid of the Jews. To have a . . . a disliking is one thing. But to go to work and put yourself out like that . . . I don't understand it. What's the answer to that?'

Mr Newman shifted his rolled-up jacket to his other arm. 'Most of them aren't very intelligent,' he said, peaking his brows judiciously.

'Yeh, but I seen some there that looked more intelligent than me. If you don't mind my saying, I think you're a man of education yourself . . .' He hesitated and then said rapidly, 'I want to lay things out on the board, Mr Newman. Not I shall ask you for favors, just man to man I want to understand. If you don't mind you shall discuss with me. Why do you want I shall get out of the neighborhood?'

He was breathing harder and was beginning to sniff.

'Well, it's not you particularly . . .' Newman felt embarrassment now, for in the face of Finkelstein's bold question he somehow could not spell out his heart's answer.

'But it is me particularly,' Mr Finkelstein said. 'If you want the Jews shall get out you want me to get out. I did something you don't like?'

'It's not a question of doing something I don't like.'

'Yes? Then what?'

'You don't really want to know, do you?'

'Why, don't you want to tell me?'

Now the man's obdurate strength hit Mr Newman in its full force, and the smile of condescension that had been forming on his face broke; his air of chieftancy shrunk before the indignity of leaving Mr Finkelstein with the notion that he was as stupid and irrational as the mob that had just thrown him out of the hall.

'I'll tell you if you want me to,' he said. 'There's a lot of reasons why people don't like Jews. They have no principles, for one thing.'

'No principles.'

'Yes. In business you'll find them cheating and taking advantage, for instance. That's something that people . . .'

'Let me understand. You're talking about me now?'

'Well, no, not you, but . . .' His right hand began trembling.

'I ain't interested in other people, Mr Newman. I live on this block'– they were approaching his candy store now –'and there ain't another Jew on this block but me and my family. Did I ever cheat you in my business?'

'That's not the point. You . . .'

'I beg your pardon, sir. You don't have to explain to me that certain Jews cheat in business. There is no argument with that. Personally I know for a fact that the telephone company is charging five cents a local call when they could make a good profit charging a penny. This is a fact from the utilities investigation. The phone company is run and owned by gentiles. But just because you are a gentile I ain't mad at you when I put a nickel in to make a phone call. And still gentiles are cheating me. I am asking you why you want to get me off this block, Mr Newman.'

They halted before the lighted window of Mr Finkelstein's store. The block was deserted.

'You don't understand,' Newman said shortly, pressing his trembling hand against his stomach. 'It's not what *you*'ve done, it's what others of your people have done.'

Mr Finkelstein stared at him a long time. 'In other words, when you look at me you don't see me.'

'What do you mean?'

'I mean what I said. You look at me and you don't see me. You see something else. What do you see? That's what I don't understand. Against me you got nothing, you say. Then why are you trying to get rid of me? What do you see that makes you so mad when you look at me?'

Finkelstein's voice was coming from deep in his chest, and Newman suddenly knew that the quavering was the sound of his fury. He had been furious since the moment in the lot. And standing there looking into his angry face, Newman's idea of him altered. Where once he had seen a rather comical, ugly, and obsequious face, now he found a man, a man throbbing with anger. And somehow his anger made him comprehensible to Mr Newman. His clear anger, his relentless and controlled fury opened a wide channel into Newman's being, just as Gertrude's had the time she had sat across the desk from him in his glass cubicle. And for a moment he felt intensely ashamed that Finkelstein, this adult and not at all comical man, was identifying him with the moronic mob at the hall. For he did not know how to answer Finkelstein as a Fronter, as a man consumed by hate. The fact of the matter was that he had no complaint against Finkelstein in particular and he could not face the man like this – and he was a man now – and tell him that he disliked him because he disliked him. Nor could he tell him that his ability to make money was objectionable, for

Finkelstein obviously had no such ability. It was equally impossible to tell him that he was personally unclean because Finkelstein was not that way. True enough, Finkelstein often let his beard grow for two days, but it seemed childish to tell him to get off the block because he did not shave often enough. And looking at Finkelstein now, Newman saw that he had not really hated *him*, he had simply been always at the point of hating him – he had passed this man each morning with the knowledge that he had in him the propensity for acting as Jews were supposed to; cheat, or be dirty, or loud. That Finkelstein had failed to live up to expectations had not changed Newman's feeling toward him. And in the normal course of such events his feeling would never have changed, however correctly Finkelstein comported himself on the block.

But the feeling changed now. For now Mr Newman realized that the only answer he could give to this man was that he disliked him because his face was the face of a man who should be acting in an abhorrent way.

'What do you see when you look at me, Mr Newman?' repeated Mr Finkelstein. Newman stared at him, troubled.

A spasm of distress began to take hold of Mr Newman's stomach. It was as though all the tokens of the known world had been switched, as though in a dream his own house numbers had been changed, the name of his street, the location of the El in relation to his corner, as though all the things that had been true were now all catastrophically untrue. He felt he was going to throw up and cry. Without a word he strode away, and before him he saw Gertrude's face and the way its foreign evilness had dissolved that time in Ardell's office ... the astonishing way she had become a familiar part of his life ...

The street beyond the area lighted by the store was dark. Mr Newman fled into this darkness as into a private room that would enfold him. The eyes of Mr Finkelstein were on his back, hurting him more. If the man would just disappear, just go away . . . for God's sake go away and let everybody be the same! The same, the same, let us all be the same! He quietly opened his front door.

The light was on in the kitchen. Mr Newman walked through the living room on tiptoe, with the shreds of his jacket rolled up under his arm, and without drawing the attention of his mother, gained the stairs in the dining room and silently walked up. At the head of the stairway he saw that the light was on in the front bedroom. He hesitated for a moment and walked along the corridor above the stairway and entered the bedroom.

Gertrude looked up from the bed on which she was sprawled with *Screenplay* magazine in her hand. He laid his bundled jacket on a chair. She kept looking at him.

He sat beside the bed on a little satin-covered stool. Her lips were parted and her eyes did not blink as she decided about him.

'You're cut,' she said, and sat up on the edge of the bed. 'Where'd you get cut?'

'I'll wash in a minute,' he said.

'What happened to you? How'd you get cut? You're all dirty.'

'I was sitting next to some moron there. He started yelling at me.'

'Why, what'd you do?'

'I didn't do anything. He saw I wasn't applauding. I never applaud, you know that.'

'Well, you should have told him,' she complained.

'How can you tell him anything, a man like that? They were all excited. You know how they get.'

'It's not over yet, is it?'

'I don't know.' He could not believe it: she was angry at *him*.

'Didn't you stay to the end? You should've stayed to . . .'

'They pushed me out.'

She blinked. An expression grew on her face that he had never seen before. It was pugnacious and cruel and her lips puffed out like swelling bladders. He was so annoyed at her being angry with him that he got up abruptly and started undressing. Her expression did not change as he shed his trousers and shoes. Every mass inside his body was floating up against his throat.

'Well, don't look at me,' he warned. 'I just never applaud.'

He got to the bedroom door with only his shorts on.

'You should have applauded,' she shouted.

'Don't shout, Gertrude,' he replied, his voice rising.

'Christ almighty, you act like a . . .'

'They're a bunch of morons!' He yelled, furiously . . . she looked so common when she cursed.

His overriding anger turned her away and she lay down on the bed with her back toward him. After a moment he went out of the bedroom and into the bathroom and stood under the shower. The soap burned his cheek, and when he got out he looked into the mirror and saw the cut. It was only as big as a shaving nick, but it was enough to curdle something inside of him and he felt his indignation again. He was not a man who was used to being handled, as some men are.

She was still lying on her side when he came back into the bedroom. He found clean underwear and socks and put them on, and then put on a gray sports shirt which she had bought for him, and then a pair of striped linen pants. She lay without moving on the bed until he had his shoes on, and then she rolled onto her back and looked at him.

'What are you getting dressed for?' she asked, merely with curiosity.

'I have to have clothes on when I go out, don't I?'

'Where are you going?'

'I'll be right back.'

He walked out of the bedroom and at the head of the stairs

slowed down and listened below. He descended with caution and turned in the dining room and went out of the house.

There was a startling moon out. He noticed it only now. A new moon, and the crickets were frightfully loud.

He crossed his own lawn quickly and got to Fred's porch. There was a light on in Fred's front bedroom upstairs but the rest of the house was dark. Mounting the brick steps of the porch he moved on the balls of his feet and sat beside the front door on a low rocking chair. He was in complete darkness. Not once did he rock.

Fred had been at the meeting. He knew it. And he had done nothing to help. But he was beyond the confusion of anger. Coldly the talons of his mind sunk into the street before him, into its ferocious silence that now seemed erected against him. There was a thing he had to do and he knew he would do it.

A car turned the corner on the left and Mr Newman followed its approaching lights with his eyes. It stopped before the house and Fred got out, but stood leaning into the rear window, talking. Finally he stood aside and the car drew away, and then he walked up the path and mounted his porch. He leaped a little when from out of the dark Mr Newman said, 'I want to see you, Fred.'

'Who's that?' Fred said, peering down at Mr Newman in the chair. It was obvious that he merely needed a moment to gather his wits, and wanted to say something that would establish his annoyance in Mr Newman's mind.

'It's me, Fred. Sit down for a minute, will you? Here.' He pulled over another rocker and Fred came around him and sat on it.

Mr Newman was glad he had planned it to take place in the dark. Both of them would be bolder with their words.

'I guess you saw what happened tonight,' Mr Newman began.

Fred bent over and tied his shoelace. He seemed remarkably

innocent of guile. 'I heard what happened, but I wasn't in the hall at that particular minute.'

'It happened after the meeting started,' Newman reminded him.

Fred straightened up and sat forward in his chair as though about to get up and go. 'Well, they didn't hurt you, did they?'

'I got a little cut,' Newman said. 'And they did manage to twist my glasses.' His voice sang just a little.

Fred seemed to realize it was not going to be as easy as he had at first imagined. 'Well what do you want, Larry? I couldn't help it, could I?'

'We'll forget that. I'm not saying you could've or you couldn't've. We'll forget it. I just don't want to be molested again, Fred.'

'Mistakes happen. They get excited, Larry.'

'That's what I figure. But they aren't excited when they spill over my garbage can.'

'Did they do that?' Hollowly the voice rose in astonishment.

'Let's stop fooling around, Fred. I told you about it.'

'Yeh, but you don't want to keep accusing a fella, Larry, I didn't know anything about ...'

'Well you must've known, Fred. The garbage was all over the grass both times.'

'All right, so what do you want me to do?'

'I want to be left alone, Fred. I want you to tell them to leave me alone.'

Fred did not answer. In the dark Mr Newman could not see his expression, and so he waited, and he felt that anything could happen. It was clear to him now that he hated Fred with a bloody hate. The man was a slimy liar, the man was a snake.

'Well? What do you say, Fred?' Mr Newman insisted. He was very stiff in his chair.

'You talk like I was the leader of the outfit, Larry.'

'You're leader enough to have them take my name off their list.'

'What list?'

'The list of Jews.'

'Who told you we got a list?'

'I know you have a list and I want you to take my name off it.'

'How'm I going to do that, Larry?'

'That's something you know, I don't.' It was too bad, but he had to say it, he had to. Nothing could proceed, he knew, unless he said it. 'You ought to have more sense than to make a Jew out of me, Fred.'

'Nobody's making a Jew out of you, Larry.'

'They don't attack a man twice unless they think he's a Jew. Not twice they don't.'

'Tonight they just got excited.'

'And somebody there didn't get excited, Fred. That rough-housing was as easy to stop as it was to start.'

'I said I wasn't there when it happened.'

'I say you were, Fred.'

'Well OK, then, I'm a liar.'

'Nobody called you a liar. Sit down, will you, I want to talk to you.'

'I got to go in.'

'No, I want to talk to you, Fred. Sit down.'

'All right, but I wasn't there.'

They sat in silence for a moment. And the silence was threatening to seal over Newman's ebbing flow of speech, so he spoke again before he would have liked to.

'I want you to tell me something frankly. Do they think I'm really Jewish?'

Fred took a moment. It was good, Mr Newman thought again, that it was happening in the dark this way.

'Well, I'll tell you, Larry.' Fred spoke as though he were only an intermediary. His guile sickened Newman, who felt like hitting him.

'Like in every big organization there's a certain element that's hotheads. You got to expect that. You got to expect that element, you know?'

'Yes.'

'Well, there's some who been noticing you. I'll admit that. Since you got the glasses you got to admit you do look a little Hebey.'

Mr Newman said nothing.

'I told them, I sez, the man's been my neighbor a long time. But they claim they know what they're talking about. I mean when you're one against ten you got to listen to them, you know?'

'But you know well enough that I'm . . .'

'*I* know, Larry. But one against ten is a very small percentage.'

Silence again. So they had really discussed him. And Fred had not dared defend him too much.

'So I stay on the list, is that it?'

'Well, tell you the truth, Larry, I was making headway for a while there. But when you brought the missus around that's when you made it tough for yourself.'

'Why should she make it tough?' Mr Newman asked angrily.

'Well, she's a Jewish girl, ain't she?'

'Christ Almighty, Fred, have you gone off?'

'You mean she . . .'

'Of course she's not. Where in hell do you get that idea?'

For one second Fred held back. Then he said, 'Well, gee, I'm awful sorry about it, Larry. I didn't know.'

And now it was the end and Mr Newman got up from his chair. Fred's fake remorse stank like a dense gas in Mr Newman's nostrils. He could not bear to plead any longer. Fred did not believe him, probably could not afford to believe him. Fred was getting up now . . .

'I'm really sorry about it, Larry. But I myself thought you'd gone and got yourself a Jewish girl.'

The heavy respect with which he mouthed 'a Jewish girl' betrayed his continuing belief. And it clinched something in Mr Newman's chest. He walked to the top step of the porch and stood looking at the houses, snug and dark, across the street.

'I'm not giving up my house, Fred . . .'

'Who gave you that idea,' Fred laughed thinly.

'I'm talking, Fred, and I'm telling you what I'm going to do.' Newman spoke low for if he raised his voice it would have started his body quickly moving toward Fred and he knew it. 'I've bought my house and I've paid for it and nobody is going to move me out of it. I don't give a damn who tries it or how many, I'm staying put. And as far as you're concerned . . .' He turned and looked at Fred, whose face he could see better now that he was standing away from the shadow of the house. 'As far as you're concerned, don't kid yourself about me.' He did not know how to phrase his hate and his defiance, and so he said, 'Just don't kid yourself about me, Fred. I can take care of myself. You understand my meaning? I can take pretty good care of myself. So don't kid yourself.'

He turned on the top step and walked down, his muscles twitching like little wounded snakes, and walking away from Fred's porch he thought his heart would crack in his chest. With a slow, measured step, calculated to demonstrate his defiance, he went down Fred's path to the sidewalk, then turned left in his time and as he came to his own path he heard Fred's screen door angrily slamming. At the sound he stopped in front of his porch.

Before him stood his house. '*Gertrude, dear, we're going to have to stand and fight it out here.*'

Turning away from his house he started to stroll. And passing the identical houses with their silent square windows staring at him he newly realized that there was a long stretch of pitch darkness here between the two street lights, for the trees hung low over the sidewalk. Here he could not even make out the curbing of the sidewalk. He was walking in a long closet. *Aleese! Aleese!* The high heaving cry flew around his head as he strolled. *Police!*

Supposing now from up ahead there, armed forms should plunge up to his face. *Help, help!* Who would come out to him from behind the venetian blinds? Who?

Strolling, he stared. Everybody on the block must either have seen or been told about his garbage pail. None of them ever mentioned it to him, even those he met on the trains going to work.

Aleese! She could have been murdered, clubbed to death out here that night. No one would have dared outdoors to help, to even say she was a human being. Because all of them watching from their windows knew she was not white . . .

But he was white. A white man, a neighbor. He *belonged* here. Or did he? Undoubtedly they all knew the rumor by now. Newman is a Jew. An attack upon him would prove it to them. Notice the name – Newman. Of course – Newman! Who would come out in the darkness of the night to fight off thugs for his sake? Who would come out, for instance, to help Finkelstein? Finkelstein. They had him hooked up with Finkelstein. He knew he would never come out and risk a broken nose for Finkelstein. He knew he would remain behind his venetian blinds saying to himself that Finkelstein should have moved away when he knew they were after him, that a beating was not so horrible to the Jew because he had been born expecting it. As it was not so horrible for that woman, who was accustomed to attack because she had never in her life been safe. It was not so horrible for them, it was a natural thing for them . . .

'*In other words when you look at me you don't see me. What do you see?*'

He crossed the macadam toward the other side of the street. And he envisioned the Blighs behind their blinds, saying, Newman is being beaten up. They found out he is a Jew. It will all pass tomorrow when he moves away. Then everything will be all right again. However close to being human a Jew might seem, he was still not as sacred as they in the blinding moment of violence. They would not come out because he would be a Jew in their eyes, and therefore guilty. Somehow, in some unsayable way, guilty. They had no evidence that he had ever conspired against or hurt them, and yet once they were convinced he was a Jew he knew they would feel he had a curse for them in his heart, and if he were lying here on the macadam bleeding, they would be salved in their conscience by imagining that curse. And if he cried out a thousand times that he did not hate them, and that he was hurt by blows as they would be, and that he was like them in every conceivable way, they would stare at his face and those who would believe him would not wholly believe him, and those who would not believe at all would despise him the more. '*In other words when you look at me . . .*'

He walked toward the yellow-lighted window of the candy store, held by the terror of his old dream. It was this that was being manufactured beneath the innocent merry-go-round. Behind these snug, flat-roofed houses a sharp-tipped and murderous monster was nightly being formed, and its eyes were upon him; he was being insensibly branded by the snarling power of this fury that would burst through the walls of these houses and surely find him.

And there was no truth to erect against it. There were no words to lull it with. It was insanity in the darkness, and it could not be confronted and calmed.

Without hesitating at the newsstand he walked into the candy store. Mr Finkelstein was sitting on a wooden backless

194

chair in front of the tall magazine rack which hung beside the cash register. The store was so narrow that he could sit with his back against the showcase in one wall with his feet propped upon a shelf in the opposite wall. When he saw Mr Newman he lowered his feet to the floor, and while his black eyes inspected, his mouth smiled.

'Good evening,' he said, pulling up on his pants.

For a moment Mr Newman seemed not to be seeing him. Then he blinked away his vision, and nodded. Leaning against a showcase, he kept his hands in his pockets as though to feel snug and at one with himself. He pretended to examine merchandise on the shelves across the narrow store from where he stood.

'How do you feel?' Mr Finkelstein ventured.

His mind elsewhere, Mr Newman said he felt all right. Then he looked at the boards of the floor, and said, 'I wanted to ask you a few things.'

Mr Finkelstein nodded willingly and turned his cigar butt around between his pursed lips.

Newman looked up at him. 'Have you thought about what you're going to do if anything ... if they start anything with you?'

Finkelstein began to look embarrassed. He took out his cigar and inspected it. 'You got some definite information they're going to start with me?'

His eyes had come to glisten now. And Newman saw that he was afraid, and was trying not to show it.

'It's coming all right. I don't know when, but it's coming.'

'Well,' Finkelstein said, and when his cigar quivered, he went to the ash tray on the cash register and steadied himself by rubbing out its glowing end. Newman felt he would ordinarily have smoked it down further. 'I can't do very much, naturally. What I can do I'll do,' he said. Then facing Newman directly, he admitted, 'Unless they shall come with too many

I'll maybe take care of myself. If there's too many I wouldn't do so good.'

'That's funny, I thought you'd know what you were going to do.'

'Well I got something, I . . .' After hesitating a moment, and smiling in embarrassment, Finkelstein went to the front of the store and opened a long drawer near the floor and took out a shiny baseball bat and came with it to Newman. 'That's what they call a Louisville Slugger. Solid wood,' he said, holding it out for Newman's view. Newman touched the smooth grain and put his hand back into his pocket. Finkelstein went back to the drawer and carefully put the bat away. Then he stood there looking into Newman's eyes.

Newman said; 'I should think that if you really made it clear to the police . . .'

'Mr Newman,' the other said, shaking his head slowly, 'you are talking like this never happened before.'

Looking at the man Newman knew now what kept him from losing his mind.

'That meeting,' Finkelstein went on, 'wasn't in no secret cellar. The police know what's going on. There just ain't no law against people hating each other. It ain't . . . there's nothing wrong with it. It's their right to make a meeting like that to murder people,' he said sarcastically. 'The only good it will do to go to the police is that a . . . a delegation should go. I tell them, but they listen and they go away. Mrs Depaw tells them but she's an old lady, what does she mean to them? If a couple of men on the block would . . . would . . .'

Newman saw himself standing beside Finkelstein in the precinct house, with the eyes of the Irish cop glancing from the Jew to him.

'Mr Finkelstein,' he broke in, 'I'll tell you what I think.'

'Yes,' Finkelstein said, listening eagerly.

Newman no longer looked at him, but kept his eyes moving

among the merchandise on the shelves. 'I think there's only one sensible thing for you to do.'

'Yes,' Finkelstein whispered, his chin raised, his lips parted.

'You've got to keep in mind what sort of people there are in the neighborhood,' he began again. 'It's a new neighborhood. I happen to know that a lot of families moved here to get away from the old neighborhoods,' he said with a tense look around his eyes, 'and they naturally resent any ... any ... well you know what I mean.'

Finkelstein's mouth opened a little wider, and he nodded just a little and stared at Newman.

'If there were just a few with that point of view I'd say, stand your ground and stick it out here. But I don't think you've got many friends around here, and I ... well, frankly, I think you ought to think about moving. That's my honest opinion.'

Finkelstein's brows drew together. Newman could not bear his puzzled gaze and looked down at the floorboards again as though in thought. A moment passed. Another. He looked up and Finkelstein's expression had changed. The man's mouth was shut tight.

'Are you a Jew, Mr Newman?' Finkelstein asked.

Newman's skin felt cold. 'No,' he said.

'You're not a Jew,' Finkelstein said.

'No,' Mr Newman repeated, on the verge of anger.

'But they think you are.'

'Yes.'

'Supposing I told you to move?'

'That's ...'

'Supposing I said to you, there's too many people in this neighborhood who are looking like Jews. These ignoramuses don't like it. Move, Mr Newman, because I wouldn't have no peace until you do ...'

'I gave you my honest opinion and you ...'

'I'm giving you my honest opinion too,' Finkelstein said, his voice quavering. His eyes were moist. 'In my opinion they got you marked with indelible ink and it wouldn't help you one penny's worth if I . . .'

'*I* don't need any help,' Newman said, his tone climbing indignantly.

'I wasn't born yesterday, Mr Newman.' Finkelstein's trouser legs started shaking. 'I thought you was buying on Sundays from that roughneck because they made you buy. I thought no matter what you did you were my friend because you are a man with intelligence, an intelligent person. But you . . .'

'I didn't come in here to be insulted,' Newman said, stiffly.

'For God's sake!' Finkelstein burst out, his fists clenched. 'Don't you see what they're doing? What the hell can they get out of the Jews? There's a hundred and thirty million people in this country and a couple million is Jews. It's you they want, not me. I'm . . . I'm,' he started to stutter in his fury, 'I'm chicken feed. I'm a nothin'. All I'm good for is so they can point to me and everybody else will give them their brains and their money, and then they will have the country. It's a trick, it's a racket. How many times must it happen, how many wars we got to fight in this world before you will understand what they are doing to you?' Newman stood like a stone. 'Move. You want me to move,' Finkelstein said, his body trying to move about in the tiny store. 'I will not move. I like it here. I like the air, I like it for my kids. I don't know what I'll do but I will not move. I don't know how to fight them but I will fight them. This thing is organized for what they can get out of it. They are a gang of devils and they want this country. And if you had any regard for this country you wouldn't tell me such a thing. I will not move, Mr Newman. I will not do it. I won't.'

He stood there shaking his head.

Newman walked numbly out the door. After a few feet he stepped off the curb of the sidewalk and headed for home, keeping to the center of the macadam street where there was more light than under the trees.

CHAPTER SEVENTEEN

But it all began to look differently the next morning. Something seemed to have happened to him during his sleep.

While he was dressing he knew once more his beloved feeling of independence and self-containment. Opening the front door for Gertrude he took note of the garbage pail standing undisturbed at the curb and walked up the street with his wife as though it could not have been otherwise, he having finally withdrawn from all contests.

And if when he passed the newsstand without taking a paper there arose in him a sense of embarrassment, it was more nearly the last drop from an empty gourd than the first of one that had now showed a crack. The only thing that needed settling, in his opinion, was Gertrude: she stood waiting for him to put the nickel in the turnstile and made everything clear by the raising of her eyebrow and repeated sighs.

The days passed that way, and when they spoke it was as though a little stone had lodged in their throats. He noticed the absence of small talk, knew she was waiting for him to acknowledge his mistake. But he had a house with a lock, and when she came to understand it she would brighten up and be happy with him there behind his door.

In a little while, however, the truth rode silently across his horizon like some hidden moon and hung there, squarely in front of his eyes. And he saw that he too was waiting, waiting to be attacked.

The garbage pail had not been turned any more violently the second time than it had the first, and yet he knew, he knew it was coming and he knew it would find him. Not because anything outside him had changed but because he had changed. In those solemn days between him and his wife, the city kept carving a new shape upon his soul. Like a current along a shore it scoured silently against the sides of his mind. It was not something that happened; tantalizingly it never took the shape of an event. He merely came to live in a state of waiting while his body carried him through his daily rounds. Work in the morning, lunch at noon, home at night. He had dinner with Gertrude in restaurants on many evenings and they went to the movies a little more often, and one Saturday afternoon, making a stab at joy, they rode along the river on a Fifth Avenue bus. But nothing drew the pressure away, for wherever he looked he saw new shapes and heard sounds that had never registered on his ears before. Often, while walking in a crowd, he caught a conversation behind him and slowed down to listen. For the sound '*ew*' had come from back there and he must know to what it referred, and trying to follow the conversation he would find his heart turned a little, and it took a moment for it to slip back into place.

Mean drunks approaching along a street made him awkward and tense. In the old days he would, if not fight, certainly stand upon his dignity and seek out a policeman to take care of the ruffian, but now he did not know precisely what rights to stand on if the man followed him to the cop calling him that name. He was at a loss as to his role in the city now. Assume he was merely another citizen? Then what if the cop happened to be the kind to take him for an alien always running to the law instead of defending himself? He knew from old experience what his own attitude had been toward such innocents. And yet if he defended himself what compassion could he expect of the passersby – while the drunk kept ringing out that dreadful name? How could a man fight alone, so terribly alone?

His mind was stuck, in these days that passed so regularly and with such seeming calm, but a mind must move and his moved in the only direction open – toward the finest dissection of violence. In the most awkward places he would come awake to the clenching of his fists, aware that he had been envisioning himself in a fist-fight. Brutal questions wormed into him. How hard must he strike to knock a man down? Could he hit a man on the chin without breaking his hand? Did he have the power to knock a man down? He moved about in the city in his usual paths and the city was new and his honor stalked him demanding its due.

And it drained away his inner ease, it burdened him with a secret new personality. He could no longer simply enter a restaurant and innocently sit down to a meal. Certain tall and broad types of fair-haired men, with whom he fancied his appearance most in contrast, threw him off balance. When they happened to be seated nearby he found himself speaking quite softly, always wary of the loudness in his tone. Before reaching for something on the table he first unconsciously made sure that he would not knock anything over. When he spoke he kept his hands under the table, although he had always needed gestures. In the glances of people, in the fleet warpings of their eyes, he sought to learn where he stood, for despite his constant self-warnings that he was becoming over-sensitive about it, that he was really not being noticed by nine out of ten people, he still could not tell what was being said in innocence and what was designed to carry meaning for him. And he felt the pressure closing more firmly on his life. Often, to destroy any impression of closefistedness, he left larger tips than he used to and was repaid amply by waitresses' smiles. He no longer dared to dally before a cashier to count his change — he had always done that, but not any more. The city, the people around him had come somehow to encircle him with their darting eyes; in the streets and public places he no longer felt anonymous. The things he had done all his life as a gentile, the most innocent habits of his person, had been turned into the tokens of an alien and evil personality, a personality that was slowly, he felt, implacably being foisted upon him. And wherever he went he was trying to underplay that personality, discarding it in every way he knew while at the same time denying that he possessed it. He felt as though he were constantly living around the subway pillars, for he kept trying to decide how many minds their violent inscriptions really represented. The secret newspapers he had called them once, the real conscience of the millions, the unedited cry of the people. But even then he had not been sure how many hated, really. How many on this avenue would come to his aid? How many on his block at home? How many would come out for his sake in the darkness of that night . . . ?

When the leaves fell and the furnace was on, Mr Newman had waited a long time. Northern man that he was, he looked forward to the changing of seasons as the time of renewal and change, and yet in the new cold of winter he had no more of an answer than he had had the night he was thrown out of the hall.

There was, however, a strange quiet chord sounding in him with the arrival of this winter. The wind came this time like a soft yet impassable fortification around him, a natural force that kept people off the streets and safely locked away in the sensible regimes of their families. Never had he thought of winter in this way, and he liked the feeling it gave him. The city and the block were turning in upon their warm radiators, and he would be left alone sitting next to his.

Perhaps he would have been content, or nearly so, to go on living without love and yet with this steam-heated peace, but one night came that was so strikingly beautiful as to bring back his longing for the extraordinary ecstasy he had once envisioned beside his wife. It was that rare, still night when the stars cast their own shadows on the ground and the sky is cloudless and the sharp air does not move. The tree in the back yard, which he could see through the panes in the kitchen door, looked as though iced by the stars. Behind his chair the radiator fizzed. Gertrude was drinking coffee across the table. His mother was having hers by the radio in the parlor. He sipped, not daring to raise his eyes to his wife's – it had become a habit. The lower in the cups the coffee sank, the lower sank their eyes, as though it should not come to pass that they find themselves face to face once no external reason remained.

But tonight, whether it was the stillness outside or the way Gertrude was made up, he thought her beautiful, and instead of rising to go into the living room where Mother would make conversation between them comfortably impossible, he set his cup down, and feeling he would cry he said, 'Gert,' in the deep-voiced way he had of letting bars fall away.

She raised her eyes, hurt before he began – having caught the plea in his tone.

He was smiling softly, kindly. 'I often think,' he said, picking at a crumb on the maple table, 'how silly we are. Really, Gert,' he laughed minutely, 'we've got everything, you know? How about forgetting everything and enjoying ourselves again?'

She agreed with him and so it seemed necessary that she appear to dissent.

'We go places,' she said with a sigh.

'I know, but we don't enjoy ourselves. Now, do we?'

'I guess not,' she whispered sadly.

'I often think of what we have,' he warmed quickly, 'a nice house all paid for, good jobs . . . How about making up?'

Her face peaked innocently, and she pursed her lips until they were soft – something he was afraid she had learned from a certain movie they had seen together – and she said, 'Why Lully, there's nothing to make up.'

He had never been able to contend with coyness, and he insisted, 'Now there is something. I'd . . . I . . . couldn't we talk a little about it?'

She saw his eyes all round and big through the glasses, his lips so red from the hot coffee seemed fat. Unconsciously she drew in her lips to destroy any resemblance. 'I don't like it here, Lully, that's all the trouble is.'

Sorry, he frowned. 'You mean Mother being here or the neighborhood?'

'The neighborhood.' Deliberately she mashed her cigarette in the saucer. 'I think we ought to move away, maybe. To another city.'

Apprehensively he lowered his head toward the table to meet her continually dropping gaze. 'Now let's try to examine things, dear. Please ...' He chucked her under the chin and she allowed him to raise her head. 'What can I do about it? Think a minute. What exactly can I do?'

'Go in to Fred. He's not some kind of a devil, he's ...'

'You don't mean that.'

'Well I do, Lully,' she said defensively.

'After the way he insulted us?'

'He didn't actually *insult* us ...'

'But he did, dear.'

'Yeh, but ...' The splotches were blooming as she struggled. 'I happen to know one thing, Lully.' Her eyes, filling with redness, disturbed him.

'What, dear?' he prompted with additional gentleness.

'They're drawring a ring around us here. Now wait a minute, they are. Every time I go to the butcher you ought to see the way they give me the eye.'

'Who?'

'All of them. Mrs Bligh, Mrs Cassidy, especially that one with the old Packard near the corner on the other side.'

'What do you mean, give you the eye?'

'I mean give me the eye. I know when somebody's giving me the eye and when they ain't. They look at me like I just come off the boat.'

'Did they always do that?'

'No. That's what I been trying to tell you. Somebody's talking to them about us. I can feel it going on. They're drawing a ring around us as clear as chalk. I'm telling you, Lully, they're going to clean out this neighborhood as sure as you're born.'

He looked down worriedly at the crumb he had forced under his nail.

'What I want to know,' she went on, 'is which end of the broom are we going to be on. We can't sit on the stick, Lully.'

Without meeting her gaze he said, 'They're not getting away with it. Don't you worry.' He looked up, determined.

'What are we going to do about it?'

'There's nothing to do but ignore them. They're just not pushing me out, dear.'

'Ignore it.'

'Yes, just don't pay any attention.'

'Well, what am I here for, then? The way you told it, it was such a nice block, such friendly people. I thought we'd have friends, parties, something to do. I'm living like a horse that goes into his stable every night after work.'

'We go places, don't we?'

'You're not the type to do it, Lully,' she said, and he felt the crunch of truth in her words. 'You can't dance, you don't know how to drink, you . . . you're just not the type.' She saw his blush. 'I'm not complaining about that; I didn't marry you for that. I really didn't. But at least I thought you'd be the other kind . . .'

'But I am . . .' he started weakly.

'But you haven't got a friend on the block. You haven't got a friend, Lully.'

'But I didn't lie to you, dear. I used to go bowling with Fred and . . .' He saw the vein in the side of her neck.

'That's what I mean. Honest to God now, could you see yourself being invited by anybody on this block any more?'

He thought.

She saw that he was convinced.

'That's what I mean,' she concluded, and leaned back successfully. 'Either we move and find friends, or we find some here.'

'Well, I'll ... I'll ...' he stared abstractly, 'I'll ... on Sunday is the best time. People are outside on Sunday. Bligh is a nice chap. We'll get something up, we'll ...' But he saw the vision of it on Sunday, and stopped talking.

'And what happens if he ain't interested?' she asked.

He looked at her now. His voice was thin as it always was in defense. 'Well, they're not all in the organization.'

She leaned ahead on her elbows, 'Lully,' she said quietly, patiently, 'people don't give you the eye that way unless they been put on to something.'

She leaned back again and watched his staring eyes. Her voice became plaintive. 'I thought you'd make a life for me, Lully. I thought I'd stay home and fix up the place for you. I ain't even had a chance to cook something nice. I'm a good cook. I ain't even had a chance to put up new curtains. All it's been is trouble and more trouble.'

She waited, but his gaze remained unbroken.

'Not that I mind working,' she put in after a moment.

He did not answer. She lit another cigarette, and looked off idly toward the door, blowing smoke.

For a long minute he studied her profile. Then, 'Dear?' he said. She turned, exhaling smoke. He saw how she was suppressing her interest in what he was about to say, and knew that what she wanted to discuss was her quitting the job. He would have asked her if that was why she married him, but whatever the answer was it would change nothing, so he let it pass. 'I want to tell you something else,' he said.

'What?'

'Supposing I went in to Fred.'

'Yes.'

'Let me start another way. I spoke to Finkelstein that time.'

'Yes.'

'I know for a fact that he's not going to move no matter what happens.'

'If nobody buys from him he'll move soon enough. They don't stay where there's no money.'

'But he's got customers for four blocks around.'

'The Front has members four blocks around, too. They'll fix it so he don't make a penny a day.'

'I doubt it. Most people aren't going to walk ten blocks to a candy store just to spite him.'

'They'll walk a mile if it gets so they're ashamed to be seen coming out of his store.'

'I doubt it.'

'Well doubt it, but I'm telling you it happens. In Los Angeles they were fixing Jews that way right and left.'

'Really?'

'Sure. Just like you're not buying from him on the corner.'

'Yes, but . . . well I'm not staying away because anybody told me to.'

'Why then?'

'Well, I just don't get along with the man, that's all.'

'You got along with him before the Front started saying not to get along with him, didn't you?'

'Well, no, I . . .' He lost his thought. Was it possible he was doing exactly what they had forced him to do? At the moment he could not recall just when he had decided not to buy there any more.

'That's the way it works,' she said. 'People just don't think it's healthy to buy from him and pretty soon he's out. The thing I don't understand is, why you don't go in to Fred and tell him where you stand and get this thing cleared up. We're suffering for no good reason. I don't understand why you don't do it.'

'Because I . . . well, I don't believe that Finkelstein is going to move until they beat him so badly that he can't do anything else but close up.'

'So?'

'Well . . . I don't know if that's a right thing to do. I mean I don't know if I want to get mixed up in that.'

'Yeh, but if they know where you stand you got nothing to worry about.'

'But I mean, is it right for them to beat up Finkelstein?'

'Well, he's asking for it, isn't he? They warned him time and again to get out.'

'I know, but . . .'

'When a man is warned it ain't as though they jumped on him without warning.'

'You don't understand what I mean,' he explained. 'I'm wondering whether it's right for them to take it upon themselves even to warn him.'

'Well . . . what do you mean?'

'I mean . . . well, take us, for instance. I guess you might say we were warned. Twice, as a matter of fact . . .'

'Yeh, that's why I say go in to Fred.'

'Wait a minute, let me finish. You've got to look at both sides. We were warned. Now do you feel they have a right to tell us where to live?'

'Yeh, but we're not Jews, are we?'

He could not press the argument. He did not know how to make her understand, and he felt then that he had become strange in his thinking, that no one but he could imagine such a way of seeing the thing. She was talking . . .

'. . . the neighborhood. Nobody asked him to move in here, did they? He knew it was a Christian neighborhood. You got to admit that, don't you?'

'Yes, but . . . What I mean is this. If there was a law I'd say all right. But it's not safe to have people deciding things like that by themselves.'

'If more did, you wouldn't have this problem. You'll see, the time will come when they'll have special neighborhoods that they won't be allowed out of, or even special states.'

'Oh nonsense. Where did you get that idea?'

'Everybody on the Coast was talking about it for a while.'

'They can't do that,' he said, dismissing the idea nervously.

She frowned now. 'I don't understand you, Lully. No kidding, I don't understand you. You got some kind of ideas.'

'The only idea I have is that I am not going to be pushed out of my house. I've bought this house and I've paid for it and nobody is going to tell me whether to live in it or not. Especially that gang of lunatics.'

'If you'd go see Fred you wouldn't be pushed out.'

'I am not going to get down on my knees to Fred for the privilege of living in my house, dear. Now that's final.' He tried to smile away his absolute tone.

She did not understand. 'You mean you don't care what happens on the block, is that what you mean?'

'Finkelstein never bothered anybody. If there was a law that said he couldn't live here, well . . . all right. But . . .'

'What do you mean, he don't bother anybody? Then why is everybody against him?'

'You know why they're against him.'

'Well, are you against him?' she asked quietly.

'Well, I . . . I wish he wasn't here, yes. But he is here and I have no right to force him to move.'

'But you asked him to move yourself.'

'I did, yes . . . but . . . well, I mean I have no right to beat up on him.' That, finally, was what he meant, he felt. And he clung to the idea, and reached over and grasped her arm. 'People have a right to *ask* a man to move, but they've got no right to *force* him to move.'

He felt his head spinning. That wasn't right either. What did people have a right to do to a Jew? Why was he so crippled in thinking about it? It used to be so clear to him that they simply had to be frightened out of a neighborhood where they didn't belong. But now the picture of it clenched his stomach and he could not even utter it, for he saw the maniacal faces in the hall . . .

He saw she was waiting for him to explain himself. It was so dreamlike trying to grab hold of her sense of . . . well . . . kindness. She was kind, he knew. She would never want to see blood, even a Jew's blood.

'You wouldn't want to see the man hurt, would you?' he asked, as though that would settle her attitude.

She kept moving her eyes around, and sat back. 'Well, I don't say it's the best thing to be happening, but if that's the only way to . . .'

He laughed. 'Oh come now, you know you wouldn't want that.'

She kept moving her eyes and opening her mouth to speak and closing it again. Something in him cried out that she must say no more or he would have to confess openly that he had been talking all along about no one but himself and her. And then there would be no arguing about going to Fred; he would simply have to go and save her.

Jolly and sudden, he clapped both hands down on the table, and said, 'I say we take in a picture.'

In reply she stared at him, calculating something that was beyond this room. 'Listen,' she said.

'What.'

There's only one thing to do. I been thinking about doing it a long time but I didn't want to. But now I think I better.'

'What, dear?'

'I'll go in to Fred and . . .'

'No, dear.'

'Wait a minute. He doesn't know who I am. I didn't want him to know. I wanted to just be a private person the rest of my life. I thought this kind of excitement blew over in California, but it's getting bigger instead of smaller. I'll go in to him . . .'

'No, dear, you're not.'

'I'll tell him who I am. I can name names he'll recognize. We'll get in with them once and for all and see what happens.'

He shook his head with absolute decision. 'No,' he said.

Her sigh shook. 'I say yes, Lully.'

'You will not go to him. I'm not six years old, and he isn't my father. Come on, we'll see a picture.'

He got up. She remained in her chair, figuring.

'I forbid it, Gert. Absolutely. I forbid it.'

She got up and with a peeved sigh replaced a strand of her hair in almost a lazy way. The outlines of her breasts showed when she raised her arms and he longed for her and for the time when he had lived only for night. He got up and went around the table to her.

'Let's forget it, Gert,' he urged softly, looking into her face.

She lowered her arms and blinked thoughtfully, then looked up at him. He took her hand and kissed it. He smiled at the foolish gesture and at himself as he let her hand go.

'Come on. We go to the movies and forget it.'

She allowed her mouth to smile and avoided his eyes. 'OK, I'll put something on,' she said, and went out of the kitchen, listless and wronged.

He watched through the door until she disappeared up the stairs. In the parlor he could see his mother in her wheelchair leaning back with her eyes closed, listening to a waltz on the radio.

He turned away and walked across the yellow linoleum to the kitchen door and looked out at the bare yard. Animation pumped into him and on the wave of it he saw that he must never lose Gert. Whatever her faults she was necessary to him; he would need another woman if she ever left him. The cleanliness of the sky and the stripped branches of the tree brought him to a sense of opportunity, as though from this barrenness a purer life could start, all undefiled by what had gone before. Tonight he would begin. Make her forget the whole nightmare, he thought, just enjoy what they had so much of. And there would be peace. If only you wanted peace enough, he felt, you could get it.

Turning from the door as she came down the stairs he felt the privacy of winter around him very powerfully, and it shut out the world beyond the tightly closed windows. He walked into the parlor to meet her, the old faint longing for happiness stirring in his smile.

Fur around her face this way softened her expression. As they walked he leaned his head over and brushed against her fox collar. She glanced at him, surprised, and allowed herself to smile.

He laughed.

The moon was down behind the houses somewhere. He looked and could not find it. 'Look at the stars, Gert,' he said.

She looked up. 'Nice,' she said.

He held her arm against his side. 'Are you cold?'

'No, it's nice out. We'll go to the Beverly, heh?' she asked.

'Fine. It's closer anyway. What's playing?'

'I don't know, but I'm sick of musicals. They're all the same. The Beverly's got that new boy . . . what's his name?'

They had passed Finkelstein's store and she had not stiffened. The store looked nice and warm. Through the door window he could see Finkelstein sitting there with his daughter, who was reading a comic magazine.

They turned the corner onto the wide, tree-lined parkway, which in this section was residential with many barren lots separating the houses. After a few blocks in the direction they were going it became a business street with two movie houses several blocks apart. He liked knowing that Finkelstein stayed open till late, thought of it for a moment.

'I know the one you mean but I can never remember actors' names,' he said to her.

She talked about the new star with enthusiasm. His comparative lack of glamor appealed to her. 'He's like a person, somebody you could meet,' she said.

They had gone a block and could now make out the lights of the stores six blocks ahead. The movie marquee which they still could not read sent up a snowy glow against the night sky. Gradually his attention fixed on a dark, broad tree trunk on the next corner. But it was out of line with the other trees ... Now it moved, became the silhouettes of several men standing in a group talking. Or were they boys?

'How would you like to take a long trip? To Hollywood, say?' he said, without moving his head.

'It's cheap to live out there,' she muttered, peering stiff-necked toward the group on the corner.

'I mean for a visit. Is it true that they have maps you can buy that show where all the stars live?'

'Beverly Hills. But we could never get enough time off for a trip like that.'

'Can't tell.'

'Unless we moved out there altogether,' she said, her voice hardly audible as they approached the group on the corner.

They were men, he could see now. He wished he could go on talking but his body was taking on a posture of intense propriety and he led Gertrude past the men in silence, looking straight ahead. They kept walking for a minute. His mind caught the rhythm of her high heels clacking on the pavement, mingling out of time with his measured steps.

Quietly, without turning her head, she said, 'What'd they stop talking like that for?'

'Did they?'

'You recognize any of them?'

'No.'

'Didn't you hear them stop talking?'

'No, I didn't notice anything,' he lied unaccountably.

'What're they standing around in the cold for?'

'Must have just come from some place together,' he said.

They walked without speaking for a block.

'Let's think about a trip,' she said.

He could not reply.

Stiffly they arrived at the box office of the theatre. He bought the tickets while she went into the outer lobby. He pocketed his change and met her there and they went into the darkness of the theatre. She kept holding her coat together near the neck even when they were inside. He noticed it as he followed her down the aisle.

She did not dispute the usher's choice of seats as she sometimes did, and took the first ones pointed out to her. He followed her past the knees and they sat. She still had not taken her hand from her coat and sat there clasping it together.

It took a moment for him to catch on to the picture, which he guessed to be half finished. Gertrude faded from his concern as the screen drew his attention, and he settled back into the darkness.

A wide field, empty in early morning.

Two low bushes show up now, come closer. A man arises from behind them. He is bruised and seems to have just come out of unconsciousness.

He feels his arm and then starts walking.

He is on a road, and comes to a house which he enters. He is walking with a limp now.

Inside the house there is one room. It is a cottage on a farm. (In Europe?) a very poor hovel.

On a bed in the corner lies a form. The man walks over to it. It is a woman asleep. He looks at her a long time.

Then he covers her face with the blanket. So she is dead. He turns and thinks for a moment; now he walks out of the cottage onto the road.

A street in a very poor section of some European city. On the boarded-up stores there are signs in Russian or Polish. (Must be Polish.) An old man with a gray beard is moving along the street close to the buildings. He carries a book and is dressed in black with a wide-brimmed hat.

He turns into a doorway and climbs narrow stairs.

In an apartment eight or ten people are sitting and waiting. Among them a priest stands mumbling a prayer to himself.

The old man with the beard now comes in and all the people look up. He comes to the priest and sits beside him.

Newman was at a loss. He did not know what there was about the picture that disturbed him. Then he noticed the unusual amount of whispering going on in the audience around him. Behind him a few rows back a woman was actually talking in conversational tones.

Now the old man with the beard begins to talk to the priest. He has found out that the Germans plan to hang 'them' in a little while. The priest thinks, and then he says it is time for them to act.

The old man gets to his feet and opens his book. The men and women in the room look at him prayerfully. He begins to pray, and he rocks a little as the foreign words came from his lips. The priest gets to his knees and with bent head also prays.

The audience was moving in a slow, continuous shifting. There was no coughing. It was a shifting that went beyond the movement of bodies. Newman studied the screen and suddenly the whole picture there swept into focus.

The old man was a rabbi, that was it. And the people in the room were Jews.

The men pray with their hats on and the women wear shawls over their heads.

216

Now the whole screen is filled with the figure of the kneeling priest. He is praying and facing directly toward the audience.

Behind Newman a seat slammed down . . .

The whole room is shown again. The priest is getting to his feet. With the rabbi he leads the people out through the door of the apartment.

Newman's eyes seemed to him to be widening across the breadth of the whole theatre. He was seeing what the people around him saw, and he was seeing it with their minds. He knew why the theatre was rumbling. The characters were Jews and were mostly quite good-looking actors. Even though dark, none of them had the hooked nose and the bent grin, and they did not like it in the theatre. The screen again reached out toward him . . .

The little band of people is following the priest and the rabbi through the streets of the city now.

They come to a square. In the center of it stands a tall series of gallows. Around the gallows many German soldiers are waiting. Otherwise the square is empty.

The procession walks across this empty square to the gallows. Now the prisoners to be hanged appear.

The rabbi and the priest stop before a German officer. The rabbi starts to make a speech. He says that the prisoners are innocent. He says that they must not be killed merely because they are Jews.

'HA!'

The single burlesque of a laugh flew like a star through the black theatre air. It came from behind Mr Newman and away to the right. Heads turned. In the third row up front a man stood up with his back to the screen. Mr Newman could not see his face, but he seemed to scan the theatre. Then he sat down.

'What're you lookin' for, Ikey?'

Mr Newman would not turn his head. All around him people were turning to see. Some sat frozen, watching the screen.

The priest in the picture leaps onto the platform of the gallows. A great confusion is starting among the German soldiers who are trying to climb up and bring the priest down.

The priest shouts that it is not Christian to murder these people and that Christian men dare not have any hand in it. The soldiers are dragging him off the platform now ... He is trying to make his words heard ... The old rabbi is collapsing with blood rushing out of his mouth ...

Two ushers were walking up and down the aisles watching the audience. They kept patrolling leisurely. Mr Newman no longer saw the screen. The shifting was massive now, a gathering of breath was taking place around him.

His fists relaxed as great flags veered onto the screen – American, British, Russian, and others. A band was playing. 'THE END' swallowed up the screen and then faded away.

'WB' in color broke out. The cartoon.

The audience laughed, mumbled to itself.

The familiar little pig on the screen is walking through a forest with a very heavy rifle. A rabbit follows right behind him on a scooter.

Mr Newman's mind surrendered to the gay and childlike colors of the picture. After a while he glanced at Gertrude. She was still sitting there clutching her coat together near the neck.

The screen seemed to tear open and the chubby face of the little pig stuck through, and with his little paw describing a gesture of farewell he stuttered hilariously, 'D-da, d-da, d-da, d-dat's all, Folks!'

And with a chuckle he was gone.

Mr Newman felt a pressure on his leg as Gertrude got up. He glanced quickly at her as she rose, and got to his feet hurriedly. They gained the aisle and he kept pace with her as she strode toward the exit doors.

The marquee lights were out now. Only a vague spray of

light from the lobby kept the night away from the sidewalk before the theatre. An old man with a hunched back was standing on the curb with a bundle of papers under his arm. Newman recognized him from the evening of the meeting at the hall. He still had on the Panama hat, but now in his left hand, displayed for the people leaving the theatre, was a paper titled *The Brooklyn Tablet*. A few yards away from him on the curb five boys and an old man were standing together, facing the empty lobby.

Newman realized the five were with the paper-selling old man. He knew it in the instant it took to take them all in. They were not loitering. They were watching the lobby. For a second his eyes lingered on the face of the older man. Then he went on with Gertrude. She was walking fast.

The darkness of the night surrounded them now. Again he listened to the clacking of her heels, out of time with his.

In silence they walked two blocks and were crossing onto the third when he spoke.

'I didn't know that was playing,' he apologized.

She breathed out sharply through her nose.

'Gert, you've got to stop being this way.'

So far he had not taken her arm. He dared to now, as though fearing she might run away from him. She shook his hand loose. They were walking quite fast now.

'Gert, for God's sake, what do you want me to do?'

She blew air out of her nose again.

'Now stop it!' he said sharply, and grabbed her elbow. She stopped and looked at him in the dark there.

Quietly, wanting very much to be believed, he said, 'Don't be silly now. Nothing's going to happen.'

She turned and walked again, but more normally now. He kept hold of her elbow, then slipped his hand under her arm and held her closer. 'We haven't done anything, Gert.'

'You don't take it serious enough. You never did.'

'I don't know what you'd call taking it serious . . .'

'Go and see Fred. I want you to go, you hear me? They're just waiting for the war to be over to bust loose.'

'I have nothing to say to Fred any more.'

'You got plenty to say.' She spoke in urgent hush, as though the dark were listening. The lots between the houses were sunk in black shadows, humped over with mounds of dumped earth. There was no traffic at all, except for a big trailer going by now and then. Her voice was full of breath. He could imagine the intensity of her eyes now, for her head was thrust forward. She was like a man this way, he thought. 'You got plenty to say,' she repeated with a quick nod to herself, 'plenty.'

He had no answer. They had come to the same old blank wall. They walked in silence.

'You hear?' she demanded.

He waited a moment, thinking out his final words. He wished now that he were taller than she instead of the same height, and could look down upon her powerfully and force her agreement. He did not look at her at all, and spoke with the regular measure of his steps, 'I'm only going to do one thing, Gert.'

She was listening. His determination had penetrated her.

'I'm going to live like I always lived. I'm not going to change a jot. I guess you realize that I don't believe in what the Front believes. I suppose I never really did.'

'It ain't a question of what they believe . . .'

'I know, but it is. They're doing what they believe. I can't act that way. Even if they decided I was all right I couldn't go along with them.'

'You couldn't?'

'No.'

They crossed the fourth street. Dimly, two blocks away, he could see the glow of light from the candy store. He took longer breaths now, mounted the sidewalk. 'I couldn't,' he said, 'and neither could you. You're too fine a person.'

220

She did not respond. He waited. He could feel her mind groping itself toward expression.

'You been talking to him too much, Lully,' she said deliberately, nodding a little toward the glow ahead of them.

'Not since I asked him to move,' he assured her quickly.

'According to them they never do anything wrong. Just like in the picture, they're always innocent lambs. They don't show you the things they done, though.'

'You're wrong, Gert. You're wrong about that.'

'You been talking to him too much . . . !'

'I haven't been talking to him too much.' His voice became high, argumentative. 'I've been thinking to myself, though. And you ought to do it too. I just don't think it's right to have people going around beating up on them. I don't think it's right and I won't have anything to do with it.'

'You don't see Fred blowin' around the streets. He's got a spot. You don't take this serious enough. I keep telling you and telling you.'

They crossed the fifth street and stepped onto the sidewalk. 'All I can tell you is what I told you,' he said. 'We've got a house and good jobs and . . . And I think if the war ends soon you can stop working.'

He had not really meant to say it, but it worked well – her arm softened in his hand and she drew him closer to her side.

'You really mean it?' she asked, excitedly.

She must be smiling now, he thought happily. 'Sure, sweet. I . . .'

The sound was light. A tap the weight of a raindrop. But it was there. It cut his words out of his teeth and left him open-mouthed. Now it came again. The gentle tapping of soles on pavement. Several of them . . . in step . . . now out of step . . .

Behind him. Possibly a quarter of a block. Several . . . he could not make out exactly how many, drumming lightly on the pavement. He counted them ... one pair ... two ... three ... lost count and the rhythm of the steps overlapped. She had her head up. Automatically they were both walking with great propriety again. Slightly – an inch at a stride – they gained speed.

Somehow it was sure, he knew it ... There was a mental wave of connection between the walkers behind him and himself. People in a group never walk without talking. Their silence behind him created a vibration in the dark and it played upon his spine.

They crossed the sixth street, mounted the last sidewalk. On the next corner they would turn left into their block. Newman saw the yellow glow of the store beckoning like the open end of a corridor in a dream. The glow invaded his head, blinded him with hope as the steps tapped on behind him. They were going for Finkelstein. They must be. This would be as good a place as any to jump him if it was him they were after. Or back there further where half the block was empty lots. It was Finkelstein tonight. Poor fella ... well, he shouldn't have moved in where he wasn't wanted. It would be bad, though, if the little girl was still in there, but it was late and she was probably in bed by now. Thank God for Finkelstein. Supposing there wasn't anyone like him on the block ... He would have to run for it now, run as fast as his legs could go ... Poor man, poor Jew ... They were strong, those boys, with their muscles curving under their sweaters that way – football kids. Who was the older man with them? That's the way they must be doing it. An older man for the strategy to keep the kids in line. *Brother*, they were quiet! Marching, almost. Why didn't they go faster, catch up and pass him and go on? Smart. Probably waiting behind him to let him get home before they went to work. No good if they had to loiter around close to the store. Arrive, and then, bang. Sure, just the right time. Nobody around on the streets. Maybe he ought to stop and let them pass, they were coming up much closer now, not more than fifteen yards if that. No, he couldn't stop in the dark here. Keep a good stride. Don't get them going with even a word said. Keep moving along. God, but Gert could walk. Her arm like a stone. Her heart . . . her heart oughtn't to thump like that, he thought . . . Why is her heart thumping like . . . ?

The corner arrived and they hardly slowed in turning it, kept moving on up their block. They were on the other side of the street from the store. The gang behind would be crossing just about now, crossing over . . . just . . . about . . . now.

Now.

Now.

Now!

'Hey, Sammy, where you goin' so fast?'

It was the older man . . . a bass, phlegmish voice. He never faltered, strode on, Gertrude pulling him faster. It was un-dignified. In all his terror he refused to go any faster, it was fast enough; if it were only raining then he and Gertrude could have run all the way home.

Running behind him. One laugh of a boy. They appeared in front of him . . . around him. Through the corner of his eye he saw that the street lamp had been smashed. Only the light from the store cast a sheen over the handsome face and the green sweater of the tallest boy . . . something glittered around his left fist. There were five of them. Two behind his shoulders, three in front. The older man stood beyond the periphery of the circle wiping his nose and watching.

The tall boy's feet were spread apart. He was smiling. 'What's your hurry?'

'I'm . . .'

'Heh?' mocked the big boy.

He felt a hand on his back. He turned around quickly, shocked. 'Cut that out!' he ordered sharply. His jaw quivered.

He heard running again behind him, turned, saw the big boy and two others running toward Finkelstein's store, saw them rushing in, and was hit on the side of his head by a fist. He fell to the ground and scrambled away, seeing feet coming toward his face. He got up with his coat flying open. The older man pushed him from behind toward the two boys who were coming at him. Without drawing back his arm Newman struck out and hit one boy's arm and the boy looked suddenly angered, fierce, and clubbed him on the ear with a hard blow. He turned around and fell into the gutter and scrambled up again. Again he felt the hands of the older man on his back and was pushed toward the two boys coming at him. He started to raise one arm when he felt his coat rolling up his back. Suddenly realizing, he stripped it off his shoulders and snaked himself out of the sleeves before it could be rolled up over his head . . . he had seen it done in the movies, was startled that it was being done to him, surged with abhorrence inside that they were doing it to him . . .

A moment, a clear moment opened before him. Where was Gertrude? He had run ten yards and turned. They were dancing toward him now, fists raised. He saw it was very technical with them, felt the directing presence of the older man who now stood between the two boys advancing, muttering to them and wiping his nose with the back of his thumb. They were coming now. He could not run away, could not run to his house with boys chasing him. It was improper and derisive of him and he stood there and he saw then that his hand was pointing, pointing toward the store.

'Go!' he shouted, heard his own shout and stopped shouting.

They disregarded his pointing. 'Go,' he muttered, his dry mouth gasping for the air. He waved them away, a silly, feminine gesture, he thought, and yet kept waving them away, backing as they fanned out to both sides of him, the older man in front. If they would just turn, go to the store . . . his knees were ready to collapse into beggary, he felt himself green and disgusting as he waved them toward the lighted window beyond their backs . . .

The store erupted. From silence to a gigantic monolith of sound from a single throat, a torrential bellowing swept out of the store and Finkelstein leaped a great leap out across the sidewalk, a bat in each hand, the three who had gone in running out after him, missing him with their fists, lunging for his clothes. Like a long-armed machine he smashed at them with the bats, they dodging almost in play, gracefully, eyeing each others' footwork, jealous of each other, half-smiling, enjoying the play . . .

Newman felt the shoe against his stomach, a heavy-soled shoe, and sprang back with the kick and could not let his belly out. The clacking of high heels. He jerked his head to the side. She was running . . . *Gertrude* . . . *Gertrude!* They were fencing him away from Finkelstein now. He sensed their change of concern now that the bats had come swinging onto the street. They were not angling any more but wanted it finished, and he rushed around them toward the sidewalk, stopped short as one of them scaled a hedge to head him off, and he went straight on toward Finkelstein, yelling for recognition. Finkelstein never turned to him, but the left bat stopped swinging and extended to him. He grabbed the head of it and felt the terrible bony knock of brass against the side of his head and danced sideways half across the gutter and stumbled to his hands over the curb. 'Son of a bitch!' he screamed in soprano, his voice coated with slime as he ran headlong away from the light, crouched over, hearing the feet behind him. And then when he had his balance and the bat was solid in his two hands he swung himself around as he ran and felt the soft solidity of the shoulder he hit. A giant wall seemed to tilt over inside of him and a great stream of silver light scoured his body. His pants were wet and

he knew it and yet he swung again and damned himself as he
missed, cried out ' *You son of a bitch* ' and headed after the boy
in the green sweater who backed away . . . The older man was
shouting now. Newman turned toward the shout and ran as
though he had been made lighter, even imagining that he had
only now gotten rid of his coat, and the older man ducked
away and he did not pursue him but kept on running toward
Finkelstein. There were only two at Finkelstein now, but the
blood was slopping out of his nose as he flung his stocky body
behind every flight of his bat. They stood together now, one
facing each way. The four remaining boys sparred in two at a
time toward the bats, and backed up as their hands cracked
against the hard wood . . .

'Hold it.'

Not even a shout. It was so astonishingly well rehearsed that
the older man only said hold it and the boys relaxed, watchfully,
kept their guard up, and moved out in a careful circle.

The older man was near the store, full in the light. He realized it and stepped to the side and into the darkness. His voice
called, 'All right, you Hebrew bastards. This is the warm-up.
Let's go, boys.'

The one in the green sweater, almost weeping, called, 'I'm
stayin'.'

The older man crossed into the street and headed for him.
'We're going, come on.'

He took hold of the boy's arm. Mr Newman and Mr Finkelstein stood sucking in air in the center of the street. Their
backs nearly touched and they still held the bats with two hands,
like fishing poles. They watched as the circle around them drew
off toward the corner. They could hear their own breathing
now and they could hear the breathing of the boys and of the
older man, who held his nostril shut and snotted onto the sidewalk. At the corner the five stopped walking backwards and
turned away and went into the parkway and disappeared.

Mr Finkelstein was facing the corner fully. Mr Newman came around now to watch the corner and stood beside him. They stood that way for a minute, waiting.

Mr Newman looked at Mr Finkelstein's face and saw the blood coming out of one nostril. He took out his handkerchief and put it to Mr Finkelstein's nose. Taking the handkerchief and holding it to his nose, Mr Finkelstein turned and walked like a drunkard to his store. Mr Newman followed him in silence and they went in.

Mr Finkelstein sat down on the backless wooden chair, and taking the handkerchief away from his nose for a moment, he saw how much was coming out and tilted his head back and pressed the handkerchief against the nostril again. He was still holding onto the bat with a grip so strong that it remained standing straight up from the butt resting on his thigh.

Newman went to him and took hold of the bat, but Finkelstein did not let go. Newman looked at his upturned eyes, his strained and helpless eyes, and stopped trying to take the bat. He could not break his gaze away and kept staring into Finkelstein's eyes. It was like seeing Gertrude all new over Ardell's desk that time, seeing her changed, human. He put his hand on the bat again, and said, 'I won't hurt you.' It was not what he meant to say but Finkelstein seemed to know and let the bat slip out of his hand. Newman tried to tilt it on end beside his against the showcase, but they started to fall, and he caught them and again tried to balance them against the glass and his hand began to shake and both bats toppled and hit together like bowling pins and then stopped moving on the floor. He felt himself sitting down and the inability to control himself started a sob rolling up his chest, and he sat on the floor, almost falling back flat. He looked up at Finkelstein who was staring up at the ceiling, and heard himself sobbing softly, as he watched the blood spreading over the whole whiteness of Finkelstein's handkerchief. The taste of vomit stung his tongue and he cried aloud against it and continued sobbing.

Finkelstein muttered something under the handkerchief.

'Nothing,' Newman shook his head and rubbed his fingers in his eyes and kept shaking his head at the way his tears were flowing.

Finkelstein turned to him with effort, trying to keep his head back at the same time. After watching Newman for a minute, he asked, 'What are you doing that for?'

Newman wiped his eyes with his sleeve and looked up at him.

'Go in the house,' he said. His stomach still had not come out entirely. 'Go on, I'll take you in.'

Finkelstein was breathing rapidly.

'Have you got a good heart?' he asked.

Finkelstein raised an eyebrow and it meant so-so.

They sat that way. Slowly Newman felt his innards unwinding, moving down from his neck. He breathed and it came easier. He rolled to one side, supporting himself against the showcase, and made his way to his feet.

'Come on,' he said, shaking.

At his touch, Finkelstein rose. His heavy arm was quivering and wet. The blood was even spreading the stain that covered the whole front of his shirt. Newman held onto his arm and they walked to the door and out of the store. Finkelstein waited dumbly on the sidewalk while Newman snapped the lock and pulled the door shut. The lights stayed on. Newman led his friend along the sidewalk and up the path of his house and onto the porch, where he opened the front door for him.

'Isn't your wife home?' he asked.

Finkelstein shook his head. 'She took the boy and the old man to the Bronx. The relatives.'

Newman took him into the kitchen and turned on the light. The shirt was too soaked to unbutton, so they ripped it off and dropped it out on the back porch. From the refrigerator New-

228

man took a tray of cubes and emptied them into a dishtowel and held them against Finkelstein's forehead. Holding them that way he made the Jew sit on a chair with his head leaning back against the white-pine table top.

Newman looked around the kitchen as he stood with his hand holding down the compress. The room was astonishingly clean. It's true, he thought, the Jews are a sanitary people. And then it occurred to him that they were supposed to be dirty. And with the side of his head throbbing and his hands still shaking he looked down at the discolored face of Finkelstein. As he turned to look his eye caught a mirror hanging beside the door and he found his image there. His cheekbone was blue. His tie was gone completely. He remembered his overcoat. The nose-piece of his glasses was dug way into his flesh . . . he must have been pressing them against his face all the time, he realized. He walked around Finkelstein's feet and changed hands holding the compress, and got close to the mirror and blinked dreamily at his face.

In all his life he had never known such calm, despite the torrent of blood rushing through him. Within his raging body a stillness had grown very wide and very deep and he stared at his image feeling the texture of this peace. It was almost a tone he seemed to be hearing, level and low and far away. He stood there listening to it.

When he had put Finkelstein to bed, he walked out of the house and went into the store and turned out the lights. Again the tone of that calm sang low in his ears and he stood in the dark store as though to draw the sound out clearer, trying to fathom why it made him feel so assured and empty of fear. He went out the door and tested it to see that it was locked and then went back in the house and left the store key on the telephone table. With his hand on the light switch of the living room he paused a moment and looked about the room. His nostrils studied the air. Again and again he turned his eyes on every piece of furniture in the room as though expecting to discover something strange.

He waited in the room. And waited a little longer. And nothing strange came to him, it was a human, ordinary room.

His hand snapped off the light and he hurried out of the house.

On the street outside he looked up and down before starting for home. There was no police car. Rapidly he crossed over to his side of the street, striding and feeling a pain under his ribs for the first time. Only now could he think of Gertrude and the way she had run off without a word. A pounding rage was deep in him and yet he said almost aloud that it was wiser for her not to scream, but to run home and call the police. It was much wiser, and yet . . . If only she had screamed and flung herself at them. It would have been a good thing, it would have been such a good thing. If only she could have done that and felt as he did now that he had fought, he would never have to explain to her why he . . .

'Lully?'

It was wrong. Instantly he knew that she was not coming out of the right house. He stood looking at her up on the porch, and then he saw Fred coming out and quietly closing the screen door behind him. He could not see their faces in the dark. She was waiting for him to come up the stoop to her but he stood there sadly. It was wrong for her to be coming out of Fred's house at this time. Or anybody else's house but his. It was so sadly wrong . . .

She came down from the porch and stood before him under the tree on the sidewalk.

'What were you doing in there?' he said thinly, knowing what she had been doing in there.

'Come into Fred's house,' she said.

In reply he reached out and delicately touched her elbow.

She grasped his extended arm. Her voice was capable, like the time in the park with the hysterical girl. 'Come on,' she urged quietly, 'I explained it to him. About the Coast and everything.'

He withdrew his arm. The hysteria of the fight seemed to be coming to life in him again and he feared he would weep if he tried to talk.

She would not let go of his arm. 'Come, Lully. Fred wants to talk to you.'

He stepped back as she began drawing him by the arm toward Fred's stoop. 'Didn't you call the police?' he asked, dumbly.

'By the time I got here it was practically over,' she explained. 'Come . . .'

'But I could've been killed . . .'

'We were just going out to stop it,' she promised, now leaning her face closer to his.

'But Gert, I could've been killed while you . . .'

'The fastest way to stop it was Fred, wasn't it? We were just about to . . .'

'Gert!' he cried. It broke from his throat. He was keening helplessly through a head full of tears, and with his hands gripping her arms he started walking her backwards along the sidewalk, sobbing, 'Gert! Gert!'

'Now cut it out!'

'You didn't even scream! You ran away . . . Gert, you ran away and left . . . !'

At the touch of the hand on his shoulder he jerked about in shock. He could not see Fred's face but he smelled the man's cigar odor.

'I want to talk to you, Newman,' Fred said, quietly.

Gertrude came around from behind him and stood facing him beside Fred. Both of them wanted to talk to him. He heard her saying it was all right, everything was all right, Fred just wanted to talk to him and apologize . . .

He could hear her calling to him peevishly as he walked. He knew he was walking but whether he had struck at Fred or not . . . he could not quite remember what had started him walking. Her excited calls became sparser, he kept on walking, and then it was quiet. Something soft brushed his ankle, and he stopped and picked up his coat off the curb, and turning the corner, put it on.

The parkway was as dark as if it were three o'clock in the morning. He was picking up a good stride against the wind which creaked in the stiff branches of the trees over his head. The wind stung his face like soap on a skin cut, and the pain swelled his chest as he walked, and he became aware of all the strength he had left in him. His eyes seemed to be open very wide and he devoured the dark with them, feeling a wild desire to be challenged. Remembering how he had tried to wave them away from him toward the store he stiffened with disgust and demanded that attackers confront him at the next tree . . . or the next . . . How he would land one on that man who had snotted onto the street! Attack, it was necessary to attack. Oh, God, if they would come at him now! If he could fight until his arms fell off . . . !

Seeing the lights of the subway station he slowed, gratified that he had walked the distance between two subway stops without knowing. An honest five minutes. A kind of proof, he felt. The first five minutes he had ever spent unafraid.

He turned off the sidewalk and hurried across the parkway and continued up a sidestreet, studying the neighborhood in an effort to recall exactly how far he had to go. Remembering, he let his surroundings fade from his mind, and he thought of Gargan and the city. The city and the millions upon millions hiving all over it – and they were going mad. He saw it so clearly that it was hardly alarming, for what he understood he no longer feared. They were going mad. People were in asylums for being afraid that the sky would fall, and here were

232

millions walking around as insane as anyone could be who feared the shape of a human face. They . . .

A spasm of shivering took hold of him and he buttoned his coat collar but the chill would not go away. His teeth were beginning to chatter. The wind was searching for his body beneath his clothes and he hurried faster, and came to a corner and turned. A few yards from the corner he saw the green lamps beside the doorway and rushed up to the building and went in.

Before him was a brown-walled room with bare steam pipes running along the walls. There were bare brown tables and a desk. It was quiet and smelled of steam and dust. One policeman in shirtsleeves was sitting at the desk in the glow of a green gooseneck lamp. Prepared and composed, he looked up from his newspaper.

Newman walked up to the desk and looked into his wind-burned face. The policeman covered him with one vertical sweep of his eyes. 'Have some trouble?' he asked, doubtfully.

'My name is Lawrence Newman. I live on 68th Street.'

'What's the trouble?' the policeman insisted.

'I was attacked and beaten up a little while ago.'

'He rob you?'

'No. It was six of them. Five young fellows and an older man. The Christian Front Gang.'

The policeman did not move. His forehead wrinkled. 'How do you know?'

'They've been threatening to do it a long time now.'

'You got any of their names?'

'No, but I'd recognize two or three of them, especially the older man.'

'Well, that don't help me much. We can't go looking for people without names.'

'Well they've got to be caught, that's all I can tell you.'

'What street was that you said?'

233

'68th.'

The policeman thought, then made an O of his mouth. 'That's the street with the candy store on the corner.'

'That's right.'

'Yeh,' he recalled, staring vacantly at the desk, 'that's a bad street.' He looked up. 'You need a doctor, or can you talk?'

'I can talk. I'm all right, thanks.'

The policeman studied the edge of the desk, formulating his questions. Newman watched his broad Irish face. 'How many of you people are there on that street?' the policeman began, trying to make a plan.

'What's that?' Newman whispered faintly.

'On that street,' the policeman said once more. 'How many of you people live there?'

'Well,' said Newman, wetting his lips . . . and stopped.

The policeman waited for the information, looking up at him. Mr Newman searched his face for the slightest trace of animosity but found none. So it would not be quailing if he corrected the man, he felt, for the truth was he was not a Jew. But the officer had assumed he was, and it seemed now that to make the denial was to repudiate and soil his own cleansing fury of a few moments ago. As he stood there about to reply, he longed deeply for a swift charge of lightning that would with a fiery stroke break away the categories of people and change them so that it would not be important to them what tribe they sprang from. It must not be important any more, he swore, even though in his life it had been of highest importance. And as though the words would join him forever to his fury of a few moments past, and separate him forever from those he hated now, he said.

'There are the Finkelsteins on the corner . . .'

'Just them and yourself?' the policeman interrupted.

'Yes. Just them and myself,' Mr Newman said.

Then he sat down and the policeman picked a pencil from

among many on the desk, and began to take down his story. Telling it, Mr Newman felt as though he were setting down a weight which for some reason he had been carrying and carrying.